BORN OF GUILT

JOANNA ELMY

BORN OF GUILT

Translated from the Bulgarian by Angela Rodel and Joanna Elmy

faber

First published in 2026
by Faber & Faber Ltd
The Bindery, 51 Hatton Garden
London EC1N 8HN

First published in Bulgarian in 2021 under the title
Napraveni ot vina by Janet 45, Bulgaria

Typeset by Faber & Faber Ltd
Printed in the UK by CPI Group (UK) Ltd, Croydon CR0 4YY

A CIP record for this book
is available from the British Library

ISBN 978–0–571–38995–7

MIX
Paper | Supporting responsible forestry
FSC® C013604

Printed and bound in the UK on FSC® certified paper in line with our continuing commitment to ethical business practices, sustainability and the environment.
For further information see faber.co.uk/environmental-policy

Our authorised representative in the EU for product safety is
Easy Access System Europe, Mustamäe tee 50, 10621 Tallinn, Estonia
gpsr.requests@easproject.com

2 4 6 8 10 9 7 5 3 1

To my mother

. . . each born in turn
upon the death mounds
of the former,
entombing themselves,
building this hill.

– John Balaban, *Hissarlik*

1

I am calm only when alone. That's what my mother used to say. As a child I hated her for this because it meant I shouldn't have existed. Now I'm frightened by how much I understand her.

A bright spot in the nocturnal amalgam of sky and asphalt interrupts my thoughts. I squint. The white shoe gleams in the middle of the highway. My gaze crawls further along the road, and I see the body. Shorts, a sweatshirt, an ankle bracelet with seashells, long hair spilling on the concrete. And the red car chewing up the bike. It must have just happened, but I didn't even notice, swept up as I was in the past. The cars have stopped on both sides of the intersection, engines roaring, the rhythm of traffic lights now meaningless in the stock-still evening.

The only way into town is Route 1, an offshoot from Delaware's massive spine of a highway that stretches all the way down to Maryland. Those not lucky enough to live in town bike to their jobs on this road. I prefer biking at night, when it's calm. In the morning everyone's in a rush, traffic jams stretch for miles, the sun mercilessly burns your flesh, the cars seethe hot air like enraged mechanical animals. At night it's almost empty. Lone cars fly past me in the rhythm set by the few small-town traffic lights, beyond which the road bursts free. The scale of America is different – everything is larger, as if the world has been distended. Most restaurants and shops are closed, with the exception of a few diners. Every day I pass through three intersections – the last one, where I am now, is the worst. To catch the green light, I need to merge from the shoulder to the far-left lane. The stoplight is on a slight hill, which my bike's rusty gears hate. I only breathe easy when I reach the flag on the other side, flapping in the wind. There are flags everywhere.

We all wait for the body to rise.

I edge my bike onto the sidewalk. I'm still staring at her but it's no longer me watching – I feel as if I'm melting away, like fog diffused by the wind. I'm here, yet no one sees me, no one sees anything else.

The night is ablaze in red and blue. A police car follows the ambulance, both braking hard and blocking the intersection. A traffic cop gets out of the patrol car and starts redirecting the backed-up cars. The paramedics flock to the body. I count three more police officers: two of them head for the car, only a silhouette visible inside. The third one waves at me.

'Miss? English?'

I shake my head.

'You all right? That your friend?'

I nod.

'So you don't speak English well? You know her? Can you at least tell me her name?'

'No.' My voice is raspy for some reason. 'No, I do speak English.' I nod this time. 'And I don't know who she is.'

'Oh . . . Sorry, my mistake. You all right? You hurt?'

'No.'

'Did you see the accident?'

'I don't know . . . No. No. I was already here . . . Is she OK?'

'I don't know. The EMTs will do what needs to be done. So, you didn't see a thing?'

'No. Just . . . Just the shoe over there.'

'Where do you live?'

'There.'

'I mean your address. You need a ride? You feelin' OK?'

I resist the urge to look at her. Out of the corner of my eye I see two of the paramedics pull out a stretcher while another two rearrange her twisted limbs.

'Sorry. I live behind the grocery store. I take the left here, then right. Airport Road. Across from Walmart.'

'Are you OK to get yourself home?' He glances over his shoulder and waves to another cop. 'I'll ask them to give you a ride. Or we'll at least come with you.'

'No, no thanks . . . It really isn't necessary. Just . . .'

'What?'

'Can I turn here? I mean, now . . . Can I go around the ambulance and turn off here?'

He looks at me, and I try to guess what he's thinking. Suddenly I see myself through his eyes: my shoes sticky with sugar and sauce, my shorts, my sweatshirt. To him I look just like her. There's no way she's American. Americans don't bike on highways at midnight.

'Sure you can turn. Would you feel better if I came with you to the other side?'

I nod.

We walk around the site of the accident – that's what the cop calls the intersection. I half-listen to the buzzing of his walkie-talkie. You can't see a thing from this side. Before he lets me go, he writes down my name and where I work. I only tell him about the one place. We know not to mention the other.

'Have a good night,' he says.

'Night. Thank you.' Then I remember: 'Hey, sorry . . . Excuse me! Sorry, will someone get the shoe?'

'What?'

'The shoe . . . Her shoe is all the way out in the other lane. Someone should get it . . . She'll probably be looking for it.'

night

We meet amid the chaos of the world. We share nothing, no friends nor continents. We don't know it yet, but this first night is our best together. We sit next to each other on the lifeguard chair that towers over the empty beach. There's no moon, it's so dark that if someone comes from the resort behind us, they'll hear only two voices narrating life. Here and now is the youngest we'll ever be for each other, at our most unexplored and thus most thrilling. Each of us will dissolve into the other slowly, a careful decantation of accrued past. Each of us is an alien in the other's universe. All we share is a language and a night's worth of time.

He holds two cigarettes in his mouth, lights them and hands me one. The smoke forms question marks in the indigo of the night.

Who are you?
Where do you come from?
How did you end up here?

birth

I will be forever blamed for this day. Here is my mother. The fluorescent lights flicker above our heads. We're still one, and the acid of her thoughts penetrates all the way to my fragile bones. She will never suspect that I will remember everything: the nasty brown hallway, the echo of each light's glassy crackle. The plastered wall peeling off in patches, the handwritten schedules taped to the doors. We've been here for hours. We're alone.

My mother owns me for the last time.
Where's my dad?
She doesn't know.
I want to wait for him.

They've informed her the child will face all the risks of a post-term birth.

Fuck, it's cold. Her naked body shivers.

Where is everyone?

I am being born into a world of deficits. Her belly blocks her view of the ward door, and she can't see a thing. The lights continue their crystalline time count: ding, ding, ding . . .

I rip her up from the inside. She curses me.

Do I even want to come into this world? Doubt courses through my body, the same doubt I must have been conceived in. Maternal exhaustion crawls down the spine, into the blood vessels, reaching the placenta. The vague feeling that something is wrong builds up in my system, along with all the vitamins and antibodies.

Won't you please come out already? she begs.

The yellowed sheet on the stretcher is soaked with blood. She's in horrendous pain. My pain.

Our pain.

My mother hears footsteps and lifts her head, a sweaty lock of hair slipping out from behind her right ear. A man in a white coat approaches. She tries to cover herself up, to close her legs. He stops next to us. He looks at us.

'What the hell are you doing out here?' he asks.

My mother whimpers. He looks around the corridor, takes a few steps toward the delivery room, turns the lights on and off again. He comes back, sticks his hand in the pocket of his coat and pulls out some dog-eared cash.

He carefully places a crumpled banknote on her overripe

belly and grins. 'Go to the canteen, grab a bottle of water, till everyone comes back. Later.'

And he disappears.

I hear her sharp breathing, the song of the glass, blood dripping on the linoleum. The note flies down toward the puddle.

No one knows where we are. She hasn't called anyone. My father hasn't been home in days. She's afraid he's started again . . .

If he truly loves us, he'll get better. The child will make him better.

And if not, at least she won't be alone anymore. I'll deliver her from her desolation. Two gentle hands throw a sheet over the wet body ready to burst.

'Did I die?' she asks.

'Hush now.'

The smell of bleach pierces our lungs. The cleaning lady rushes into the room – she is probably trying to press the button to call the head nurse. My mom tells her that those buttons don't work in most hospitals.

'How do you know?' asks the other woman.

'Because I'm a doctor,' she responds.

She tries to swallow, but has nothing to swallow. She knows she's dehydrated.

I just want to make sure you have all your fingers and toes, she tells me. She's not afraid of dying. She even feels relieved. She only wonders, *Who will look after the baby?* Some time ago the head doctor had told her that *whimpering women are the worst*, that they make him sick. She tries to escape the pain and think of something else; she dives into the shadows of definitions and terms, burrowing deeper and deeper into a thick forest of memories. She squeezes her eyes shut – the words appear one after another in red ink, engraved on her eyelids. She has always been a straight-A student.

Good job, Doctor, good job . . .

Herds of 'A's start running before her eyes. So many of them . . . and all of them are fat and pregnant, 'a', 'a', 'a', their bellies bursting with smaller 'a's coming out.

. . . her grade will go from 'A' to 'F', and then everything will be over.

A.

Where is he?

B.

Where?

C.

Somewhere something is ringing.

D.

F.

She's hearing voices.

Hypovolemic shock. Sudden drop in the circulating blood volume.

A shock means a jolt. What was it again? *When left untreated, the patient goes through several stages . . .*

Initial stage.

They meet at a party in 1992: music, shit alcohol and cigarettes are the poor man's meal. Tall, a hiker, works out, has a long scar on the left of his chin, slightly darker than his skin – he burned himself with a cigarette during his army days. His movements are premeditated, like a cat ready to rip prey apart. She loves him, or that's what she thinks. She can't breathe when they are apart. Sometimes he disappears and doesn't call and then she doesn't know what to do with herself. But then he comes back, and all is well. And she's too afraid to ask where he's been.

Second stage of shock, compensatory.

He makes her feel graceless. Like a child who wants to be praised but is unable to speak. His mother and father have travelled the world. They show her souvenirs: precious gems from Brazil and empty bottles of Chanel N°5 perfume.

She and her brother have never been to the seaside and her mother's hands are so rough . . . She doesn't remember her own mother ever wearing perfume. She's consumed by hatred for herself . . . She will cut away the past. She will become someone else.

Followed by the progressive third stage.

It's the little things that drive her crazy. Why is she like this? He always eats standing up, never sitting at the table, crumbs falling everywhere. He doesn't know how to run the washer. He hasn't ever helped her around the house.

On the phone her mother asks her why they haven't bought new furniture – aren't they newlyweds, how can they live in such indigence?

His mother constantly criticizes her: her nails aren't done, her hair needs cutting, her legs are too thick, she doesn't take enough care of herself for him to want her, and this is the most important thing for a man.

She suspects that he has never wanted to be a doctor. He's erratic; he lacks determination. He reminds her of a fly trapped in life's webs. She observes his chaotic collisions with hardship, watches him wasting energy, making the same mistakes over and over. A fruit fly drowning in colorful poisons: amber, crimson and a bit of ice.

Lily, Lily, where is Dimitar?

Why have you let him go out drinking yet again?

Refractory stage.

Hush, be quiet,
don't talk,
you're not well,
not well,

not well . . .

I don't want to have a child, he tells her, touching her growing belly. *I can't be a good father.*

He whimpers.

He tells her about his great-grandfather, the Party Secretary, and the two sixteen-year-old boys he used to live with. About his great-grandmother who slept in the other room.

He talks about his time in the military:

There were three of them,

he sobs,

thirteen months of service, no women, no nothing, stuck down at the border, the most horrific border, not a living soul around, no one allowed there without a special pass. There were three of them and they laughed and laughed and laughed . . .

It hurt so bad.

My great-grandfather hung himself in this very kitchen, right here. My great-grandmother didn't cry.

Why don't you take him to acupuncture, her mother-in-law asks, for his nerves.

He'll need medical treatment, my mother answers. He's an alcoholic.

How could he be an alcoholic, don't be stupid, Lilia. I gave life to this boy . . . I know him better than you could ever imagine. You won't understand until you're a mother yourself.

Only breaking the vicious cycle, the repetition of each stage, can save the patient.

Initial, compensatory, progressive, refractory. He loves her, she promises to do better, he disappears, he has a disease and she can't help him.

Initial . . . he loves her, she believes in him, she can help him; *compensatory* . . . she'll find better doctors, support him more, he just needs to be loved, needs someone to understand him, what will happen if she leaves him too, as if he hasn't suffered enough already; *progressive* . . . where is he, why does he abandon them, if he loves them why does he need to drink;

refractory . . . he comes home, vomits everywhere, pisses in the sink and the urine reeks of alcohol, the child is heavy inside her and she wakes up at night because she has dreamed that the baby is dead. His side of the bed is empty.

They don't let her hold me, they carry me away straight after the birth. She is in pain, she feels her body melting on the table, she's cold, she just wants to be left to die in peace. At least that.

2

It's around 4.30 a.m. when I drift off to sleep. I googled: 'incident', 'Bethany Beach', 'Coastal Highway', 'supermarket', 'intersection'. Nothing. Maybe something local, something small? Nothing. Twitter, Facebook? Nothing. The search engine spits out old results.

14 August 2011
On Sunday night, a twenty-four-year-old Polish girl who lived with a family near the beach was hit by a car while on her bike. She was riding against the flow of traffic when a car pulled into the emergency lane to enter the Kmart parking lot, the police reported. The woman was not wearing a helmet and was taken to Christiana Hospital in Newark with severe head injuries.

7 July 2014
. . . the accident happened around 8 p.m. on Sunday, 6 July 2014. A middle-aged truck driver from Bethany hit a nineteen-year-old Hungarian girl who was biking on the shoulder of the Coastal Highway . . . At this time, there is no information as to whether the victim's family has been notified.

20 September 2014

Andrea Beatrice Roman arrived in the United States from Romania in the summer to work at Bethany's Country Club, where she bussed tables after the golfers' dinner. She biked to her seasonal job, just like hundreds of foreign students who work on the beaches of Bethany during the summer. Cars and trucks significantly outnumber bicycles on the highway. Her modest red bike was also her means of transportation to the beach, restaurants and shops.

She had planned to stay here until October to work and have fun. 'She was a very active girl,' recalls her summer roommate, twenty-eight-year-old Andra Vale. 'She was always busy. Always looking for something to do.'

On 27 August, a near-fatal accident put an end to Roman's carefree American summer. She is now in critical condition at Christiana Hospital, where she was transported after her bike collided with a scooter on the highway near Kmart. Her loved ones and her colleagues, who are spending hours and days by her bedside, say that the accident led to brain injuries, which forced the doctors to perform three neurosurgeries, due to which Roman has lost her ability to speak. Nevertheless, Roman can answer questions and give indications of her state by writing notes or by moving her arms and legs.

Most of the people supporting Roman during her recovery come from Central European countries and are working overtime to pay her hospital bills. Nearly five thousand foreigners work at the beach resorts every year. Businesses count on them during the busy summer. Having arrived as students, some of them make a life in the US. However, they say that biking is becoming more and more dangerous. They try to warn their younger compatriots, albeit with little success – biking remains the cheapest means of transportation.

'Every year there is an accident. Every year someone dies.'

I fall asleep feeling that this must be impossible. Things like this don't happen in America.

night

How can I tell you what kind of childhood I had? You wouldn't understand a thing.

It's far easier to create an inventory of deficits.

I didn't have a big shelf with Disney VHS tapes, like Lina, who on top of that was blonde with blue eyes, as if on purpose. All girls in Bulgaria want to be blonde and have blue eyes. And all boys like blondes with blue eyes.

I didn't have a beautiful pony like she did either, from McDonald's, that lived in a pink, heart-shaped house. It was an expensive treat, McDonald's – my grandmother used to take me there once a month, after getting her pension. So I found a plastic toy horse, flat, almost two-dimensional, probably from a set of toy soldiers or something, and I made a house for it from an empty *Zdrave* box, this moisturizer from the Communist era that was found in every house. Lina was so impressed that I tricked her into trading with me. Then I refused to give her pony back to her, and we didn't speak for a long time.

We didn't have a car (my father had an old East German Wartburg, which he later sold – I rode in it once; then he had a blue Citroën, which didn't last even that long). It was a big deal to own a car in Bulgaria in those days. Other kids got a ride to school while I froze on the streetcar. Only one boy from my class traveled with me, his father had died of cancer. I don't know if it was the streetcar or the fact that we both didn't have dads, but I was in love with him until I turned fourteen.

We didn't have money for chocolate. We didn't have money for a vacation at the beach. We didn't have money to go skiing.

We didn't have nice plates or glasses. Just lone survivors from broken sets. We saved the wedding china for a special occasion that never came. After the divorce my mother threw it in the dumpster.

Along with the colorful, ragged bedsheets and the old Rhodope woolen blankets, reeking of time and strangers' skin.

Nice shoes, nice clothes, Friday nights out with friends and their kids (my mother didn't have any friends, my father didn't have any friends), beautiful Barbie dolls . . .

We didn't have cable. We didn't have a computer. There was an old radio with only one working speaker – my mother would play this station that only played Bulgarian songs, and the two of us would sing and dance our hearts out.

We didn't have new furniture – the neighbors would give us their old stuff and my mom would cover them with sheets of vinyl in fake wood grain to make them look new.

They also gave us their daughters' old Mickey Mouse comic books. That's how I learned to read – I must have been four or five. When my mom sold them at one of these paper recycling points that would give you a few pennies a kilo, I was so angry I cried. We used to collect all sorts of paper back then, supermarket leaflets full of stuff we couldn't afford, my old childhood drawings, we even sold some books from the library.

We've had the same childhood, you in Bulgaria and me here, you say.

Mickey Mouse, McDonald's.

A second-hand American childhood.

Rice, potatoes, cabbage, pork chops and rabbits from the countryside, sent by my grandparents. Oh, and *popara* . . . Do you know what that is? You don't, how could you. Water, bread, cheese. Or linden tea instead of water. If you're lucky – milk. I used to make my grandmother squeeze the chunks of bread until they were packed hard, like little balls when you chew.

How disgusting, you say. *Have you tried eating that now?*

No way. You have to be five or it won't be the same . . . But still, I was happy.

I had no idea how poor we were until I grew up.

Now my mother sends my grandparents money from Germany and she gets mad because when she asks them on the phone what they're eating, they say popara.

I send them hundreds of leva, she tells me, and they still eat bread and water.

They didn't have anything for so long that now that they actually have something, they have no idea what to do with it.

Lily

Will there be warm shoes for the winter?

Will there be bread?

They will 'release' the shoes in the stores, they used to say. They will 'release' the bread. Who is *they*? *Where* are they *releasing* it from?

Yana, I hope you never have to ask these questions.

Babyboo, Babyboo, my little crescent silver moon, my father sings.

I'm hungry, so my mother goes to one empty shop after another.

My merciless crying reminds them of the mistake they made having a child in this time and place. Or at all.

My father feeds me stale bread, carefully unstitching the crust until all that's left are frayed clouds of bread.

Misery grows on life like mold – they can taste it, they can feel it in the sheets, in their shoes, in the pipes. My mother can't stand the idiots who talk of a new coat of arms and new national values. She has her own suggestions:

She wishes my father would get angry and smash a glass or something. But he's silent, smoking old cigarette butts and staring dumbly at the screen as she roams the streets for food. When she screams, he is silent. So she doubles down. There has to be something alive inside him, something that can fight. Because she can't be the only one doing the fighting.

The same tobacco-yellow faces on TV, bodies in black coats. There are strangers in the apartment, some friends of his father, former Secret Police. They both know something is going on but they don't ask what. They don't care, there are more important things to worry about. They have a child now, they have to use their heads.

She can't stop thinking about the glass. Wishing he would break it, just to show he still has a spine. Kick those stooges out of the living room, if he's such a rebel. The door opens and closes constantly; I squeal, restless in the shadow of strangers. My mother has so much milk – she pulls her breasts out of her graying vest top with cheap lace just as several beefcakes in tracksuits mistakenly barge into the kitchen. They recoil in disgust while she explains coldly that these are the living quarters. Then she hangs an old hospital bedsheet across the hallway where it turns into the kitchen, which is where we sleep.

Another one of my mother's national values:

Squalor

The load-bearing beam in my father's spirit is cracking. He has nightmares about the past catching up with him. He hadn't imagined a crying child, nor this woman with purple streaks on her breasts, with lips already framed by wrinkles, with gray hair at twenty-seven. He had not imagined such a world.

She looks in the mirror and thinks that this cannot be her, it has to be someone else's body, a stranger's, a foreigner's, because she couldn't bear it for a second if it turned out to be hers.

Third word:

Prison

A TV journalist catches a cabinet minister at a beauty contest while people are killing one another in the streets. My mother cannot take her eyes off the models, who slip away from the table one by one. Tall, beautiful, white bodies, shiny hair and moist eyes, faces heavy with make-up. One of them returns with a drink, sits down on a chair next to the minister and starts fixing her hair, staring off into the distance.

'The minister has resigned,' my father tells her a few nights later.

She is breastfeeding; his eyes are once again pinned to the screen. 'Big deal, he resigned. Another bastard will replace him.'

Those girls are probably sitting at that same table with a tasteless tablecloth, my mother thinks, where another future hero, stinking of cigarettes and salty sweat, makes his way unhindered to their perfect pussies.

3

The rain has driven away the people who would otherwise have been cramming cotton candy, greasy donuts, pizza with extra-thick crust and sodas in giant cups down their throats. Even the seagulls are hiding. From the store I can hear the beeping of the games in the arcade next door. Only a few bored tourists are left, waiting for the downpour to end, heads drooping over their phones. They look like tired flowers.

There are four of us. The store is at the end of an avenue that terminates at the beach. We sell sweet caramel corn and saltwater taffy, which, according to my grandfather, is complete idiocy. Sooner or later everyone swings by Sally's Candyland to buy a box or two of taffy and a bucket of caramel corn for the road. At the end of my shift, the sprinkles, greasy streaks of oil, ketchup, mustard and mayonnaise on the sidewalk out front resemble a Pollock painting.

When it's slow, as it is now, I watch the dune grass sway in the wind. The cop left an hour ago but I can still feel everyone's stares on my back. The accident had made its way around town before noon.

'Hey.' One pimply pre-teen interrupts my train of thought, his eyes somewhere behind my back. 'What kinda popcorn do you have?'

I direct his attention to the plastic tubs arranged to the right. 'Hi. There's the small, which is five dollars, medium is seven-fifty, large is ten and jumbo is fifteen dollars.'

'Uh-huh . . .' He contemplates the buckets for a while, mouth agape. 'How much does the jumbo hold? Compared to the large, I mean. Like approximately.'

'Sorry, I'm not sure I'm following. I can get you an approximate weight, it says it here somewhere . . .'

'Nah, I mean, like, how many?'

'In terms of kernels?'

'Yeah.'

'Um . . . Could you wait so I can ask my manager?'

'Sure, no problem,' and he is back to staring at his phone before the sentence is over.

'Stan, can you watch the front?'

Stan is lighting a fire under a copper kettle so that he can make another batch of popcorn. I head toward the back of the store, where the entrance to upstairs is.

There I find Alina, the boss's wife, alone. She is absorbed in her usual pastime: sketching new chocolates and chocolate figurines. All of them are equally ugly.

'Alina, I'm sorry. A customer wants to know how much popcorn a bucket can hold.'

She always looks at you as if you work at a nuclear reactor and have just committed a fatal error.

'What do you mean? Didn't you show him the sizes?'

'No . . . I mean yes, I did, but he's asking how many kernels . . . as in the number . . . a bucket can hold.'

'Morons. Tell him we fill the buckets to the brim. Then he can go fuck himself. No, actually, tell him he can count it and come back to let us know.'

I have to wait for her to laugh at her own joke. If I say anything of the sort I'll lose my job.

'Wait, wait . . .' she finally says. 'I'll come down with you.'

There is nothing more important to Alina than selling popcorn and candy. I attribute it to a catastrophic mix of American capitalism and Eastern European greed. We are only allowed to take the shortest breaks possible, they monitor bathroom breaks (the camera is just in front of the bathroom), and if you want to sample the saltwater taffy you can use the generous 5 percent discount. Every mistake is punished, and since I am usually the one to err, mostly in my complete failure to demonstrate enough enthusiasm for selling popcorn and candy, I am the most familiar with the punishments. I actually prefer spending my time glaring at the toilet bowl – perhaps in the company of other outcasts like myself – to pretending to care about questions such as 'How many kernels of popcorn are there in a bucket?'

All sorts of rumors are circulating about Alina, most of them true. I don't care. What annoys me is that she always schedules you to work on the days you request off. One of the first things you learn when you start the job is that Alina came from Romania ten years ago and a short time after that the boss, Sal, left his family, which – according to the only two Americans working there, a boy and a girl around fifteen – is the typical behavior of an Eastern European slut.

Sal often works with us; Alina never does. But today she is uncharacteristically gentle with me.

We simulate busyness while she deals with the customer. It's important to pretend there's work being done even when there's none. The cameras are watching. I have undertaken the sorting of two shelves under the counter where we keep bags, rubber bands, small boxes and all kinds of trinkets. I rearranged it last week, so next week I'll have to stretch my imagination and find another target. I lift my head for a moment and notice Alina staring at me.

'She died. The girl. They called an hour ago, and I wondered whether to say something, but you'll hear it somewhere anyway.'

At first I don't understand who she's talking about.

'If you want to take the day off, that's fine. You can make up your hours later.'

I wonder if it's worth telling her that this is not exactly *taking the day off*. I decide to pretend I am touched.

'What about the family?' Stan asks, having finished polishing yet another copper kettle.

Alina shrugs. 'I don't know. They didn't say. But I guess they'll call them. They'll send the body to them. That's what they usually do.'

'What about the driver?' I interject.

'The cop said she was biking with no lights on. Nothing they can do. Even if she did have lights, what are the chances of a foreigner winning in court?' Alina decides to move the boxes I have just arranged. 'They pay the insurance money, and it quiets down because no one wants to deal with courts, let alone from the other end of the world, let alone from *Moldova*.'

We're silent.

'It's big money for the family. Most of them won't ever see that much money their whole lives. I'm not saying it isn't hard . . . It's just that these things happen. You have to be realistic. At least she had insurance.' She slaps her thighs and stands up. 'Could you please rearrange these boxes? They have to go from the smallest to the largest, the lids here are full of crumbs. And also, there are ants on the fudge in storage, and it needs to be cleaned. I won't dump the entire batch, so when you're done, go to the cooler and get to it.'

Before she goes back up to the office she says over her shoulder: 'Unless you want to go home and rest. But decide fast so I can fix the schedule while I'm down here.'

I like the cooler now even though it made my skin crawl at the beginning, its silver walls and frozen vapor reminding me of the place where the psychopath keeps the chopped-up bodies in horror movies. Then I got used to the quiet and the cold, in complete contrast to the summer outside. I open the fudge box. Numerous ants are crawling in the chocolate-vanilla swirls, the big kind, the ones that bite. How did they find a way in? I feel bad killing them, so I get a jar that I shake them into with the help of a sheet of paper. I hope Alina doesn't make a surprise visit because if so, I'll be cleaning the crapper until September.

How did the girl from Moldova spend her last day? Was

she also removing ants from fudge, or was she scrubbing toilets, or frying donuts, or did she arrange magnets with names like Stacy, Katie and Ashley alphabetically? And what for: a pair of Nike shoes and Victoria's Secret underwear, to go to Vegas in September or to pay for college? Did she call her mother that day? What did they say to each other? *What are you up to, how's my father, we let the dog get out and now she's having pups, your grandmother is making preserves, your grandfather got drunk last night and got into a fight with the neighbor, we miss you, have fun, be careful, I love you.* Could they imagine where their daughter was staying? I hope their last words were just like that, humble and familiar, like the heel of warm bread with butter and colorful salt, that traditional mix of savory, paprika and other spices.

The ants bite me as I change their trajectory. I'm itchy but I keep cleaning because what else can I do? I wonder if all this – how nice it is here in the West – wasn't made up by our parents, that maybe it was just a mirage they glimpsed from behind their iron curtains.

night

The resort still roars behind us, but it will all quiet down around one, when the beach closes. In America, even nature has closing hours. We alternate between laughter, smoking and shared silence.

My father taught me the constellations. Can you see them?

Did my father teach me? Or was it my grandfather – who was actually my father's uncle but raised him, since his real father left when he was a child; I barely remember my true paternal grandfather. I like to think it was my father. I used to be crazy about the stars and the planets as a child – my room was covered in star maps, and filled with books about aliens and astrology. Now it all seems distant, like someone else's story.

I point at the sky. This is . . . I don't know the names in English. Language paralysis catches me off guard; he pulls out his phone with a smile.

I keep talking while he looks them up and translates. I lean toward him as if by accident. He smells of cigarettes, salt, faint cologne.

You probably miss them . . . How long has it been? Your grandmother?

I pull away reluctantly as he puts his phone back in his pocket.

The last time I saw her I had just gotten my driver's license, and I promised to take her to her native village so she could see her childhood home. She had begged my grandfather to do so for years, then my uncle, but they never found the time.

As if the waves have just started crashing ashore, the noise of the ocean barges into the conversation uninvited. The lights behind us go out like flames extinguished in the wind. The world sheds its skin.

I don't know if I miss them. I want to say something more but nothing comes to mind.

Lily

My mother and father say terrible things to each other. I am a baby, I don't understand words, but I can perceive the delicate vibrations of thoughts, like radiation.

My daughter needs a father, not a drunk;

I need a man, not a parasite;

One day I'll grab my bags, I'll take my child and I'll run away, I'll never look back, you hear me?

He slams the door, runs, my mother cries, he comes back, they fight, they make up.

They know her at the corner store, the woman whose sweaty red face appears in the window to buy him a bottle before his shift because his hands are shaking – he can't go to work like that, and what will people say if they see him, what will his colleagues say, what will the neighbors say. Thank God the little one doesn't understand a thing . . .

The babies cry constantly on the Pediatric Ward where she works, and her milk soaks through her scrubs. She apologizes, slips away to clean up, pumps in the lab room, in the bathroom, in the nurses' room, donates her milk. Where are you now, my milk siblings? Life is an endless cycle of washing scrubs with crusted yellow stains. No one told her that having a child would be so difficult. No one told her two doctors wouldn't even be able to afford nappies.

Sometimes when I'm colicky and crying, my mother wants to run far away and never see me again.

Sometimes she imagines taking the pillow and placing it over my face.

Sometimes she lets me cry for hours, powerless, unable to get up from her bed. Then she atones for her guilt with tears.

Now I am asleep. My father has gone to the protests – not because the prime minister has again bankrupted the country and caused hyperinflation – but because he has heard they give out free tea and coffee. They haven't had coffee in months, and the tea is still warm – he will pour it in the thermos and bring it home to make popara. They are so hungry they are either constantly constipated or have diarrhea.

'What one thing do you want to eat the most?' Later the three of us snuggle on two of the old spring mattresses, trying to keep warm.

'Freedom.'

My father laughs because he finds my mother banal. Sometimes he tells her that she speaks like a provincial poetess.

'You can't eat freedom.'

I shift between them. It's nice.

'It's not so much that I'm hungry. It's the ability to eat. If you want, you can eat; if you don't, you can starve. That's what I miss most. The freedom to choose. Now I'm only free to die.'

He embraces her, and they drift off to sleep while I dream of clouds made of bread.

My father takes to the streets to chant for democracy, equality and so on – he tells my mother he's doing it for me. She keeps quiet, telling herself over and over that she'll endure it all, if not for herself, then for the two of us. In our house everyone lives for the sake of someone else.

Both of them wonder why everything wasn't fixed after 1989, like they believed it would be. Why is tomorrow's world as empty as yesterday's . . . ? My father's face hovers right above me. I follow its changing expressions as he tells me fairy tales about the Christmas trees set on fire on the central boulevard in Sofia, Tsar Osvoboditel Boulevard; about the columns of smoke supporting the leaden sky; about the hungry crowds throwing chunks of ice at those who've gorged themselves for years.

As if they give a damn about some clowns hurling snowballs at them, my mother mutters aloud. Their lined pockets will protect them.

Dad comes home after a student blockade, he brings back bread and cheese – some old man brought them for the students – my father didn't eat his share and he gathered up the leftovers, too. This is the one and only time my mother allows the world to be lifted from her shoulders, but she is afraid to admit to herself that the lightness frightens her.

The revolution is safe on a screen. They show those arrested on TV – they march them out with plastic bags over their heads. My parents find this extremely funny, and they laugh until they cry, out of breath, hands clasping. I wave my hands and try to imitate them.

My father bounces me on his knee and sings the protest anthem to me:

Someone built you a world of gray concrete . . .

Someone made you from colorless dreams . . .

You must bravely leave a trace,

To show that you are here,

That you did not run away,

No, you did not run away . . .

Not someone, my mother thinks. *They* made up those dreams. She wants to run away more and more frequently. She's fed up with being proud of destitution.

My father puts me to bed with tales about the carnations the protestors give to the police. Carnations are for the dead, my mother adds. My father calls her a cynic and goes on to tell me about the piles of stones, about the buses and trams forming cordons, about the barricades, about the chants 'Elections! Elections!', about the siege of Parliament, about how they whisk the MPs far away from the people. The news comes live, described over the telephone, because the authorities control all video transmissions. My mother isn't surprised when a frenzied crowd storms Parliament – you can't eat propaganda.

And everyone is so hungry. During the nineties in Bulgaria, there wasn't even anything left for the cockroaches, she once told me.

My father is convinced that only good things will come from now on.

My mother opens her mouth, and her mother comes out:

'We saw them bringing "The Radiant Future for All Mankind" to fruition once, pray we don't live to see a second time.'

My father strikes back: 'For the first time, after all the humiliation, people have decided to fight for something better.'

My mother starts gathering up the dirty laundry and doesn't say that the revolution's greatest hero is the empty stomach.

4

'How come it's Bulgaria's fault that we always get shafted?'

I took the bus to work, I couldn't muster the courage to bike. I had counted on someone giving me a ride back home, but before I knew it everyone had gone. I left on foot – I don't mind walking at night, it's a good time to wander through your thoughts. When I was near the gas station, I heard someone call my name – I saw Stan waving, then splitting off from the big group he was with and running towards me to convince me to join them. They were all Bulgarians and were on their way to a party.

The gathering is at a first-generation immigrant couple's house. They live just off the main Route, in a place called Oyster Bay. Everything in the area is named after oysters: the Big Oyster restaurant, then one which is just called Oysters, then another called Oysters and Friends, the Oyster House and so on. The houses look glued together; the home of our hosts, Dancho and Sylvia, is seemingly like the rest, but crossing the threshold is like walking straight into Bulgaria: brown mats and rugs with animal prints, fridge magnets from the Belogradchik Rocks and the Black Sea, the folk singer Slavi Trifonov blaring from the TV. Everyone is hugging and kissing, the living room is a buzzing hive of languages. I immediately pick up Macedonian and Serbian, Romanian, Russian, Ukrainian, Polish . . . there are probably over fifty people in the house. I grab a bottle of beer to blend in with the crowd and join three men and one woman in the kitchen – their group is closest to the door and farthest away from the TV; everyone is talking at the same time, which means I won't have to say much. They are in the middle of a conversation and pay me little mind. I join as the baldest of the three men is talking. They're rehashing history, or at least their own version of it, the endless game of who's to blame for our country's demise – the Communists, the Ottomans, the Byzantines . . . 'Why should I spend my whole life feeling guilty that I didn't steal for five centuries, while others stole from me?'

'I'm not saying it's our fault. I'm just saying this is how things turned out. The strong and the weak. It will only change if we all die out. Hi, my name is Emil, Emo.' He startles me by stretching his hand toward me as a greeting. He looks around thirty and is wearing a shirt and jeans like all the other guys there. Most of the women are in ultra-short dresses.

'Yana,' I reply.

'This is Dancho' – the baldie whose tirade I have interrupted lifts his can to say cheers – 'Sylvia and Chris.'

Sylvia directs her greeting at the huge soy sauce stain on my jeans. Chris drawls out a *Hi*. He is also balding, but has the face of a thirteen-year-old – he looks like a cartoon character. Sylvia reminds me of the seagulls that eat fries on the boardwalk. Her nose takes up the majority of her face, her eyes are slightly slanted, even her voice reminds me of that prolonged *yeow, yeow*.

'So? You one of the new ones? First year? How's it going?' Emo asks.

'I don't know. How is it supposed to be going?'

'Where do you work?' Sylvia chimes in.

I say the name of the restaurant and the store. Sylvia is one of those people who loves to talk and knows everyone. I feel at ease with people like her because I don't need to do much other than add fuel to the conversation with the occasional: 'Oh, really?', 'And where is he from?', 'And what did she do after that?' and the like. The usual questions follow: do you know this person, do you know that person, what about their cousin, plus a detailed description of the people in question. I always wonder if anyone can tell how ill at ease I feel, if everyone thinks I am a complete tool.

'Where do you live?' she continues.

I won't get away until I am added to her address book, so I oblige her.

'Is it something organized, or?'

'It's Tony's house,' Emo adds.

'Aah, Tony's. And so, how is it at Tony's?'

'Like everywhere else, I assume.' I shrug. 'A bit far, but no big deal.'

Tony is something of a legend. Instead of doing shitwork – no one says it openly, but we're all doing shitwork – he managed to graduate from the local university and now works as a programmer in one of the bigger towns in the state. Every Friday he arrives with his car filled to the brim with beer and snacks so that he can drink and smoke weed with my roommates until he passes out on the filthy living room couch, where I find him in the morning. Sometimes his girlfriend comes along, a pretty, thin girl who always ends up upsetting him. Every night ends with everyone awkwardly slipping away from the table while he yells at her and she looks at her feet. Tony frightens and repulses me. I feel that his life is frozen in an eternal *brigade*, which is what we call the Summer Work and Travel program. Our parents and grandparents used the same word to describe the forced student labor demanded from them by the Communist Party: *brigada*.

'Yo, didn't a car crash happen near that house yesterday?' Dancho joins in. Everyone's ears perk up.

'It did.'

'The Moldovan?'

'Aaah, yeah, yeah, Nelly told me.' Sylvia takes the reins. 'They worked together at the store. They didn't know each other, I mean, but everyone is shocked. She was a pretty girl.'

Would it be more bearable if she were ugly? I don't say anything.

'Some girl saw it, the cops went to . . . Hey, was that you? You work there! And you live there . . .'

I hesitate for a second, thinking about lying – no, it wasn't me – but then I imagine her grilling me for the next half hour, trying to figure out who exactly it was.

'Yes.'

'Jeez . . . And so what happened? Are you all right? What did you see?' Another beer hisses in Dancho's hands.

'Ugh, we don't ask those kinds of questions, you . . .' Sylvia slaps him on the shoulder. 'Sorry, he's a bit like that, a little wild . . .'

'No worries. I didn't see a thing. I got there after it happened.'

'Ugh, that sucks. And it happens every year, I mean . . . This is why I always tell my students, when I explain about the house, that it's not near the highway so it's safer.' Sylvia scans me from head to toe. 'You . . . If you want, I have too many people here now, but at some point, if something comes up, you can move in. To be honest, I am an *exceptionally* good judge of people . . .'

There's eight of us at Tony's house. How many have they got crammed in here?

'. . . and I'm talking quiet, clean people,' Sylvia rambles on. 'Although we also like to party, as you can see, we get together, with our people . . .'

'How did you end up here?' Maneuvering the conversation away from me is difficult, I have to scream over the pop-folk songs (*I am hell and heaven, I am a master and a slave*) to avoid Sylvia's next question. Emo laughs.

'What? Did I say something wrong? I apologize, if . . .' I try to take back my words.

'Nah, no, don't be silly. No worries.' He giggles.

'We clean, we have a cleaning company, we're the owners. With Dancho,' Sylvia says proudly.

Dancho interrupts her: 'You see, Emo laughs every time someone asks, because our situation is such a . . .' Sylvia looks at him from the corner of her eye. 'What? Whaddya want?'

He sips from the can, then points to Emo. 'He and I are high school friends from Karnobat, we graduated in 2002. And Sylvia, she's from there too, that's how I know her, high school sweethearts' – she shoots me a sugary smile – 'then he won a green card and moved here, we came on a brigade one summer and the following one . . . and finally decided to stick around. Like everyone does.'

'Emo and I are married,' Sylvia tells me and points to a faded photo on the fridge. She and Emo are hugging and laughing – she's wearing a white dress.

I feel like I must have misunderstood. I start to say something, but Emo intervenes: 'This picture has to be there, so everyone can see it and in case there's a surprise inspection. Get it? Do you get what the deal is?' He glares at me. It must be obvious that I don't get it. 'Not that we don't all know each other and each other's business, so it's not an issue and we're open about it, we're honest people. You see, if you marry someone and live together for five years, then you can divorce and they can keep their citizenship. And then these two will figure things out on their own. Of course, this is 'cause Dancho is my best friend, I've known him since we were born. I wouldn't marry just anyone, you know.'

'Buy one, get three free.' Dancho cackles.

'Otherwise the going rate for a marriage is around ten grand.' Chris ogles me.

'Cut it out, dickhead,' Dancho tells him. 'You'll have to pay someone to marry your ass, if it comes to that. The poor girl would have to be pretty damn desperate.'

'That's not true, Chris,' Sylvia consoles him. 'Jeez, you get so nasty sometimes, you know! Man, I freaking love this song!' She leaps toward the center of the living room with hands in the air, snapping her fingers.

'For real, if something frees up here, you can move in. We have about twenty students, four or five people per room, but it's close to town. I don't know if anything will, but it could . . . In the small room there's two, in the big one six, in the other bedroom three more . . . But if you want, you can clean with us. Ten bucks, no taxes, nothing. Instead of working for these American morons, you can make good money. Not do their dirty work for pennies.'

'C'mon now, for pennies,' Emo interrupts.

'Damn straight, I won't do their shitty jobs for them . . . I'd rather work for myself.'

'So what if you won't do it? There's ten more who'll do it and who will keep their mouths shut while they're at it. Or Latinos'll come and do it three times faster and twice as cheap. That's why there are Miguels, Angelos and Josés everywhere. Because of people like you.'

'Fuck 'em! That's because they come from some godforsaken tropical swamp full of bugs! They can work for five cents an hour if they want. I've seen them, I've hired Latinos before, can't clean a toilet to save their lives. In the end I always have to send one of ours, we're the best cleaners and that's the truth.

Anyway, I'm not having them exploit me, I'm not a n

They've told us not to use that word, but no one cares. With a nod I leave them. As I walk around the house, I overhear bits and pieces of the ongoing conversations. Everyone seems happy. The heavy make-up on their faces and the lacquered curls, the slightly overdone shine and glitter give their backgrounds away. There is something strange about this house, about all these people who have transposed the Balkan way of life to this foreign space. All of a sudden I understand why a faint déjà vu has troubled me all night – I feel as if I'm at a high school party. The drowsy drumming of the voices grows into threatening noise. I'm relieved to find an empty porch.

I've noticed everyone insists on the proper pronunciation of their birth names. 'Stan' was imposed on Stanislav by Alina, but the poor guy always clarifies: *My name is not Stan but Stanislav*. Who gives a shit? I have two names: Yana and *Jane*. I can feel the distance growing between the two, like a conversation between friends that dries up over time.

No one calls the girl by her name. They call her The One Who Got Hit, The Dead Girl. Are her friends here? Does anyone use her name, or has she been transformed into something new, into gossip? The cold ocean breeze whistles across the neck of my beer bottle. Crickets chirp in the grass. The wind's embrace brings a crushing nostalgia for every voice, smell and touch that my mind has possessed for even a moment, before being let go forever; nostalgia for the life that's passed so far, a life that is still trickling by with every second, running like sand through my fingers.

night

When I was a child, I would often watch my grandmother repot flowers. She had green fingers. She would plant her seedlings in old plastic yogurt containers that we were always collecting at home until they formed high towers, which were then shipped to the countryside.

She would grasp the young plant by the stem and shake it with a gentle movement until the dirt loosened in the pot. Then she would tilt the pot sideways and deftly pull the stem up, with a dark lump in the shape of the pot hanging from it. She would clean off the old dirt, and roots would emerge from the brown-black clump. She would then place the plants carefully in holes in the garden or in larger pots she had prepared in advance.

Some of them had strong roots, others were frail, like a single strand of human hair. My grandmother never gave up when it came to her flowers: after repotting or being moved to another corner of the garden, some that had dried out would become unrecognizable; others would droop for a week or two, then get used to their new surroundings and return to growth; it happened rarely, but sometimes one would die, and my grandmother would not be able to hide her anger when explaining that they couldn't get used to the new soil for some reason, no matter what she did.

The first few days, weeks, months in a new place are like repotting. The banal: being able to ask someone on the street for the time or where something is, striking up a conversation with a stranger, knowing how to read your electricity bill, bumping into an acquaintance at the market, knowing exactly what there is at the store, listening to the news on the bus driver's radio – all of it is your soil without you knowing it. And as you roam the streets uprooted, you glance through the windows of houses and wonder how it is possible that these people have lived here their entire lives, beside their neighbors who are also locals; how can anyone know by heart the names of these local schools and the way to these workplaces? And the news here is different, the ads, even the trash is sorted differently. The foreign is most visible in the familiar: grocery stores, hospitals, administrative buildings.

In America I understood for the first time that knowing a language is not only a door to the world, as my grandmother used to say, but also a prison. I talk to cleaners and dishwashers who turn out to be teachers or nurses paralyzed by a foreign language they can barely speak, with a heavy accent. Among their own they laugh loudly, they flirt with their long lashes, and they toss their heads back coquettishly, showing off their plunging necklines; among Americans they shrivel, stammering in a reedy voice, eyes on their feet. The same happens to the men, who look down on everything foreign with spiteful contempt, while the bitterness of their ignorance pools in their mouths, only to end up on the sidewalk as heavy, hocked spittle.

If I were a plant, my roots would be thin, like silken hairs. I thought the poor, barren soil was to blame. All I needed was to be replanted. The older I get, the more I worry that the place isn't the problem.

Yana

The last time I see my grandmother and my grandfather is before my departure, when I leave my cat with them. It's sad that I have to run away from people in order to love them.

They never allowed me to grow up. Or maybe I didn't allow myself to. As I step into their apartment, the years melt away and I am nine again, it's always summer, time stretching into an endless day, like back when my grandfather would lock me inside the house as a child while they canned produce in their 'villa', if you could call the *lozé* that: a dilapidated house with adjacent vineyards or *lozi*, hence the name. He did this because he was paranoid that I would escape, that I would go slutting around with boys, and he couldn't be raising a whore. I watched from the balcony as kids gathered in front of the apartment building, and we would agree to meet when I could finally come out and play, and I always optimistically promised the earliest possible time that I could expect freedom, around five thirty or six. But the old people never came back on time, something always held them up. I would go out at nine, sometimes ten o'clock, when the games were already in full swing and an extra person was a nuisance, an interruption requiring boring questions like which team I should join and whether the game needed to be restarted. In the end I just stopped going out. But I still remember those torturous three to four hours, when the sun melted into the horizon and the city gave a cool sigh of relief as people flocked to benches and gazebos.

The apartment hasn't changed a bit from my childhood, from my mother's childhood – the familiar stuffiness seizes me, and I must force a smile, embrace my grandfather, leave my bags in the bedroom.

'He doesn't think you should go to America at all,' my grandmother says. 'He's worried that the plane will fall from the sky on the way there.'

The table bends under the weight of the food. Food and objects fill the hole where their warmth should be. I stuff my face and keep quiet. I have developed the habit of not listening to them. After the third shot of *rakia*, the fruit brandy my grandfather makes himself, like any self-respecting Bulgarian, he starts lamenting my uncle's fate. After the fifth shot – his own. The Communists are to blame for everything.

'He could've been a soldier, they can't find any soldiers now, no one wants to be a soldier, fuck 'em, fuck 'em all. A fucking cop makes more money than a soldier. And the cop is at home with his wife, sitting next to her bare arse. You, you don't know shit, you haven't served . . .'

He speaks in a heavy north-western Bulgarian dialect – the words fall harder, vowels agape. My grandmother has been embarrassed by him her whole life. Or at least I used to think so. When I was little, I thought she forced herself to laugh at his words. Now I am not so sure.

'You're speaking rubbish,' she cuts in. 'For twenty years I've walked back and forth between the clinic and the barracks, for work . . . So I know what they were like back then . . . And now they say "Oh, it used to be like this, it used to be like that . . ." Lemme tell you how it really was: a high-ranking officer showed up, a Communist who was in charge of a pig farm. My co-worker disappeared, so I followed 'er, I saw 'er taking the officer and leading 'im from the room. And what was that about? Turns out this top brass couldn't stand the sight of blood. He got sick, started staggering around. There was a bench in the hallway, and I went to him: "Good job, savior of Bulgaria! Are you going to faint? And here we thought that you, an officer, were meant to lead us!"'

'A real man, a real man, a real man . . .' My grandfather's fist continues to pound on the table.

In my memories they always talk like that: telling parallel stories, simultaneously, but never speaking to each other. Two versions of the same life.

'I went to the Military School in Shumen, they went and sent me, four of us, I figure.' He pours himself another shot; my grandmother sucks on a chicken bone. 'And the platoon commander came around: "Spassov, they'll ship you off 'morrow, come to us an' we can get you dressed." But before all that – gymnastics, you don't know what it's like to be a soldier and you see the kind of warm-ups they made us do, for the love of Christ . . . And I got scared, I thought to myself: *Why don't you go and fuck yourself* . . . And I took off running. Straight home. And my dad asked me: "Ignat, what in God's name happened?" "Dad, tatko, listen, it's like this . . ." But boy, did he jump on me! "I'll take this stick and break your head with it!" And he brought me right back.'

'He was the grandson of a tsarist officer, your grandfather. His grandfather was a royal officer,' my grandmother says proudly and grabs another bone.

'Who the fuck wasn't a tsarist officer!' he barks. Then he continues unperturbed: 'Y'know where they sent me? Border guard, nineteen months at the Greek border. It wasn' like the usual army bases. Down there, it's like a restaurant, there's women who bring you food!' He looks at me, disappointment swimming in his watery gaze. I am not impressed, I don't ask him anything. He dismisses me with a wave: 'You're young, 's hard for you to understand all this, I reckon. Bein' a soldier, now that's where you learn discipline, not doing what you want but what you've been told!'

He gets lost in the past for a moment. I get lost in my thoughts.

'I could've been a major . . .' Seventh shot. 'Had I stayed in artillery school, waited it out 'til I was forty-five, now I'm eighty . . . How many years ago would I have retired? But you couldn' just do whatever you wanted back then . . . The real pricks, they came from Western Thrace, on the Aegean. There was this Georgi Stamatov, a commie partisan, a *pustiniak*, a waste of space. When he even bothered to come to school, he was too lazy to study, and the French teacher, her husband a lawyer before the changes, rich, well they took away his property. And she was a good woman, a kind woman! There used to be these coal stoves in high schools . . . And Stamatov, he would kick the stove, the pipes would come crashing down and the stove would choke, and the woman couldn' do her classes. Years later . . . I met the same guy at the gas station. Four stars! A decorated captain! Now, you tell me, how does somethin' like this happen? Only now does it come to me that they were doin' it on purpose, to torture this woman, on account of her husband . . . When I saw him – him, a captain! – everything shriveled up inside . . . And I was thinking – I should've made colonel way before him! But I wasn' a piece of shit. In this country, to have power you have to be a piece of shit.'

'What kind of colonel could you've been with a fascist wife!' my grandmother interrupts him with a forced laugh.

'A fascist . . .' He points at her as if it's the first time I've met her. 'Fascists, her father and her uncle! What fascists, goddammit, what fascists, tell me . . . Accountants! Her father was in the reserves, even joined the kolkhoz, but it didn't work . . . And so they write it down, there, they write it down: there's one here, he's on the shitlist! And his kids – they're on the shitlist! But their kids . . . take any one of them, may be the dumbest fucker you've ever seen, but at least he isn't on the shitlist! So it'll be him we'll get for the job.'

He's drunk. I can still taste the childhood fear that prevents me from joining the conversation, from revealing my thoughts, from leaving the table.

'Fuckin' interesting lot, these people' – he turns to me as if I have reminded him of something – 'America . . . There's a guy, a chemistry teacher, damned if I know where, he graduated university but both his father and his mother were commies, active resistance. And now, their grandchildren – both in America! And he was the Party's point man in charge of the Momin Brod collective farm! And I've been tellin' him: "Listen, there's fodder for the animals delivered here, but lots has been stolen! Whatcha doin' here?" And he'd turn to me, grinning, and he'd say: "Hold up, now, what am *I* doing? What're *you* doing is more like it!" And now, can you imagine, both his daughters're over there, and isn't he there, too, in America! The fuck he doin' there? But he was a Communist, y'know, a father in the resistance! A Bulgarian can switch between three hundred parties! Everyone just wants to be in charge!' My grandfather's giant hand falls down on the table and the cutlery rings in unison. 'Fascist, Communist, no difference. Everyone wants to crack the whip and make you work while he watches! It's the same all over the world. But these other nations, Americans, English, they're more . . . they've killed so many people, slaves, and Spaniards, too. But they have laws. They have police. They've an army!'

He stares into the jug – there's a bit of wine left at the bottom. After a brief internal struggle he pours it into the same glass from which he drank his rakia. Slowly his words start to get entangled, to trip on his tongue, and his head droops to his chest.

I look at my grandmother who nods at me to save myself – now or never. I quietly slip away from the table – he's deaf anyway, he can't hear, even when you're screaming at him; she follows at my heels. While I get ready for bed she tells me her stories in the usual way, as if for the first time. Does she really forget, or is she engraving her legacy upon my memory? Her silhouette draws an outline on the colorful wallpaper. She has told me that she waited for nice wallpaper her entire life – everything was in dull, ugly colors, as if for a funeral home.

When I was a child, I pictured Communists as huge monsters with sharp teeth and tentacles, with twenty ears that could hear everything, and nine brains – like octopuses have multiple hearts – with which they remembered and knew everything. I feared them, then I hated them in a childish way, the way only a parent can teach you to hate what you don't understand. I wonder if two days from now, when I step onto the plane for America, I will board alone or if they will all flock around me – my grandmother and grandfather, their fascist *kulak* parents, my grandmother's grandmother who died when they burned the churches . . .

I approach the check-in desk, place my heavy bag on the conveyor belt and, by force of habit, stare at the scale reading that is supposed to tell me everything is fine. The digits rise slowly, then speed up: 10, 15, 20 – I am above the allowed 21 kilograms – 30, 75, 100, 187, 200, 260, 400 . . . The employee looks at me in surprise, and I panic. I say that I have no idea what is going on, probably some issue with the scale; she doesn't hear me, the digital counter goes nuts: 2,000, 3,000, 5,000 . . .

We'll have to open the bags, she tells me coldly.

Of course, I have nothing to hide, I really don't understand, I mumble as her experienced hands search for the pink suitcase's zippers. She turns it toward herself, opens it, and her top half disappears into its gaping mouth. A second later she pulls out my grandfather, who starts looking around the airport and cursing. Then my grandmother emerges, dragging after her all her cousins, uncles and aunts whom I know from her stories; then she pulls out my uncle, who says the only thing I ever remember hearing him say: *Do you know, Yana, that children aren't people? Before turning fifteen, children aren't people . . .* His voice echoes in the airport, people turn around and shoot me disapproving looks, and all of a sudden there are hundreds and thousands of bodies around me, they've all come from the suitcase, and I shrink, I look at the glass behind the check-in desk and see that I am no older than ten years old.

We can't let you travel to America, the woman from the desk tells me. *You'll have to stay. You're too young. Do you have a parent or a guardian? Go home.*

I hear my childish voice trying to convince her that this is impossible, that I don't even need all this luggage, that I'll get new clothes, whatever it takes.

You can't travel because you're not a person, she cuts me off, and I answer that there is no way I am not a person because I even have a visa, I passed an interview at the American embassy, would she like to see my passport? And I start searching for my passport, but I can't find it, it isn't in the pocket of my jacket, maybe in my purse, but my purse is gone and all of a sudden I realize I am stark naked, everyone who has come out of the suitcase is looking at me, embarrassing me in front of the people at the airport while the woman tells me again that I cannot travel, and I scream back at her that I am a person and I have a visa.

I startle – I've dozed off. My grandmother hasn't even noticed, lost in the embroidery of her stories.

night

She told us one story more than any other: that she loved only one man in her life. And this man wasn't my grandfather.

This man's name appears somewhere between the tales about the hellish life after 1944 and the hellish life after her wedding.

They gathered the livestock for the collective farm and left them behind a fence in the middle of the field, with no heat or food. They bellowed for days – the entire village was listening and everyone was waiting for someone else to take action first. The bravest ones killed their cattle before having to give them away. Her father couldn't bring himself to do it.

They set the church on fire. My great-great-grandmother – a God-fearing village woman, with only a fourth-grade education – watched the church burn and cried, repeating over and over that sacred places mustn't be destroyed.

They managed to save three icons, wrapped in white cloths embroidered by the village women. Once upon a time such cloths were used on holy days, to collect food and money as offerings. My great-great-grandmother took to her bed, holding the cloth-wrapped icons close to her chest, never letting go; the cloths turned gray and she was no longer able to recognize her nearest ones – her mind had crossed over and left her body behind. She called the saints depicted on the icons by her grandchildren's names. They buried her with the icons. It's good she didn't live to see her last surviving son sent off to the Belene labor camps.

Recently she told me about the other man again. I was here, on the beach, just like we are now, it was windy and people were out flying kites. There were plenty of grandparents with their grandchildren. And, you know, usually she does the talking. I can't translate this world to her, it's too foreign, too real, too present. We meet only in the past.

5

'Bulgaria? Wasn't that in Russia?' The red face grins idiotically.

Who the hell wears flip-flops to a restaurant? This place is the American idea of elegance, a portrait of Queen Victoria to top it off, with a Sharpie mustache drawn on her upper lip – the servers scribble on her; the manager Greg cleans her up. The interior is dark pink and green, the colors you would find in the stomach of a cow. But as far as the locals and the tourists are concerned, the prestige of the place is indisputable – the Victorian surroundings are proof of a *fine dining establishment*. The big shots from the surrounding states reserve rooms with an ocean view in the adjoining hotel – where they can die under medical supervision. The last such client was a fifty-six-year-old woman. They brought her up to her room with an automatic crane, rented especially for the occasion, because she didn't fit in the elevator. This is the first time I have seen people dying from abundance.

'No,' I answer with a rattle-brained smile, mastered to perfection. 'It's close to Turkey. But it's a former Communist state.'

Communism – guaranteed exoticism in America.

'Oh, Turkey? Then it's in Africa.'

I thought these people only existed on TV. I can barely keep myself from looking around in search of a hidden camera.

'No, sir, but you've got the hemisphere right at least. Turkey is in Asia, on the border with Europe. And Bulgaria is just on the edge, the Iron Curtain went right through it.'

'How interesting!' his wife joins in. Do they think that the Iron Curtain is an actual curtain made of iron? 'George and I met a girl the other day, at the T-shirt shop . . . where was she from?' While she thinks, the busser comes and pours them ice water. Bussers rarely speak English, not that they need to, their job is just to carry plates around and pour water. Sometimes I'm jealous of them.

'Thank you, darling.' She goes on: 'From Moldova? Or Slovenia? Or maybe Slovakia?'

'Whatever. There's many of your kind around here.'

'Yes, sir, it's a summer program. We work in the summer, and then we travel around America before going home. Cultural exchange.'

It would be much more unpleasant if I said cleaning toilets or washing dishes in America . . . I use the official government name. Their eyes light up.

'I can only wish you the best of times in the best country in the world, young lady!' He winks at me. 'I myself should travel more, to be honest. There's always something to see.'

'Yes, we are lucky, there's so much to see here. Plus, they probably pay you better . . .' Her eyes flash with the contemptuous compassion of the fool. Suddenly I think of the ghetto

I pass by on my bike every morning, the black kids perched on porches like crows.

'Yeah . . . Well, call me if you need anything. Enjoy your lunch!'

They always ask *Where do you come from?* Some have never even heard of such a place and some have been to Eastern Europe years ago, for work, and they ate the best feta cheese and tomatoes of their lives; everything was so cheap they couldn't believe their eyes; the people were poor but hospitable; the natural landscape left them breathless, even though it was horribly dirty. Gradually I get to know the clientele: Delaware is a flat mosaic of beaches and chicken farms, its low taxes mainly attracting retirees and a variety of legal and not-quite-so-legal companies. The big leaguers gather either at the Country Club, a bit further inland, or at Selmer's Victorian Hotel. Mr Selmer often visits the restaurant, depleting its stock of Pinot Gris without paying a dime, while telling the personnel how his parents and other real Americans like them have made our American dream come true.

With the exception of George and his wife, the place is empty. The piano is in the no man's land between the dining room and the bar. As in every small town, there's one of everything: one photographer, one musician, one painter, all of whom have no choice but to be famous. Every weekday, the local music star John plays, the quality of his performance deteriorating as the line of whiskey glasses placed on the lid grows. After the fourth drink Greg usually announces that John has exhausted his repertoire and puts an end to the live show.

When it's warm out, John plays on the terrace, a debatable choice when one considers the goal of attracting customers.

The servers Tim – the only American who works here, if we don't count Ken, the bartender – and Laz are folding napkins on one of the tables at the highest of the restaurant's three levels. The bussers are gathered in front of a cupboard on the second level where they are polishing silverware and tossing it into the drawers. The clear metallic ringing measures the time passing. I am ready: the flowers in the little vases have been changed, candles are lit, the reservation list has been updated. The portable phone is in my back pocket in case someone calls for room service. I am getting better with the menu, I don't have as hard a time understanding people on the phone, and I am learning more about the food. All my life I have eaten only five spices: salt, pepper, savory, paprika and mint, in four elements – dough, rice, potatoes and meat. And now, all of a sudden, so many new smells, names, combinations – I had never heard of such foods before. I build this new vocabulary through taste, not through my native tongue: each aroma, color, texture – a new word.

I lazily direct myself toward the low hum of the bar. The TV is always on, maybe muted if there are more patrons, as if everyone is possessed by the fear of missing out on something important, of remaining isolated from mass fury or joy. Ken is wiping glasses behind the bar, eyes glued to the screen.

'Hey.' He smiles at me, his eyes exhibiting a rare calm. Tim has told me he takes coke. Indeed, Ken's gestures become more chaotic as the night goes on, his enthusiasm for talking to customers morphing into awkward extroversion. In the afternoon, we set aside about ten of the pink napkins so that he can wipe his sweaty head when the bar fills up. Alcohol, heroin, cocaine – at first it was scary, but I don't care anymore. Everyone's high on something in America.

'Hi, Ken.' I lean on the bar. 'What are you watching?'

'Oh, just some bullshit.' He places the wiped glass above the bar and grabs another. 'We missed the debates last night, it was busy. I'm catching up on who said what shit.'

'They were the most-watched debates in history. That's what I read.' Tim comes in, balancing a huge tower of folded napkins. 'Where do you want these?'

'Really? How many?'

'Twenty-four mil, I think. Something like that.'

'Go figure!'

'OK, tell me where to leave these.'

Ken points to the POS station. Tim doesn't miss a chance to mess with me: 'Hands off the bar, or they'll slap us with a fine before you know it!'

I shouldn't even touch the bar – I'm not twenty-one yet. The camera centers on a blond man with a bright fake tan. I don't know where I recognize him from.

'That pig . . .' Lazlo joins us as well. 'I watched videos online, I can't believe a hick like that could be part of presidential debates in this country. Even we don't have dumbasses like that.'

'Who is he?' I ask. It annoys me that I can't be part of the conversation.

'Trump.' Tim leans on the sink near Ken. He hasn't had a drink yet, his blue eyes are clear. His hairline is receding, but a halo of white, fluffy hair surrounds the rest of his head. He must be around sixty, if not more.

'Have you heard of Trump? His wife's one of yours.' He laughs.

'She's not one of ours.' Lazlo the Hungarian takes offense. 'She's Slovenian. Or Slovakian. Whatever.'

Tim bursts out laughing. 'You the same guy who talked my ear off about the differences between Romanians and Hungarians?'

Lazlo is one of those people whom there's no talking to unless you share his opinion. He digs his hand into the bowl of mint chocolates behind the bar and starts eating them one by one, tossing the wrappers back in the bowl.

'Hey, easy there, asshole.' Ken laughs.

'They gave him the most airtime.' Tim looks at the TV pensively. Sometimes I wonder how Tim ended up working here, why he stays. He doesn't fit in. He turns to me, smiles: 'If you need to know one thing about America, it's that TV wins you the election.'

'As if that's not the case everywhere,' Ken chimes in.

'It isn't,' I dare to say. 'In some places people still just waste ink.'

On top of everything, Lazlo always argues just to argue: 'Bullshit! Maybe before, but it isn't like that now. At least it's not that bad . . . You're young, you haven't lived under Communism so you don't know what you're talking about.'

The Communism card is the ace up every Balkan person's sleeve, proof of the supremacy of their suffering. Even if Lazlo lived during that time, I doubt he remembers much of it. I roll my eyes, making sure he can see me, and shift my attention back to Tim: 'What does he want? Trump, I mean.'

'To make America great again,' he answers. I can't tell if he's joking or not. 'No one knows what he wants.'

'Doesn't matter, 'cause no one's gonna vote for him anyway,' Ken adds.

'Don't be so sure.' Lazlo shakes his head. 'People like Welch will put him in office in no time.'

The manager Mr Welch has worked for Selmer's for at least twenty years, most of which has been spent in a service room-turned-office in the underground car park. Inside there's a desk, a chair and a cork board with millions of documents and paper notes pinned to it with thumb tacks. The room doesn't have any windows, so the smoke from Welch's permanently lit cigarette hangs from the ceiling and gathers in clouds in the corners like a poisonous spiderweb.

'Welch? But he's the one who hires . . .' I start.

'Welch is an old-school Republican.' Tim winks at me in response. 'Do you know what a Republican is? Don't worry, they don't either . . . Anyway, here, on the seaside, most of them are rich and pro-business . . . But you know, profits make a business, and there's no profit if you're paying and insuring white Americans – you'll be paying benefits out your ass. So immigrants wipe American asses and plates, build the roads and collect the garbage, so then someone like this guy here' – Tim nods to the TV – 'can spew bullshit.'

'Still, so many are out of a job and barely making ends meet,' Ken says. 'No offense, Jane, but why can't an American girl, one of ours, do your job?'

I shake my head, I am not offended. It makes sense to me.

'Because American girls don't want to do Jane's job. And Welch won't be able to treat them the way he treats Jane,' Tim replies.

'Tim, what if he comes . . .' Lazlo cranes his neck and looks toward the hallway, then the other way, toward the exit.

'He can come in here for all I care, he can suck my dick.' Tim snorts, but still lowers his voice. 'Welch's paying at least twenty people under the table, off the books. And that's how he keeps them, making them work overtime without pay, because if they don't keep quiet he'll kick them out. If they don't want to work, they can go try their luck elsewhere, he'll find others. Who knows if someone will hire them after him, not everyone hires illegals, and if they lose their job . . .'

The door that separates the bar from the hotel opens – bits of conversation filter in from the hall. The sous-chef Norma's husband Almandeto greets us with his strong accent and tell us that they have to clean the carpet before the second shift starts at four. I turn around one last time before I leave. Almandeto is holding the door for the cleaning girls who enter one by one. Most of them are Latina.

I half-close the door to the bar and head toward George, who wants more bread.

Eva

Sometimes I call my grandmother after my shift – it's four or five o'clock in the morning there. She tries to convince me that she's always gotten up this early. The conversation usually starts with a news announcement. Everything that she describes as news I have already read several days ago online. I never tell her.

'Your grandfather's completely panicked because of the TV, but, to be honest, I look at these refugees now, these folks, I look at them and somehow I can't wrap my head around it. And on the news they talk about disease, infections . . . Once upon a time we were like that, too, your great-grandmother – they were war refugees, from Serbia, Romania . . . I remember when we moved from the countryside to the city . . . at first they looked at us like we were outsiders, no one greets you, no one helps you. But I don't know . . . these folks don't belong here . . .'

'You've told me that, Nana,' I say.

You've told me everything.

* * *

The other man's name was Ivan. He was the adopted child of refugees – after the second Balkan War redrew the borders,

Bulgarians from Bosilegrad suddenly woke one day in a part of Serbia, unwanted in what was now a foreign country. The Spanish flu came for anyone the Serbs couldn't get their hands on, and so Ivan's adoptive father and his two little brothers were left as orphans. Then cholera took those brothers, and Ivan's father apprenticed in the neighboring villages until he grew up and met the woman he would marry. Their children died one after the other and were buried by their mother under the linden tree in their yard, and the sweet smell of honey and hardship smothered the entire village until the Gypsies came and picked the tree bare, carrying the heavy blossoms away to the markets. In the end, the couple took Ivan in.

You and I, son, may not share the same blood, but we share the same fate, his father used to tell him.

One spring as they were leading oxen across a ford in the Tsibritsa, the river swelled and carried both his adoptive parents away. Ivan buried their empty clothes.

* * *

That night in the graveyard, he could have done anything with her, but he didn't even try once. That's how she starts her story, every time.

But she wants him to try, just so she can tell him no. The moon shines like a coin in the dust of the scant clouds. She tries to catch up to him, shorten the distance between them.

They enter the village cemetery. In small places like these, everyone knows by heart where the living and the dead are, so their feet lead them. He cleans the graves, whispers something to them that she doesn't hear.

'They raised me on work and honor, they didn't have nothing else,' he says.

They stand and look at the tombstones. She wants to touch him but she doesn't dare.

'Eva, I'm going to run away,' he says after a while.

She doesn't respond.

'I'm going to Europe, somewhere . . . I thought, after everything . . . I thought something would change after the war.' He shakes his head. 'Peace isn't built on blood. These people are just the same as the others.'

She doesn't understand.

'Gradually you become what you fight against.'

There's no crickets chirping, not a whisper of a wind.

'Ivan, what . . .' she finally says.

'Come with me. It'll only get worse here. You can see it, so many people . . . You can see it . . . And your father . . .'

'What about my mother?'

'Later, when you and I figure it out, we'll send for them.'

Impossible. Her father would never leave the village.

'I don't know . . .'

'Think about it.'

She reaches out to him, takes his hand. They kiss. Time stops for a moment, but then starts back up again, a wind blows in from somewhere, scattering the clouds. The trees' naked branches pierce the sky and the light of a thousand stars trickles through the holes.

'You need a boy with a mother and a father,' her mother proclaims the next day, when she shares what has happened with her. My grandmother doesn't keep secrets from her.

'Mama . . .'

'With a mother and a father.' She is unrelenting. 'One who won't try splitting you from your family. When folks don't have roots, it's easy for them to always be running back and forth.'

'Mama, I love him,' she dares to say.

Her mother doesn't even look at her, she just scoffs.

'Go and get me my yarn from the chest,' she says, 'and see where your brother is.'

My grandmother obeys. Her mother's voice reaches her as she's about to close the door: 'With a mother and a father, you hear me? Don't be talking nonsense and no more fooling around with this boy.'

* * *

In the next few days, her father is supposed to be returned to them. My great-grandmother kneads sorrowful ritual breads, but the flour is bad and they come out doughy. There are no more pigs to feed, so in those hungry post-war years she takes a sin onto her soul every time a loaf is thrown in the trash. My grandmother's father was crippled. He couldn't go to war and so he became a wartime mayor – and with that, without his knowledge, a fascist. His refusal to join the kolkhoz didn't help, even though he was a conscript and had done his state labor.

The sound of it: returning home from concentration camp. They set off to retrieve him at five in the morning in the ox cart. They looked like a funeral procession, all dressed in black. Her brother, heartbroken that they wouldn't bring him along, has been given a slap goodbye. My great-grandmother doesn't know what she'll find, she's afraid of the child seeing something bad – boys must respect their fathers.

The locomotive pants as it enters the train station; my grandmother feels as if it takes an eternity to stop. Smiling faces protrude from the windows, numerous hands stretch out toward the sky, looking like naked branches. Finally it halts, the doors open with a bang; bags, sacks, baskets tumble out from inside, squawking and cries fill the air. You can tell families like theirs from afar, those waiting for the Party's shipment, because they are standing apart from the crowd. Eva feels like a black-and-white cut-out sloppily glued onto summer's hot colors. There're no embraces, no tears, no kisses; no customary baskets full of brazenly ripe grapes.

The train station empties out – the only people left are a few locals. It's quiet. In the doorway not a person but a memory appears. Her mother lets out a scream, her uncle rushes in to support the skeleton that falls from the train, groans, and begs them not to hold him up under the arms.

'You've grown so much, Eva,' the ghost says, reaching out to touch her face with a dirty hand from which she recoils and falls back, off the narrow platform, onto the tracks. Her mother turns her back to her and embraces her father. Eva stands up and approaches the memory, but his hand does not reach out again.

At home her mother takes off his shirt – my grandmother cannot take her eyes off the brownish-black buboes that cover her father's body. He screams at her to leave the room.

'Skin tuberculosis, with ulcers,' the doctor says. 'Nothing special given where you've come from. I've seen worse.'

During the next few months he's silent, he doesn't eat well. He seldom goes out, only to walk around the village slowly so that everyone can get a good look at him. He looks them in the eye, all of them, and his eyes and body say what words cannot. He passes the empty houses and listens to the echoes of those who are gone. The decision ripens in her parents' minds and the night when my grandmother will have her last dream in her childhood home comes closer and closer.

They gather their things quickly, after sundown, so that people aren't watching, gossiping; they stuff chests and suitcases with carpets and blankets, old pots and pans, clothes. They leave their first steps, their first words behind.

'My mama said it had to be someone with a mother and a father,' she tells him. She doesn't keep anything from him, either. As his shadow melts into the night, her mother's voice reaches her from the yard.

It's time to go.

'I absolutely obeyed my parents when I was young. My mother's word was carved in stone. And I regret some things to this day,' my grandmother used to say.

When my mother and I had vicious fights during my teenage years, my grandmother was my confidante. She repeated those words to me so often that I finally took an oath to never listen to these women, to do the exact opposite of what they had done. If they had followed their own advice and were this unhappy, something must be wrong. Their complacency filled me with terrible fear. I rejected them, I refused them the right to live inside me. And the more my real fathers – my father, my grandfathers, my uncle – failed, the more bitter and cruel they became, the more these dreamed-up men became flesh in my mind. I was a foreigner in my own blood.

He lights another cigarette and hands it to me. He doesn't say anything.

Gradually the nervousness brought on by the memories recedes in the face of the present. I look at his face, the beach, the black ocean. The ghosts go back to their home, to the past. I listen to the sounds of the warm night, the wind blows the grains of sand and they rustle, the air smells of sea.

If you don't want to talk about it, we can talk about something else, he says.

Actually, for the first time I do want to talk. For the first time someone is listening.

6

Without realizing it, Diana and I have adapted to seventy-two-hour work weeks and our schedules are consistently different, but this time we manage to meet. We live far apart and neither of us has a car, so we go on long walks, even if the weather is bad. The first few times we hung out, we realized that in America – or at least in the America we found ourselves in – there were no cafes where you can just sit and talk for a few hours; the coffee is to go, you take your drink in a paper cup and leave, probably on the way to or from work. This is how you can spot the foreigners – they are the people sitting for hours on end over a cup of coffee in front of the Eastern European store and at the Jewish deli up the highway.

Benches are also a sign of this different rhythm. At home, they form a natural continuation of the environment, sprouting like rose bushes or chestnut trees in front of building entrances, in city squares, along the sidewalks. We had never considered the necessity of a bench for a conversation – here you find them only at bus stops, on the boardwalk or in a park nearby. They don't host any grannies asking us the customary Bulgarian questions of who we belong to and what we're up to; no teenagers furiously making out; no one says, 'Let's sit down, let's take a break.' We talk about how in Sofia, they replaced the benches in the park next to my apartment and then these same new benches were stolen and stealthily placed between buildings, furnishing the playgrounds, the DIY gazebos and plots-of-grass-turned-football-fields.

'I see how foreign this place is because of what's missing,' Diana says.

I tell her about my third job. Sylvia and Dancho liked me – I had caught the American virus of pride in a job well done and did my work more and more conscientiously. They ascribed it to Bulgarian diligence, although most Eastern Europeans I worked with were negligent: they either didn't know how to clean or just didn't care – maybe because they were supervised by other Balkan people or because they were hired illegally, which gave them back a bit of their power over the boss; often someone wouldn't show up and, naturally, there were no consequences. The two of them gave me more hours and saved me for the houses of the richest, mostly elderly people from the gated communities where women organized poker nights and such activities, like in the movies.

'And for those poker nights, it's not like someone casually coming over to your place, seeing your dirty underwear or an open book in the bathroom. Or your neighbor calling to ask for some sugar, so you invite her in, and you end up drinking coffee for three hours . . . Before someone is allowed in the house, we have to turn it into a mausoleum, I swear. Not a single hair or anything else inside, as if people don't live there.'

'It can't be that bad,' says Diana, the kindest person in the world. 'I think they're just being polite. I'm not scared to walk down the street here and talk to people. What more do you want?'

'I don't know, sometimes I feel like all this politeness is just hypocrisy.'

After we hit a dead end with the cafes and benches, we tried going to restaurants. But that didn't work, either – the food comes out quickly, you eat fast, they bring you the check right away and if you linger, the waiters give you dirty looks as if you are stealing from them. Besides, ever since I started working in a restaurant, I've developed an intolerance to eating out.

We often go to the Cape Henlopen State Park. This time we enter from the eastern side on our bikes. We come here rain or shine, animated by the desire to speak in our native tongue, the proximity created by a common past. Most tourists prefer the beaches or the Fort Miles Museum, so the trails here are less crowded. The park is situated on the tip of Delaware, where its nose cuts into the ocean. The coast stretches from Delaware Bay down to Maryland, and on the other side of the Delmarva Peninsula – which is shared between those two states and Virginia – lies Chesapeake Bay, separating the farmland to the east from the politicians and lobbyists in DC to the west. The Chesapeake and the surrounding rivers – the Susquehanna, the Potomac, the Nanticoke, the Choptank, the Patapsco, the Pocomoke – have old Native American names, a world completely foreign to us. Tim told me that the Oyster Wars, battles between oyster pirates, were fought in the bay during the eighteenth and nineteenth centuries; today, it is uncertain if the habitat will survive.

'There used to be so many oysters, the water would be filtered in four days, now you need at least a year,' I repeat what Tim has told me.

Diana nods: 'This whole peninsula looks like a slimy oyster to me.'

What is so magnificent about Americans is their ability to turn everything into a symbol, symbols into marketing, marketing into profit.

We take the path around Gordon's Pond, the salty lagoon separating the wooded part of the park from the beaches. The cirrus clouds look like creases in the folded fabric of the sky. We pass several photographers hidden in shelters, waiting for herons, colorful warblers, gorgeous red cardinals and all kinds of sparrows. There are thousands of birds nesting in the park whose names I do not know or know only in English. Same goes for the plants, flowers, trees. The smallest details are different in a foreign place, even the structure of the ocean salt probably differs and – in contact with air that is similarly different – produces a variation of the salt-infused Black Sea air that I keep in my memories.

How I wish I could see the shores of Delaware the way the Dutch, the Swedes, the English saw them for the first time: unyielding, untamed. I want to believe that before baptizing the new soil in blood, they stopped for a moment in humble contemplation of the unknown. That they stroked the tips of the pale pink grass orchid in wonder, that their native tongue got lost among these unknown forms and bodies that had seemingly followed different laws of metamorphosis.

Tim says that the American gift of turning history into a fairy tale with heroes and villains is a European legacy: they called appropriation 'Grand Discovery', they called the suffering of others 'the process of civilization', while their own continent agonized from her never-ending internal divisions into allies and enemies. The United States was supposed to rectify the error of Europe. I look at the lakes, the cattails, the beach and the boundless blue beyond, the dark green and the yellow of the shores . . . Nature, beauty, and in all of it so much forgotten history, tender to the touch. I once again get the feeling that I have missed the right time to be in America, the right age altogether – is this what it feels like to be born after history has ended? I will never see the fabulous fifties and swinging sixties, nor the glorious thirties. The world is hot and bristling with anger, illusions are melting away, and people seem the same to me everywhere.

Diana and I have entered the pine forest without me even realizing it.

'I talked to my mom.' She pulls me away from my thoughts.

'How is she?'

'They're fine. My dad's disappeared again.'

Diana's mother and her father's lover have an unspoken agreement to share the same man.

'Alexander's mom and dad are getting a divorce,' she tells me. Alexander is her boyfriend.

'Really? How come?'

She waves her hand. 'It was only a matter of time. Ever since we moved into our own place, his parents have been fighting. She can't get over the fact her son has left her house . . .'

'Sure, but after twenty years of marriage? And at that age? Why bother . . .'

'At that age? They're young, like forty-seven or eight . . . They probably have that many years again. Why live out the rest of your time with someone you hate? Life doesn't end at thirty.'

'Can you imagine your mother turning her life around like that?'

She thinks about it.

'No.'

'Right?'

'I don't know . . . Look at Olya's father . . .'

'What about him?'

'He's blown all this money again.'

The ocean sighs in the distance.

'A generation of miserable women,' I say.

'What do you mean?'

'These women who carried everything, everyone, on their shoulders. I don't know how they can live like this. Can you name one – my mother, your mother, our mothers – one woman that age who is happy?'

'You're being too dramatic.'

'Maybe it's all in my head. I don't know, but there is something really sad about that generation.'

'No sadder than any other generation elsewhere.'

'You think?'

'You see your mother in every woman. You taint everything with her sadness. Including yourself.'

I kick around a pine cone.

Diana continues: 'I just . . . I just think your take on things is messed up. You're looking for something that doesn't exist anywhere.'

I don't know what to say. I disagree, but I don't know why.

'And besides, look – your mother is an example of someone who changed their life after thirty.'

'My mother didn't change her life. She just ran away from it.'

'Well, if your mother has run away from her life, you've done the same with yours. Otherwise, why are you here?'

'Bullshit. I'm here for the same reason everyone else is.' I'm getting irritated. 'It's not the same. My mother has the same issues she had before. She left holding a grudge against Bulgaria, whereas I . . .'

'Look, I'm not trying to piss you off or anything. It's just that when you say *happy* – that they aren't happy, I mean – you say it as if you've got some monopoly on happiness. Not everything is so . . . You haven't lived their past. How many daughters have judged their mothers' mistakes before making the same mistakes themselves?'

A storm blows in from Jersey. The wind makes waves in the soft grass. The clear ocean blue turns to metallic gray, the heat charges the air. The roar of engines reaches us from afar. I imagine beachgoers running toward their cars, dragging all their metal lawn chairs, inflatables and coolers behind them, stuffing everything into trunks and taking off to their hotels. The rain does not spell the end of the fun, just its relocation to outlet malls and restaurants; I smile, a reflex – we'll have plenty of work tonight.

A first muffled clap of thunder comes from the cape. Somehow I hear an echo of Diana's words:

How many daughters have judged their mothers' mistakes before making the same mistakes themselves?

Lily

The whole ward has gathered in front of the TV – only my mother and a nurse walk up and down the corridor, shoes squeaking, checking on patients.

Clearly we will gradually let go of what has been happening to us for fifty years, says a news anchor. My mother half-listens, the other half of her attention is focused on the old folks' complaints. The Mausoleum was supposed to implode all at once, but something went wrong. The reporter's words haunt her, burrowing into her thoughts and remaining there throughout the night.

One of the old men in room 23 waves her in. 'Did they blow it up, did they blow it up?'

'No,' my mother says, 'it didn't collapse.'

'Of course it didn't, and it won't,' he rejoices. 'You're young, you don't know yet. But I heard it, they said it on TV, most people don't want it to fall. They want it to keep standing. This is our history, goddammit! They have no shame! Traitors! Not like the Russians, did the Russians let their Mausoleum get knocked down? Of course not! Scum . . .'

He keeps cursing, she nods, asks him about his blood pressure, tells him to calm down, to watch out for his health. She throws out a plastic cup full of spit from his nightstand; she no longer feels nauseated by things like that. She does not want the old people to suffer in squalor, so she makes sure to keep things clean for them. She sees her parents in them and prays that one day someone will show them the same compassion.

'Have a nice night,' she says as she leaves.

Her anxious thoughts churn endlessly.

What has been happening to us for fifty years.

But who did it? Who made it happen, if not us?

What we did to ourselves for fifty years.

As if it had all fallen from the sky. Times don't make people, rather people make their own times.

What was brought to life over fifty years.

People don't want it to fall.

She can't shake the feeling that there was something she was supposed to do but didn't. That she has missed something that would only happen once in life.

A probable error, they say of the tilted mausoleum. They wanted to blow it up safely – a revolutionary act, but done safely. Good luck finding anything more Bulgarian than that. She hears her mother's voice. *Fifteen years we waited for an apartment. And they built the Mausoleum in eight days, damn them all to hell.* On top of everything, they used limestone from Vratsa, from her home region. My mother wants to laugh and cry at the same time.

When did her mother stop resembling the beautiful woman she remembered from her childhood and start reminding her of her sick patients? Perhaps her mother also missed that once-in-a-lifetime unnameable moment . . . And now her own guilt and lost time are devouring her, making it impossible to let go of everything that *had happened* to her, to them, for fifty years.

She turns off the TV, she turns off her thoughts and barks at the nurses to get back to work.

Yana

A flock of sparrows twists in the sky, disappearing behind the jagged line of the pine forest and then reappearing again. The Wartburg trundles up the paved road – the sun reflected in the mirrors throws little flames onto the shag rug covering the backseat. The child is jittery: what if she misses it? Up front, her mother looks out at nothing in particular, with a gaze too empty to reveal a mood. The fatigue of the night shifts turns her thoughts into thick, milky fog. Her father holds the wheel with one hand, the other hangs out of the window, a cigarette between his fingers.

Her mother always complains about how tired she is. Her

father never does. Mom always says how much she does for them. Dad never does. Mom is words. Dad is silence. Dad smells of smoke and tension, as if he is waiting for something that may happen any second but never comes to pass. Mom has the scent of safety. The little girl holds the birds in her gaze, then sets them free, and they fly off to Lyulin Mountain.

They round one more turn and there she is: the white stone bear! The little girl screams with joy.

'Pull over,' the mother says.

'There's nowhere to stop, we've already passed it,' he says. 'I thought she just wanted to see it.'

'It doesn't matter. Turn around and pull over. Let her have a bit of fun.'

He purses his lips. She does not look at him, but she knows his mannerisms. He's more nervous when he's not drinking. Quieter. A little further down the road the car turns around, drives back downhill and pulls over onto a small gravelly hard shoulder, pebbles scratching the tires. They let the little girl climb out from the side away from the road. Her mother pulls out the new camera with film.

'Do you want to ride the bear?' her father asks.

'Yes!' The little girl stretches her hands in the air. He grabs her under the arms, lifts her up and places her on the statue's back.

'Do you want me to take your picture? Stand still so I can take it,' her mother says. The shutter opens, the camera clicks, time imprinted onto film. 'Another one with your dad? Stand next to her.'

The father obeys.

'Come on, hug!'

He places his palm on the child's shoulder.

Click.

'Yana, now take a picture of your father and me.'

The two of them stand next to the bear – she tries to put her arm on his shoulder, he tries to do the same with hers; then both of them go to wrap their arms around the other's waist. The mother exhales sharply, grabs his hand and places it on her shoulder. She places her own on his hip. The click of the camera echoes in the valley.

The three of them linger by the bear for a bit longer in silence. The father lights a new cigarette, crosses the road and stands on the edge of the gully that offers a vista of the blue-hazed valley. The hawthorn's claws grasp onto the rocks, the river murmuring below. He finishes the cigarette, steps on the butt and turns to urge them to get back in the car.

'Do you practice regularly?' the mother asks while the father starts the car.

A spark of hesitation in the little girl's eyes. She looks at her mother, then looks at the back of her father's seat.

'Sure.' Half-voiced.

'Are you sure?'

'Sure.' This time with exaggerated confidence.

'Tell me: when was the last time you sat down to practice?'

The car crawls on the road. The back of the little girl's head burns.

'The other day.'

She plays with the broken window crank.

'When your grandmother was at home?'

The child thinks, knits her brow and looks at the car ceiling. 'Yes.'

'Then why did your grandmother tell me you didn't play?'

Tiny hands curl into fists. They relax. 'Because I played when she was at the store!'

'Right . . .' the mother quietly responds. 'And how long does your grandmother take at the store? What do you think' – she turns to the father – 'twenty minutes? Half an hour? Yana, what does the teacher say, how long do you need to practice?'

'At least an hour a day,' mumbles the little girl.

'Right. So even if your grandmother really was at the store and you're not lying' – the little girl's eyes water, her lips betray her and curl into a frown – 'that still means you didn't practice as much as you should have.'

The father coughs.

'Yana, how many hours a day does Asya practice, do you know?'

'No.'

'At least three hours a day. Her mother says so. Soon they'll be sending her to competitions.'

The little girl doesn't want to cry in front of her mother.

'Yana, do you know how much it cost me to buy the piano? To find you a teacher? If it wasn't for Vanya—'

'Leave the kid alone,' the father intervenes.

The words freeze on the mother's lips. She turns to him.

'Don't look at me. We're about to go hiking, and you're nagging her about stupid things—'

'It isn't a stupid thing!'

'So she hasn't practiced, big deal, she'll play tomorrow. She's a kid. Why are we always looking to pick a fight? Why do we always need to be miserable?'

'We don't. We don't,' she snaps. 'I'm just trying to explain something.'

'Explain away!' He waves his hand. 'Where are my cigarettes?'

She hands him the pack. He lights up. Her mother turns to her.

'Playing the piano is a sign of intelligence,' she says. 'Even if you don't become a virtuoso! Imagine that someday you will have guests and you will want to entertain them. Remember, we saw that American on TV, Condoleezza Rice? Well, she can play the piano! That's why I'm telling you that these are good things to do, because I care about your future and I want the best for you. We don't have much money, but at least . . .'

'Mom?'

'Yes, sweetheart, what?'

'What do you do when we have guests if you don't play the piano?'

The father bursts out laughing and coughs, tiny clouds of smoke shooting from his lungs. The mother turns with a sniff and settles sulkily into her seat.

'Well, very funny. Hilarious.'

'It *is* funny,' he says hoarsely. 'That's what you get when you do something to try to impress someone. Your psychological complexes are so obvious.'

'So what should I teach her?' she responds. 'How to hold her drink?'

His eyes darken, a furrow appearing between his brows. His hands squeeze the wheel, then relax.

'Come on, big deal.' Her voice soon fills the silence. 'Don't be mad. I'm simply saying, I might be whatever, but you're also—'

'Oh, no, no. Nothing is ever simple. The kid this, me that . . . It's the way it is. There is no happiness. You have to be unhappy. You're allergic to anything else.'

'That's right,' the mother snaps at him and turns around to the little girl. 'I just want a better life for you than the one I've had. Someday, when you're older, I'll tell you everything and you'll understand. Promise me you'll play, promise me.'

The little girl is still fiddling with the crank. The mother grabs the child's arm. 'Promise! For me, promise you'll play!'

'OK, I promise, I promise.' The little girl wrests her arm from her mother's grip and starts fiddling with the crank again, face pressed up against the window so that no one can see her tears.

They leave the car near the sign for the national park and begin hiking in silence. The little girl forgets quickly, the sadness settles down somewhere deep inside her, and she runs giddily ahead or falls behind to look at a flower or a bug on the road. The mother pants in her big puffy jacket. The valley is covered by clouds, only a line of conifers is visible, with the open meadows sprawling toward the summit in the distance. A river flows beside the path, little fish darting in its clear waters. They stop near a deeper pool – the little girl immediately splashes into it.

'Mom, can I go for a dip?'

The mother shrugs. The little girl doesn't need much more than that – she undresses, leaves her white undies on and wades into the shallow pool. The two adults sit on the yellowing grass. He lights yet another cigarette. She lies down on the grass and half-closes her eyes. Soon she's asleep.

He can stop whenever he wants to, he thinks. And still, the thought won't leave him alone . . . Back in the day, they studied together. Back in the day, they laughed together. Back in the day, they did everything together. Now he is ashamed to admit to himself that he wants to run away from them. In his mind he runs through symptoms and diseases . . . But it isn't so bad yet. If he is able to diagnose others, he should be able to do the same for himself. But how does she manage to open the bottle, take a sip or two and then leave it – she just doesn't feel like drinking anymore . . . Well, some people drink more than others, he has a taste for it. That's it. No need to complicate things like she does, always looking for something to pick at . . . That tiny voice whines in his head, asking him whether he really could leave a bottle half-empty, without finishing it. Let the voices whine all they want, let them talk. The clouds race toward Cherni Vrah, the Black Peak. His daughter bends down, struggling to keep her face close to the water with her eyes open, hands roaming the bottom in search of the smooth stones she pulls out and throws downstream – they bounce off the large river rocks, the noise echoing in the surrounding hills before they land back in the river with a loud splash. He is afraid of himself. He is ashamed of himself. They went to see psychiatrists, with Lilia, to see colleagues – they told him he was 'fine'. Then why this torment? Or has she planted her own doubts inside him, her own hatred of him . . . His mind sprints through a hundred thoughts an hour and only strong alcohol brings quiet. No, there is nothing wrong with a little drink, to calm his nerves . . . As if his work isn't hard enough already, as if he isn't holding on to human lives with the tips of his fingers. The drink also kills the memories, which pulse like infected wounds that his wife is ready to rub salt into at the first opportunity. But that's also his fault. What more could he ask of her? To forget? They think he's mediocre at work, too. And if he's destined to fail anyway, why not have some fun along the way . . .

His wife tosses in her sleep. He looks at her black hair, her sharp features, the dark circles under her eyes. When, at which exact moment, did it die, what they had? And did they have anything at all, or did they both throw themselves into this game of a family, each to escape their own nightmare? He sees nothing in his daughter – nothing of himself, nothing of her. She never cries when he leaves for work, she only cries for her mother. He knows himself and her well enough to be fearful of whatever they have left in the little girl, wherever it is lying dormant, whenever it is bound to wake.

For the first time he understands his own father. His father never spoke to him unless he was tipsy. His father wasn't interested in talking, just in crude jokes about his mother. Then he grew up, he started high school, and they would meet over a beer. They got to know each other. His father told him of his travels, of all the other women he had slept with – before, during, after his mother. He kept telling him he had to be a free man, not to let anyone order him around. His father, the sea captain; his father, always hidden by an aura of silence; his father, the man he could not impress. When he thinks about happiness, the two of them are not in the picture. No women, no children, not his mother or his father – no one. But he isn't like his father – he won't run away. He's tired of carrying the guilt over the mistakes he's made and over the people who've suffered because of them.

'Daddy, can you take a picture of me?'

He hadn't even noticed the child coming up to him. The little girl goes to hand him the camera. The mother wakes up, reaches out and takes it from her hands.

'I'll take your picture,' she says. 'Let your father rest.'

'Daddy, what are you thinking about?' the little girl asks.

His wife turns toward him.

When he thinks about happiness . . .

'Don't ask stupid questions and don't bother me, go and play,' he says, lying back on the grass; now he is the one closing his eyes. The sun sinks toward the horizon, the shutter clicks.

7

I do everything I can to avoid looking into his eyes. But the hazy irises are like a magnet whenever I go to pour him water or he calls me over for some reason or another. He surely sees me, he isn't blind, his extravagant vanity gives him away. He is wearing a red-checked suit, a tie and a plain white shirt that glows on his black skin.

'One of the first things they tell you before you arrive is not to call them . . . you know,' I say.

'For real?' Tim and I are sitting on the restaurant patio, watching the ocean. Tonight I'm the outside hostess, and he is looking after these tables. 'The n-word?'

'I'm dead serious. It's not a big deal where I come from. No one realises it's a big deal.'

'Words are not bad on their own.' He tilts his head. 'But sometimes they amass a history of their own.'

'No one taught us your history. Or at least, I didn't hear it. I didn't pay much attention in school, I read books,' I say, and Tim laughs. 'I'd like to see you if, for twelve years in a row, you had to listen to how a thousand years ago one of our kings drank wine from the skull of his enemy. You can't possibly give a damn about the world when you believe your country is the cradle of *Homo sapiens*.'

'Don't think it's just you Bulgarians who act like this.'

'Oh, by the way, I brought you candy.' I change the subject; Tim loves saltwater taffy.

'I'll explain later, my food's ready.' He winks. 'By the way, Lazlo believes that civilization started in Hungary. Ask him sometime. But please, do call me over first.'

He laughs out loud as he walks toward the kitchen.

An elderly black woman approaches me from the boardwalk, asking for Mr Barrow. I glance at the reservations list: yes, that's him, follow me, please. She smells of lavender and something else, sweet but not pungent. He senses her from afar, smiles, she smiles as if to herself, and suddenly I see them in their youth – their beauty has aged well, with none of the hideous rot we often see back home. She thanks me, he just nods, his whole being turned toward her.

'You're stunning,' he says before I turn around to grab the water pitcher, and I feel instantly uncomfortable at being present at such a personal moment. In reality, the discomfort comes from the fact that I've never seen such a casual display of love before.

'Fifty-three years of marriage,' he tells me. 'It's our anniversary today. Four kids, thirteen grandchildren. With all my heart, I wish you find the same thing!'

'Thank you. Anything else I can do for you?'

'No, thanks, young lady.' His words are careful, gentle, falling softly between us like ripe summer fruit. People don't talk this way anymore: 'Let the order stay as we discussed, please.'

Fifty-three years. More or less the same as my grandparents. The busser brings freshly washed and polished silverware, and as I arrange it, I glance at Mr and Mrs Barrow. He asks Tim for a blanket, which he wraps around her; she spreads some butter on a piece of bread, splits it and gives him one half. The comparison occurs against my will: my grandfather interrupting my grandmother while she eats so she will bring him more bread; my grandmother taking my grandfather's blood pressure; my grandmother washing my grandfather's clothes by hand, because he is too stingy to buy a new washing machine; my grandfather coming up with another name for my grandmother, a stupid smile on his face.

'They're cool cats, Mr and Mrs Barrow. They celebrate their anniversary with us every year, at least since I've been here.'

It now dawns on me that Tim's name was noted down next to their reservation.

'Wow! Same place, every year?'

'You need all sorts of shelters as time goes on, to hide from the world. Especially this world.'

'Tim, can I ask you something?'

'You, in particular, can ask me a-ny-thing.'

'Mr Barrow . . . Is he blind? I feel like he can see me.'

'No, he's not blind. Does the name mean anything to you?'

'No . . .'

'Well, I guess that's how it is for most people, I'm not surprised. But around here everyone knows him. He was part of a big news story back in the seventies, when I was young and wet behind the ears – and quite handsome, however difficult it may be for you to believe it.'

I giggle.

'Barrow's story is like a movie, he told me himself. His father is David Barrow, patient number 025 in the Tuskegee Experiment, in Alabama.'

He looks at me with expectation.

'You've never heard of Tuskegee, Alabama?'

'No.'

'Never?'

'Not as far as I can remember.'

Tim is surprised and says nothing.

'What, do you want me to pretend like those people who say: "Oh, yeah, right, I've heard of it, but I can't quite remember . . ." in an attempt to look smart?'

'No, no.' He laughs. 'Sorry. It's just amazing how one world's tragedy is completely unknown to another.'

I shrug.

'Anyway. In the 1930s in Tuskegee, Alabama, four hundred black men with syphilis were studied to see how the disease would develop – there was no cure back then. You at least know what syphilis is, right?' I nod. 'Right. And keep in mind this was about ten years after penicillin was available, but the doctors didn't say a thing, they didn't treat them, they even took serious measures to prevent the men in the experiment from being treated elsewhere.'

'Wait, how so? Didn't they ask? You always hear something from somewhere . . .'

'Hear from where? You can't imagine how miserable their lives were . . . Keep in mind this was all happening before the sixties, before anyone even cared, and I don't think much improved afterward . . . Anyway, during that time the black folks called all sorts of diseases "bad blood" – they died from bad blood, which could have been anything . . . And the doctors told them they were curing them of bad blood, and they believed it. Some even fought in the Second World War – the military doctors told them they had syphilis and gave them penicillin, but not enough to cure it completely . . . The doctors who were tracking them actively tried to prevent the other medics in the army from treating them.'

'And Barrow was one of them?'

'Not Barrow, his father. I don't know whether he fought or not. But you know, over all those years folks still got around. They gave it to a bunch of women who gave birth to dozens of syphilis babies – they were lucky to have even survived. Barrow was one of those kids. His father died from complications sometime after he was born. Most of them went mad, blind . . . His mother was from somewhere around here, she came home and took her baby to the doctor, he had issues with his sight, his hearing was impaired – he still has a hearing aid, if you look . . . And the doctor said: congenital syphilis. The mother was sick, too, but in the early stages, so they both recovered. But his eyes stayed that way.'

'What about the others?'

'I can't remember how many others were still alive when

the whole story came out. But it was a big deal. Most of them had died by then, lots of women and children . . .'

'What about after word got out?'

'After word got out . . . They donated some money to the survivors, they changed a few laws, they treated the families and some others who had been infected for free . . . They promised to pay for their funerals. Clinton apologized, I don't even remember when. Don't think apologies can fix Barrow's ears or eyes. I gotta go, I have tables.'

Mr and Mrs Barrow are finishing off their banana bread pudding. This story doesn't fit Barrow; it is incompatible with his kind features, his gestures as he steals the last bite from his wife's plate, their laughter. It doesn't fit this country, at least not the America from my childhood fairy tales. Could people who have suffered so much laugh like this? My grandmother and my grandfather can't sit at the table without their salt and their sorrow.

Eva, pass the salt . . .

Eva, pass the past . . .

And don't you go off and marry some black guy, my grandfather warned me before we parted. Like most Bulgarians, they are both suspicious of people they've never even met.

I've seen those people on the TV, and they have these amazing white teeth, but they still make me nervous, my grandmother says with a shrug.

Mr and Mrs Barrow get up from the table – she folds the blanket with care, he places the bills in the little booklet and wipes his lips one last time. He helps her make her way through the chairs and tables before holding his hand out to say goodbye to me.

'Thank you for a wonderful evening, young lady. I hope I'll see you again.'

'Thank you for spending your anniversary with us, sir. Have a wonderful evening!'

At twenty years of age, I touch black skin for the first time. I feel Mr Barrow deftly transferring something from his palm to mine. When they turn away, there is a neatly folded five-dollar bill between my index and middle fingers.

No one has ever tipped me before.

night

Whenever anyone returned from *chuzhbina*, that vague word for any country outside Bulgaria, any place our parents could never go, they would always go on about how clean the streets were. How there was not a single piece of trash.

When we were young, they kept telling us: run, run toward the *Zapad* – the West – run while you still can, while there's time. Get out of this country, there's no life here. Make sure you sort your future out, get yourself to a better place.

No one ever asks me what I do in America. It doesn't matter. The more the Communists hated it, the more our parents loved it. But which America? The America from the Korekom hard-currency stores filled with magical Western goods, Kennedy's America, the America from 1969 and the Moon Landing, the America of fully stocked grocery stores and colorful diners, the America of cool jeans and hairstyles, of rock 'n' roll, pop and disco, of those other things you can't eat: *Life, Liberty and the Pursuit of Happiness . . .*

Everyone back home wants to be either American or Russian. No one wants to be Bulgarian.

My folks live in the America you described, you tell me. *They still expect gratitude from the world for things that happened eighty years ago.*

People love the sales pitch for the American dream. The horror of every fairy tale lies hidden in the fine print.

Yana

They give her a green Brick Game with yellow buttons, a *Tetris* knock-off. She has to arrange the curiously shaped pieces so there aren't any spaces left between them. To her, the city resembles these brick constructions. She imagines how the gray Soviet panel-blocks would look if they were rearranged so that the space between them disappeared. The slabs of the pavement – where there are any – dance under her feet. People dump plastic bags, peels, rotting chicken bones and eggshells into the grass underneath their balconies. The bushes reek of cat piss. A giant stray dog approaches the little girl and recognizes something in her; she bends down, pets it – the fur is matted and dusty.

You'll get worms if you touch stray dogs, her mother has told her. Shaggy and dusty, the defiant beasts approach her with puppy-dog eyes and wagging tails – she lets her eyes linger on them a moment longer than necessary.

Mama, Mama, let's get a dog.

Who's going to look after that dog, she answers, *you or your father?* No, her mother has enough on her plate and never misses a chance to tell her this.

Yet she touches the dogs and does not get worms. The suspicion that her mother doesn't know everything germinates inside her.

When you grow up, her mother teaches her, *you shouldn't go to clubs, because they're full of junkies who scratch little girls with used syringes and give them AIDS*;

She should never cross the street before looking at least twice, because the cars don't stop and they'll run her over in the road;

She should never go out when it's dark, because she'll get raped – there are all kinds of psychopaths roaming about;

She should not open the window in the winter, because she'll get sick, she'll get pneumonia and die;

Come and see, her mother tells her – they're talking about a little boy on the news who was walking across the bridge over the river, on Pirotska Street – *the same route you take from school* – and someone came from under the bridge, snatched the boy – *and his parents never saw him again, he was probably sold in a human trafficking scheme*;

Never walk on the outer edge of the pavement, because a

car might stop, someone might pull you into it and sell you into sex slavery or harvest your organs;

Don't talk to strange men. Run if someone speaks to you;

Always run up the stairs to the lift, because the door of the building doesn't lock, they'll catch you inside and they'll trap you within seconds, and you know that no neighbor will come out to help you;

Does your dance teacher touch you, her mother asks her. *Be careful with him, if he ever talks to you about sex you'll tell me, right?*

Yes, Mom, please, let me go, leave me be . . .

She wanders about in the muddy rain, apartment blocks surrounding her like dangerous reefs, like crooked teeth in the gray mouth of the sky, ready to chew her up and swallow her. Other people's glances are a threat, they conceal troubled thoughts, only the eyes of the stray dogs and cats are kind – one small rebellion, a second of warmth.

The hubbub of the open-air market swallows her up. At the entrance, Gypsies chant incantations to the passers-by: *cigarettes, cigarettes . . . perfume, perfume . . . watches, watches . . .* Merchants sit on thrones made of cardboard boxes and crates, their faces frozen into grimaces; their fingers, protruding from cut gloves, hold dying cigarettes. Stubble covering their yellowing faces, hands covered with black cracks, they shoot bloodthirsty stares at yesterday's customers who have dared to choose the competition today. Radios and portable transistors blare from the dark-green metal sheds, the news trying to drown out the oriental pop music and disco.

The crowd carries her toward the street, where bottles clink in dozens of plastic and fabric bags. She knows what's in the bags – beer and white bread. This is what her father buys, this is what his friends buy on their way home; this is what their fathers used to buy, too. A whiff of sweet-and-sour decay comes from the metal rubbish bins. They've put carp out in front of the fish shop: its blood trickles onto the ice and gathers in pink puddles at the bottom. The blue letters FISH remind her of the only time she has tried shrimp. Crunchy and meaty at the same time, it tasted like the Black Sea. She began pestering her mother and father for shrimp every day, but they didn't have any money, so they never bought it again. They hoped she would forget. She didn't forget, but she learned not to ask.

Pirotska is the saddest street in Sofia. The old, elegant facades are adorned with ugly signs, under which nestle greasy bakeries and pawn shops. An aromatic cloud of tripe soup and grilled meats wafts over from the tavern on the corner, whetting the appetite in the autumn cold. The damp asphalt reflects the traffic lights with red, yellow and green sparks flying from under the car tires. She waits at the junction, the straps of her backpack cutting into her shoulders. Two trams pass each other on the boulevard. The saddest time of the year – the holidays – is near but there is still school before that. The green man on the pedestrian light finally lets her walk, and she runs as she was taught to, because she is afraid of traffic lights. Behind her the light stays green for a long time.

The rain strips the last autumn leaves from the trees in the park – their naked branches tremble in the cold. The benches are empty. Time has creased the asphalt of the alleys; chestnut shells have fallen everywhere. When she was a little girl, her grandfather used to hide coins under the leaves and say that little elves had left them there. The fairy-tale creatures have long left the park, only the stray dogs sleeping under the church awning remain. The air is filled with grief and freshness. The puddles spit dirty water at her shoes. The street lights glow like orange suns in the indigo sky. The little girl wants to reverse the day, like the scales she plays on the piano – do, re, mi, fa, so, la, ti, do . . . ti, la, so, fa, mi, re, do – for it to be morning again, to be heading out to school. The cars dart like ants on Tsar Simeon Street, going left and right onto the side streets, the panel-blocks fill with life after a long day. She enters the labyrinth of the buildings. It rains harder.

The bakery is still open. When she was very little, they had only three desserts: *Garash* cake, chocolate balls with coconut flakes and baklava. There are many more cakes now, with white cream and oranges, eclairs with various glazes, tube-shaped shells filled with cream, petit fours, pyramid-shaped cakes. But they don't taste as good to her anymore. The saleswoman turns the lights off behind the glass. The little girl continues past the grocery shop that her mother goes to after work, when her father has forgotten or has spent the money on other things. She will never forget the one time when she lost the last of her mother's money. She crawled around in the dust by the building for hours hoping to find it, and when her mother finally came down to get her she told her that she wasn't even surprised: after all, who ever appreciated all her hard work – not the little girl or her father.

After taking the last turn, she sees the crooked number 204. Habit forces her gaze to shoot up toward the fourth floor. A familiar warmth tingles at the back of her head. Her father has lit candles; her mother won't be home until the next morning. In her mind, the soft light is fused with the smell of alcohol, the dancing gaze, the clumsy movements, with the glass, full and placed in front of her, with her mother who screams and begs, with the words: *You will either drink all of it, or I'll beat you senseless.* Her stomach convulses.

The little girl takes a few uncertain steps towards the entrance before darting in the other direction. In front of the panel-block apartment building, only the rusted skeletons of the animal-shaped jungle gyms remain.

8

When you speak another language, you put on a different skin. Like being born for a second time. And when the hands are hard at work, the mind is quiet, which is why there is a particular kind of liberation in cleaning toilets. My whole life in Bulgaria consisted of people forcing me to listen to them talking about how a person needs education so that they can make something of themselves in this life; the catch is that no one ever explains what this 'something' is. My mother is educated, she has had the most prestigious education, and we have always been poor. My grandmother and my grandfather are educated and every month they make an educated choice: medication or food. And here I am, half a day of scrubbing toilets – almost a hundred dollars. My rent is three hundred a month. Check and mate, education.

I like Sylvia and Dancho, who were the first to help me when I told them I was going to stay in the US illegally. I'm afraid of being dependent on money from my mother if I go to school, of the generous interest rate, paid in guilt, that she would collect. Like everyone who has no idea what to do with themselves, her favorite thing to tell the world is: 'You should.' This illegal job is my spiritual vow, a complete crushing of the ego in return for a reward that seems fair to me – that someday I will get to be someone else. My mother was always telling me that I didn't know the cost of money. Well, at least now I am free to learn.

They pick us up from our housing early in a rattling minivan full of rags, buckets and cleaning supplies, rubber gloves and sponges, newspapers and vacuums. The inside reeks of cigarettes because we all smoke, collectively prepping our lungs for the chemicals we will soon inhale. American homes are organized into 'communities'; in this one all of the neighborhoods have nautical names to match the resort's spirit of happiness, which can be purchased for a price. These islands of identical homes are the last fortresses of a dying America. Here 'neighborhood watch' and 'vigilance' are practiced, there is only one entrance, trimmed lawns, white teeth, cabinets full of antidepressants and TVs to watch the presidential debates. They are protected here, far from the restaurant kitchens where no one speaks English, from the vans filled with cleaners and gardeners, just like the one I am riding in now; in sum, they are protected from all the places where the *others* are, where the American dream writhes in agony. There is another America, inland, away from the golden beaches and the smell of fried sugar. There lie the bare bones of Jefferson's farms; the poisoned soil spews corn and soy for millions of mutant chickens, crammed in giant factories with no windows, their smell stretching over the DE 24; there, people have their heroin dreams inside their trailers, reveries of a great past they just happened to miss out on. These are the two Americas: one of resort-style happiness, of outlets, full grocery stores, beach arcades and minigolf, one hundred and thirty-two flavors of ice cream, caramel corn and vinegar fries on the boardwalk, luxury hotels and large trucks . . . And the other, of creditors, *America made in China, India, Bangladesh*, of ghettos, frigid earth, fanatics in their decrepit churches, overdoses in the bathrooms of highway McDonald's.

But there is no time to suffer. The real motto of the country is: if someone isn't paying you to think about something – don't. And I am paid to polish the facade until it's sterile. Without a speck of dust – the breadcrumbs from the toaster, the marks from the morning's coffee, the dried splashes on the cabinets, even the drops on the spout of the kitchen sink – everything must go. Then the couches, the decorative pillows with empty phrases, the futons and the chairs need to be fluffed and dusted manically. There are rarely paintings on the walls, most often generic scenes of sunsets and exotic places or ten-buck decorations made of plywood and plastic with alternating combinations of the words 'happiness', 'home', 'family', 'love', 'blessing'. I dust shelves covered with shells and conches, cheap sculptures made from all sorts of materials, collections of all kinds, once even taxidermied cats, and pictures, so many pictures from the life my grandmother and mother were denied: vacations, vintage luxury cars, mobile phones, neon leggings, aerobics, beautiful jewelry, bags and perfumes, modern kitchen equipment, college, 'baby showers', 'bachelorette parties', huge weddings with happy guests, beautiful babies with toys and clothes . . .

'We're going to the black doctor's house, you haven't been there yet. You have to pay attention, she really looks, don't halfass it,' Dancho mumbles as he smokes. I look at the two cleaners behind me. They're new, I'm more seasoned, I have been working with Dancho and Sylvia for months, so I have a certain degree of confidence. These new guys aren't any different from the rest. They all have the same meaty cheeks and necks, eyelids, ears, tongues – as if their flesh is made of *banitsa* and the doughy buns they stuffed down our throats as kids. They all stink of the same sour sweat from the morning, which gives away the fact that five people sleep in the same room, that they don't have time to shower after they come home from work late at night, because there is always someone else in the bathroom or because they immediately drift into an exhausted sleep. Their athlete's foot steams in the same Adidas or Nike sneakers they bought with their first paycheck, 50 percent off. They all scratch their balls in the same way, through the same shorts they all wear, with the same short, fat fingers with black under the fingernails.

We pull up in front of the house – it's massive. It's going to take us all morning.

'I won't clean where these people shit, Dancho, just so you know,' one of them says while unloading the equipment. 'We never talked about crap like that.'

Dancho and Sylvia have a legal business, and as for the question of how they manage to clean forty houses a week with five people as registered personnel – it's the same as everyone else's answer: the entrepreneurial spirit, effective management.

'You're gonna clean whatever Yana tells you to clean, she'll deal with you. I'll be in the kitchen if you need anything.'

Dancho goes straight inside and starts talking to the doctor in broken English. I hear 'Für Elise' from the door. The television is always on, everywhere, even when there is nobody in the room. When I was a kid and my mother worked nights, once we were living on our own, I left the TV on all night – it was the only way I could fall asleep. Now I can't stand its constant drone.

The hallway is spacious. There is a small room to the left – through the glass door I catch two tiny heads bent over a book. The staircase to the upper floors starts in the front of the room and under its arch I can see a part of the couch in the living room. I finally comprehend that the huge black piece of furniture, in front of which a tiny man with curly salt-and-pepper hair and a young boy are sitting, is a Yamaha grand piano, the same as the professor's.

'Hey, what'd you say your name was?' I yell at one of the guys.

'Nikolay.'

I just want to leave the room, to not hear the piano.

'Nick . . . I'll clean the bathrooms. You can stay here.'

'Great, thanks! You're a cool girl, y'know that?' He flashes me a grin.

I head toward the bedroom. The piano lesson continues as if we do not exist.

Yana

'Do you see this sign here?' the professor asks. 'It's like an arrow, but without the shaft, just the tip?'

'Yes.'

The Yamaha's black polished wood stands out against the fading, rotting wooden floor. The doors of the rooms are covered with frayed leather, yellow foam sticking out of the slits. The walls in the music academy are not soundproof and in the afternoon the instruments' braying echoes in the surrounding buildings.

'Do you know what it means?'

The child shakes her head.

'It's a diminuendo. It means you need to gradually play quieter, to grow softer. Can you think of the difference between the diminuendo and the piano pianissimo? Or the piano?'

The girl continues to shake her head.

'The diminuendo is more delicate. You can also see molto, like here' – she taps on the sheet music – 'then you need to reduce the volume more noticeably, like so.'

Her hands, spotted with age, crawl over the keys. The sound fills the room, then slowly fades. The professor continues to speak as she plays.

'You can also have poco, or poco a poco, meaning little by little. Yana, are you listening to me?'

Summer strips white tufts from the poplars. For her it's

hardest during the warm months, when the days are endless. All of her friends are in the park, laughing and sharing secrets that she is missing out on, climbing trees, throwing green wild plums at each other and waiting for dusk to fall so they can play hide-and-seek. She longs to be there, but she isn't. Her grandmother puts her on the tram, they spend about an hour crossing Sofia – she looks out the window and dreams of the freedom to solve this city on her own, freed from the cage of parental desires and schedules. She doesn't want to play the piano, but her mother is unshakable.

From the tram stop they take a narrow street filled with Sofia's cats. If not for the cacophony of instruments – tubas, pianos, violins, violas, lungs and larynxes – the so-called New Building of the National Music Academy would seem abandoned. The facade is covered with graffiti; mountains of rusty metal rise in the weed-grown parking lot. The same rust chews at the roof. White drifts of cigarette butts cover the pavement under the windows.

The professor is a tiny woman and resembles a benevolent bug: thick round glasses, a toothy smile, slightly hunched over with bony hands. But the moment she starts to play, her back straightens, her chin proudly shoots up, the delicate hands come out of their cocoon and flutter over the keys like butterflies.

*   *   *

They met four years ago, in September, when the little girl was five and autumn had started to weave its flames into a tapestry. On that first day, her mother led her into the room. The professor was playing with her back to them, effortlessly, as if her hands had a mind of their own and it was instead the body that was an appendage to them. She teaches pedagogy at the Academy. At the start of every year, each child is assigned a college student – they have to practice together on their own once or twice a week. But often the students either don't show up or they make it known they are doing it for the grade alone. Yana has to be understanding – none of them are there to become a piano teacher in this thankless country, her mother says. They're in their last year and most of them have other plans, elsewhere.

The little girl can't play when her mother is at home, nor under the supervision of her grandmothers. Why can't her mother leave her alone? With the professor it's different. As she listens to her, the little girl finds another meaning in the sounds, sounds that appear forced and ugly at home.

The kids at school make fun of her because she plays the piano – most of them take contemporary dance or some other sport. The boys say that she has a big bum already, bound to get bigger by sitting in front of the piano too much. When she tells her father, he laughs and says that big bottoms run in the family, on her mother's side. And despite all of her pleading, her mother pushes her to play at school concerts, putting her in front of the class. Her father never comes to watch.

*   *   *

The sound of hard brakes coming from the street outside brings her back to the present.

'Yana,' the professor says. 'What's on your mind?'

The child hesitates for a moment. She doesn't like asking questions – she is embarrassed by not knowing.

'Miss, during the first lesson, when mom and I came . . .' She gathers up her courage.

The professor thinks back for a moment, then nods in encouragement.

'What were you playing?'

The professor smiles, her cheeks lifting her glasses. 'When I'm by myself, I always play a nocturne,' she replies. 'So, the first time we met, I was playing a nocturne. Did it sound something like this?'

The little girl nods.

'Yes, this is a nocturne by Czerny. Do you like it?'

'I only like the sad songs,' the little girl says. 'Like this one.'

'Really?' The professor looks at her with surprise and stops playing. 'Why?'

'I don't know.'

For an instant all the instruments in the building take a breath. The warm wind ruffles the leaves of the poplars.

'Well, then I guess from now on we are going to practice only sad pieces.'

'Yes,' the child agrees. 'If we can, let's play only the sad ones.'

Eva

The city saddens her. The noise, the people – all this life aggravates her loneliness. Their house is at the end of the main street, near the old Cavalry – and current People's Military – barracks. She has to delay her graduation, and her brother has to start school. Her mother finds work as a seamstress, her father starts at a factory because no one else would hire him. Sometimes strangers storm into their house, appearing out of nowhere, even in the middle of the night, rummaging through the drawers and the cupboards, questioning her father and her mother, and their glares leave a trace on her skin, sticking to her like filth. One Holy Thursday – they still celebrate, in secret – she hears children's voices coming from outside. The chant splinters the May day, becoming clearer as she crosses the kitchen – she discerns an eerie thirst for blood in its childish lilt. She may have heard her father's name – what could they want with him? Her parents have come home for lunch and also head for the door. In front of the low fence that separates the small yard from the main street, there are children dressed in white shirts, black skirts and trousers, no more than ten years of age. Front and center is the comrade-teacher, holding one of the boys by the hand. A wave of hostile shouts engulfs them: 'Georgi, you are an enemy! Georgi, you are a kulak! Georgi, you are an enemy! Georgi, you are a kulak! Georgi . . .'

Her mother slams the door.

. . . *youareanenemygeorgiyouareakulakgeorgiyouareanene-mygeorgiyouareakulak* . . .

My grandmother glances at her father. All three of them recognized the boy holding the comrade's hand. When her brother comes home from school and they sit down to eat, her father does not leave the bedroom.

*   *   *

My grandmother graduates high school with an A average, due to that damned D in Russian – she refused to learn it. She goes with her classmates to the dance pavilion on the town square; she loves dancing, and most of the boys want to dance with her. She sips on a lemonade with her only friend Emilia, standing apart from the crowd. Emilia wears heavy make-up – her father is a Party member and brings all sorts of colorful rouge and kohl back from abroad; my grandmother never wears make-up, because her mother does not let her – she says that make-up only ages the skin, that only harlots wear make-up.

'Emilia, do you remember I lent you *The Hunchback of Notre-Dame* at the end of last summer?'

The book was a gift from her father, a final remnant of her childhood saved from scattered travels and everything else. One of the old editions, with a beautiful leather binding and gold embossing, that was printed before the language reforms.

'What?' Emilia says as she exchanges glances with a sweaty young man across the dancefloor.

'*The Hunchback of Notre-Dame*. I want to take it to university with me.'

'I gave it back to you months ago.'

'No, you didn't give it back. Please, it's very—'

'Yes, I did. Check your place.' Emilia smiles and heads toward the boys, turning around to wave at her one last time before disappearing into the dancing crowd.

She returns home, crushed with guilt. She feels as if the bookshelf is looking at her with an empty socket where Hugo's book should be. She doesn't say a word to her mother.

*   *   *

Her mother wakes her up early in the morning, a few days before she is to leave for Lovech.

'Get dressed, quick,' she tells her.

Her mother leaves breakfast on the table, and the two of them leave before the men get up. The merchants along the main street have already taken up their positions under the linden trees, arranging jars of honey, pulling big chunks of feta from vats of brine, cutting up the yellow suns of *kashkaval* cheese. The crowing of roosters comes from the surrounding villages, the heat's battle to wrest the city from the night's coolness is only just beginning. Breathing hard, her mother leads the way without looking at her. When they reach the old *chitalishte*, the community center, she waves her in. The two of them enter the cool entrance hall that smells of mold and old books. Her mother turns to her and looks her straight in the eye: 'Because you're a grown woman now and you're going off to university far from me, I want you to see some things today and remember them well.'

My grandmother wants to ask her what, but by the time she manages to, her mother is already entering the room. The librarian greets them, they say hello, make some small talk, then her mother whispers what she needs to her. The librarian glances at my grandmother before disappearing between the shelves. She returns shortly with a large, brownish volume. Black letters spell out the title on the cover:

Dr Luben Hr. Popov, MD
Dermatology
and
Venereology
Vol. 1
Sofia, 1947

Her mother grabs her by the sleeve and leads her to the furthest table, throws the book onto it and takes a seat across from her.

'Eva . . . I've said many harsh words to you, don't you think I don't know it. I'll probably say twice as many before I'm through, that's what it's like to be a mother, someday you'll see for yourself – it's a bitter pill, but you swallow it, because it's for the best.'

'Mother, what . . .'

'When you were out roaming around the fields with that snot-nosed boy, I could barely contain myself, but I kept my mouth shut. Thank God, it sorted itself out. What you can find in this book right here' – she nods toward the volume – 'I heard 'bout it the first time when I was in Stara Zagora, many years ago. Now the doctors know more, so you can see it like this, written down, our teacher, Mrs Slavova, told us . . .' Her mother startles, looks over her shoulder. 'Comrade Slavova, a very cultured woman, she'd studied in France, told us, but whatever she told us was enough in any case. I'll leave you here for the day to read, I've talked to the woman . . .'

'Mother . . .'

'Read! If you move, I'll know. And to think what you'll be doing in Lovech. You've got a big mouth, and you're stubborn to a fault, you need to weed out some bad habits, otherwise I don't know. There are many things you don't know – here, learn now.'

Her mother grabs her bags and leaves the reading room. My grandmother doesn't move; the book is waiting to be cracked open.

She finally braves the volume. She flips through a few pages and is immediately seized by embarrassment – she lifts her gaze to see if the librarian is looking. Inside, it talks about the relationship between a man and a woman, the most intimate things. She's grasped the main idea – from what she's learned, from watching the village animals, from friends, from her mother, who had quickly explained what happens after the wedding. But her mother had leaned into the *why*: because women were created to bear children, she says, much like a cow is meant to have calves, just as a hen is made to lay eggs. In several places she catches a glimpse of horrifying pictures, as if of burned, hanging flesh. What kind of book is this? She stops at page 616 and reads.

LUES S. SYPHILIS

> *Lues venerea* or *syphilis* is a chronic spirochetosis of degenerate provenance . . . caused by *Spirochaeta pallida*. The disease is either transmitted congenitally through infection of the fetus *in utero* or acquired during life . . .
>
> . . . the history of syphilis is of great interest . . . scientifically it begins at the end of the fifteenth and the beginning of the sixteenth century, when this new and heretofore unknown disease suddenly appeared and infected large swathes of society. This event coincides with the discovery of America. With the arrival of the first of Columbus's ships in the port of Baiona in the Galician Bay in 1493, an epidemic of syphilis broke out in Spain as well. Once it had spread to Europe, syphilis quickly developed into a widespread pandemic due to poor hygiene, liberal sexual activity, ignorance of treatment methods and prophylactic measures, wars and other events . . . the Spanish called it 'the Galician disease', while the Italians, Germans and the English referred to it

> as 'the French disease'; the Eastern nations and the Turks labelled it 'Frenga', or 'of France', and so on . . . brought to Calcutta by Vasco da Gama's sailors in 1498 . . . From there it quickly spread to India, China and Japan . . .

She gets bored and quickly flips through a few pages. She wants to see the pictures. A human curiosity about pain and horror awakes within her. The pages continue in succession, revealing to her a secret world that has been so zealously concealed from her. She's had so many questions; she has touched it in secrecy, with a guilt-ridden pleasure; she has been told it is a sin in the eyes of God; she's had enough of the old women and their babblings about children and lineage. And now – everything so out in the open, in this brazen scientific language.

No wonder they have been protecting her. Her mother was right: you should only go to bed with a man to continue the family line. Every act of closeness with another body carries death within it, and what a death at that – a hideous, decaying death. The more she reads, the more she can feel a thin layer of dirt on her skin, something dusty, sticky. Is she imagining it, or did it itch there before . . . Is this scab on her leg just an abrasion, or did she sit somewhere, perhaps she touched someone?

> Syphilitic ulcers . . . cicatrix . . . syphilitic sores . . . herpes simplex . . . reduced immunity . . . necrotic tissue . . .

Enough, she can't take it anymore. She flips through more pages and finds new and terrifying pictures – what looks like a bloody, raw mass of minced meat between the legs. It's the first time she has seen a male . . . She's only seen drawings so far, but this is a black-and-white photo, and it's all covered in ulcers and pus – she reads the line underneath: *Neisseria gonorrhoeae, Gonorrhoea* . . . She leafs through all sorts of wounds, rashes, scabies; her head spins from all the Latin names – *Mycoplasma genitalium, Trichomonas vaginalis, Chlamydia trachomatis* . . .

When she leaves the library, the sun is already descending toward the river. The city seems smaller than before. She greets people from afar, taking a longer look at their faces, their hands. She itches everywhere – she wants to go home, to wash her face, her hands, to close the windows, to chase the noise of the world from the room. She feels dirty. She can't believe that only a few days ago she held strange men by the hand, danced with them, roamed about in the night. Had she really done that so recently, or does it only seem so . . .

She quietly shuts the door. Her mother is already home.

'D'you understand now?' she asks.

'I do,' my grandmother says without looking and scrubs her hands until they're red, above the bucket with suds, as her mother pours water over them to wash it all away.

9

Bulgaria, France, Italy – increasingly these names become abstractions, and I start to think of them the way Americans do: some shapeless Europe somewhere out beyond the ocean, where the people are different. The same magazines have different covers depending on the continent, the news also flows differently – if the European is used to hearing news from other places every day, the American has fully conquered his continent and rarely lets intruders into his daily routine. But this year it's different. When there's no work, we watch shots of wet, ragged clothes rolling around beautiful Greek beaches; swarms of tiny silhouettes grasping onto an even tinier boat, fighting to come ashore; people in orange life jackets anchored beneath the Mediterranean sun – you can hear seagulls, shouting and crying; tents set up on the asphalt in European capitals; when they show footage of a child's body spat out by the sea, Tim turns off the TV for the first time.

'Towelheads,' Lazlo says. 'This is not good at all.'

I instinctively look at Tim. I don't know how to react. News words whirl around in my mind: 'invaders', 'crisis', 'refugees'.

'I talk to friends in Hungary, they're worried. No one knows what to do with these people.'

'Some people here don't know what to do with people like you,' Tim answers.

I trade glances with Harry and Bruce, who are seeking refuge in the restaurant from the unbearable kitchen heat.

'What do you mean?'

'I meant what I said.'

'It's not the same.'

'Why not?'

'I came here legally!' Lazlo backpedals.

'And did you stay legally?'

Lazlo doesn't respond.

'Laz, you're cool, but sometimes you say some dumb shit,' Bruce chimes in.

'How come it's dumb shit?' Ken joins in as well.

Tim turns to face him.

'What?' Ken shrugs. 'Lazlo . . . And Jane, actually' – I don't want to be dragged into this conversation – 'they've come here to work, they speak English, even if they did something wrong along the way, they sorted it out' – Lazlo nods – 'whereas these people, just look at them . . . I feel bad, don't get me wrong, but . . . they're totally different.'

'Is that so?'

'Yeah.' Lazlo is back in the game. 'They probably don't speak a single European language, and . . . they're not Christian.'

Tim laughs. 'Once upon a time we Americans were scared shitless by Catholics, you know that? Irish, French, Austrian . . . We thought they'd ruin our Protestant republic.'

Lazlo shakes his head. 'It just ain't the same, Tim.'

'I have to agree with Lazlo here, sorry, guys. Although we've got our own problems,' Ken adds.

'What other problems?' Tim asks. Then his mouth gapes open in surprise. 'No, you've got to be fucking kidding me.'

Ken puts his hands up as if he is surrendering: 'Hey, I'm just listening to the other side. You can't have some people coming in legally to work, while others . . . you know. They should take care of their shit, just like we should take care of our own.'

Tim shakes his head.

'The problem is,' Lazlo continues, 'that it's all too easy to move around. They didn't have these problems once upon a time, because people knew their place.'

'I think I've heard this somewhere,' Tim interrupts him mockingly. 'There were these people, once upon a time, who even built a wall so that you couldn't move around too easily.'

'It's not the same, man, hear me out . . .'

Tim gathers the dirty dishes from the bar and heads toward the kitchen: 'Of course it's not the same, Lazlo, because now you're lucky enough to be on the other side.'

Yana

The bike is blue, scuffed in places. It is waiting on the black mosaic tiles in the hallway for her to get home from school. The first thing she sees is her father in the living room, kneeling on a huge sheet of plastic with tools scattered all around him.

'Well?' Her mother comes out of the bedroom. 'What do you think?'

They dress her like a boy and keep buying her things for boys. They cut her hair short – her mother entrusts her to her father, and he takes her to the barber and tells him to cut her hair like Nadezhda Mihaylova, the no-nonsense leader of the democratic opposition party. The other mothers braid their daughters' long hair, tie it up in ponytails with beautiful bright-colored clips and hair ties or let them wear it down, swaying long and shiny across their backs as they run around the park. They buy her baggy second-hand clothes, three leva a kilo, so she can grow into them, but she fails to grow to fit the clothes. Her mother gets cheap cotton underwear from the open-air market, which falls down and bunches into sticky layers beneath her clothes. There are no changing rooms at school. Everyone changes for gym in the classroom. The boy she likes catches a glimpse of her ballooning underpants. The class starts calling her Baggy-Bum Yana. Her mother dismissively says that someday she'll understand how practical these decisions were – what does she care about some bratty kids? The teachers won't let her change in the bathrooms and never fail to remind her that she doesn't deserve any special treatment. Finally, she starts to lie, saying she forgot her sweatsuit so she can't join in; she'll explain the Fs later, at the end of the semester. She gorges herself like a predator – food soothes her. She hates the shapeless packaging of her body.

A second-hand childhood. Second-hand clothes, second-hand toys, second-hand furniture.

A second-hand life. And now this bike. Her best friends both have brand-new bikes, one purple and one red. The purple one even has white tires. The bike in front of her is old with worn pedals, and on top of everything, it's blue . . . blue, blue, blue, for a boy.

'A co-worker gave it to me for free, it's hardly even been ridden. I just need to tune it up, I bought some training wheels, too, 'cause you can't ride without them yet,' her father tells her.

They never fail to point out to her what she can't do.

'It's raining today, but when it stops, you can go out to the park and give it a try,' her mother chimes in. 'Your dad will take you.'

'With Daddy?'

'Yeah, when I go out running, you can ride alongside me, so I won't have to wait for you, you little pain-in-the-bum.' He ruffles her hair.

Maybe the bike isn't so bad after all. The little girl sits down on the plastic next to her father and watches him wipe it with a rag – the metal shines, little scratches are visible here and there, but only up close. Then he grabs the training wheels and presses hard until the metal gives and curves up slightly; he bolts them on tightly.

'You'll learn quicker this way,' he tells her. 'See? They'll touch the ground only if you start to tip over, the rest of the time you'll have to keep your balance in the center.'

'Won't she fall like that?' her mother worries.

'She won't.'

'But what if she does? She needs to keep her hands safe for piano . . .'

'If she falls, she'll get back up, dust herself off and get back on the bike. And with time she'll learn not to fall. Just like a grown-up, right, Yana?' he replies, then gathers up his tools and goes to get ready for the night shift.

Gradually the two of them create their own ritual. At first, the movement is difficult for her overfed, childish body, but the little girl quickly gets used to it. Her father jogs in cheap white netted shoes, the only ones he has; he takes her to the park, walks to the market, runs, goes to work in them – so she insists they buy her a pair just like them. The salesman at the market says they're boy's shoes, but that doesn't stop her, and five leva later her little feet are pushing the pedals in miniature netted shoes to catch up with her father. She vaguely senses the struggle between the two bodies from which her own has been kneaded: one body energetic, whose skin hungers for sun and wind, for movement, and the other sluggish, that fears the unknown.

She likes her father's silence. If he doesn't love her, if he isn't happy with her, at least he doesn't tell her. She likes that he knows the park, all its secret paths, twists and turns, every wooden gazebo, the little brook, every bridge and hill . . .

She always asks him to take her to the abandoned amusement park hidden in the small woods. The skeletons of the rides both frighten and entice her; a sparse green haze swirls around the rusting metal. The Ferris wheel looms above them like a memorial to the children who have long since abandoned the park. Her father doesn't remember ever seeing the rides working. For whom are these ghosts being preserved? The place hints at a past that holds the answers, but she is still too small to ask the right questions.

When her father gets tired of running, the two of them walk along the paths and she asks him: *What are all these monuments?* Her favorite is of a father hugging his two children. She imagines that one day she will be like the stone girl: in a dress and braids. Right now, she looks more like the little boy in the man's arms.

A partisan father returns home from an armed struggle, her dad says with a sneer, and she decides that partisan fathers must not be so bad if they hug their children so nicely.

Daddy, hug me like a partisan, she tells him once, and he and her mother laugh, and she feels good that she was able to make them laugh.

Another time, they sneak into the park through a small gap in the thick brush by the railway tracks. She stops in front of two white pillars – three terrible faces have been carved into one of them. *Who are these guys?* she asks her father. He makes her read the inscription, sounding it out syllable by syllable.

HERE LIE BURIED THE CORPSES OF
13 REVOLUTIONARIES

KILLED BY MILITARY ACADEMY CADETS ON 28 SEPTEMBER 1918 DURING THE VLADAYA SOLDIERS' UPRISING

The little girl imagines a bony hand clawing through the dry earth and grabbing her ankle. She almost bursts into tears and runs off toward the path. Her father laughs.

Someday she'll understand.

What? she asks.

That history is written in blood. Corpses are sleeping everywhere. She's used to those two words: 'blood' and 'corpses' – that's what her mother and father talk about at home.

Just our history? she asks.

No, everyone's, I guess. He shrugs.

Her father tells her about the first big war and says that *Bulgaria was always on the wrong side in both wars.*

Why? the little girl asks.

Because that was just their luck. My great-grandfather was one of the first partisans, he says. *In Macedonia.*

What's a 'partisan'? she asks.

At first it meant a person who believed strongly in a beautiful but impossible idea. But then, as with all ideas, it turned into something else: a nightmare. Someday she'll understand these things. Not now. Now it's enough for her to know that after the first war, many of the soldiers were unhappy and hungry. Many were crippled, not only in Bulgaria, but all over Europe. She thinks about the big map of the world in her bedroom. It has drawings of the Eiffel Tower, the bears in Russia, a big mug of beer with a sausage in Germany and roses in Bulgaria, but there are no sad soldiers anywhere.

Were they like zombies? the little girl asks.

He laughs. Like zombies. Only they weren't lucky enough to die, they had to live their whole lives like that. People would avoid them in the streets and scare their children with stories of them.

She feels sad. Her mother would call such people 'ingrates'. Some of those soldiers didn't want to have a king anymore. They wanted a republic and even put Stamboliyski in charge – *Have you heard of Stamboliyski?* he asks.

She has. The big boulevard downtown!

He laughs again. She'll learn about that some other time as well.

So what happened? she asks.

Nothing happened, as usual. Later someone thought to prettify the story a bit and use it for *brainwashing*. Brainwashing – she imagines someone pouring a drop of Vero dish-washing soap in her ear, then grabbing the long wire her mother uses to unclog the drain, and . . .

Daddy, she says after a while, *Grandma says that before the Communists* – she is particularly proud of that word, she lets the letters roll off her tongue like ripe grapes, *c o m m u n i s t*, never mind that she's little and this is a word for big people, she doesn't have to wait to grow up to understand it – that before the Communists everything was fine, that the king was very good to the people and everybody lived better, but then Grandma had everything taken away and she had to flee to the city to survive.

People always think that what they don't have is better than what they do have, he tells her, and they confuse the good times of their youth with good times in general . . . *Your grandmother suffered, but before that, others suffered, and others after her will suffer as well. It all comes down to luck. That's all there is to it.*

She doesn't understand but doesn't ask a second time. She doesn't want her dad to think she's too little and stupid, she likes it when he talks to her and tells her stories.

On the way back from the park, her dad stops at the convenience store.

Can you keep a secret, Yana? he asks her.

Of course she can, she's a big girl. She won't tell her mother about the empty bottle that her father throws away before they get home.

night

Perhaps it was the winter of 2011 or 2012, I was walking toward the apartment on Tsar Simeon Street with my first boyfriend – the largest snowfall in God knows how many years, huge snow drifts, ice, a hellish landscape to navigate. From the subway station you had to pass the bus stop near the building, and there was this homeless guy there, stinky and disheveled, drunk as a skunk. I thought I recognized him, I had probably seen him around the neighborhood.

I didn't understand what he said, I didn't even understand if it was directed at me. I just saw my boyfriend lurch toward him. He had done some boxing as a kid – not anything special, he was nothing special in any case, I didn't believe I deserved something special. In broad daylight, in front of everyone waiting at the bus stop, he punched him one, two, three times in the face. Nobody moved, nobody said a word. The tattered shape gathered its bottles and ran into the park, yelping.

I can barely remember anything from that day apart from the few drops of blood on the cigarette ash in the snow.

Afterward, I thought about the homeless guy for days. I hadn't seen my father in over ten years. Had he quit drinking or had he gotten worse? How much worse? After he left, my mother was constantly harping on about how I would meet him on the street, and he would kidnap me. In order to prove my love to her, my loyalty, I had to hate him, to fear him. She called me constantly, didn't want me to go out, cried in the morning after having nightmares, kept repeating how I had to take care of her, to be better, to not be like him.

Gradually I stopped being afraid – even if we did pass each other on the street, he wouldn't recognize me. But I never look away from the homeless drunks, always wondering if their daughters are looking for them somewhere.

10

'You go ahead, I'll walk home,' I tell Dancho.

'But why? Are you sure?'

'Yeah, I'm sure. I feel like walking.'

It's a pretty long way from the doctor's house to ours, but I need fresh air, time. I watch the car drive off and have only taken a few steps when I feel my phone vibrate in my pocket. I hesitate between picking it up and leaving it. In the end I swipe the green circle to the side with my finger and find salvation in my grandmother's stories, far away from 'Für Elise'.

* * *

She met my grandfather in the town of Lovech, where she was studying to be a vet tech and he to be a feldsher. She was twenty-two; he was twenty-seven. He was tall, passed for handsome, had good manners – men wanted to be his friend, women liked him. She was never known as any great beauty and has always joked with me that she is a descendant of Genghis Khan, with her broad face, big rounded cheekbones, dark-blonde hair and hazel eyes. No matter what she might say, I've seen enough photos from before she was married, before she had kids. She could've had any man she wanted. Why him?

'It was time to settle down, he liked me, I didn't find anything not to like in him, my mother and father liked him too, and so that was that. His mother said I looked like a magpie – I weighed all of a hundred pounds soaking wet – how could I carry sacks of corn? I don't know how I didn't realize it even back then.'

As a child, and even years later, I could never manage to find a photograph from their wedding. I've hungrily pored over the familiar faces from the past in those brownish photos with tattered white edges. There are shots of celebrations – birthdays, village fairs, baptisms of Lord knows which cousins, aunts, great-aunts, third cousins twice removed . . . But not a single one of their wedding. She has bequeathed me so many dates and years, but never the year of their marriage.

It's obvious, however, which photos are from before and which from after the wedding. Suddenly her long hair has been clumsily cut off and has turned dark; the mischievous look in her eyes has died out. Beautiful dresses are replaced with dark suits and simple shoes with low heels. There are no more friends, young and just graduated, smiling in front of some cave or in a city park. Instead, I see her in village yards, under trellises, alone with the children – the only other figure is her mother-in-law.

Even after all these years and with thousands of miles between us I don't dare ask her why she didn't try to find the other man. I am afraid to name the prison sentence she has long been serving.

'Oh, sweetie, you can't even imagine how times were back then . . . A person couldn't just run off, to say nothing about getting a divorce. Plus, we'd just bought the apartment, we needed to finish it and then pay it off. Besides, I'd already more or less learned how to wrangle him, I was wiser, and we didn't fight as much as we did when we were young . . .'

She got pregnant after the wedding. They went to live near Veliko Turnovo, in his mother's village. Her mother-in-law was infamous in those parts, but my grandma didn't pay any attention. People always repeat the rumors they want to hear, and in most cases they are far from the truth, she tells me. It hadn't even been a hundred years since Bulgaria was liberated from the Ottoman Empire, there were still old people in the village who had lived under the Turks, the old customs were still alive, the Communists hadn't managed to root out old traditions, even though their efforts at changing things had already borne fruit and the houses were starting to be abandoned one by one – people were running off to the cities.

'When a man took a wife,' she tells me, 'she only took his last name in official documents. Otherwise in your grandpa's village, they'd call her by her husband's first name: if he was Peter, then she was Petrovitsa, if he was Ivan, then she was Ivanitsa. Except for your great-grandfather, who was Spas Ivankin, after your great-grandmother Ivanka. That's the kind of woman she was.

'And she was a large woman, no two ways about it,' she goes on. 'And until the very end she would wear old-fashioned woolen aprons and skirts that made her look even bigger. With hands about yay big, and some nice fat legs. As tall as your grandpa . . . He and I couldn't be together like other young couples. We'd sit down on the sofa to talk about something just the two of us, and she'd come over and start jabbering on, saying stuff she had no business saying aloud. But your grandpa listened to her about everything, always did exactly what she said. And when she'd rile him up, he'd never say a word to her, but me with my big mouth, I'd pay the price for speaking out. So me and him started fighting, he'd come at me, and she'd go into the other room and sing folk songs.' My grandma laughs at the other end of the line.

Then she clicks her tongue and finishes the phrase with a sigh.

There are two different stories about that marriage: my grandmother's, who has long since gotten over it and has turned everything into an awkward joke, and my mother's, who will never forgive the past as long as she lives.

Eva and Lily

When I was a child, your grandmother, all black and blue as she was, would drag me through the streets, and people who saw us would turn away or cross over onto the other pavement. And she would ask them: why does Ignat do this, haven't I cooked and cleaned for him, haven't I washed his clothes, why does he do this?

All the while I was dying of shame.

The first few times my grandmother couldn't believe it.

Huge bruises blossom purple on her ribs, on her shoulders – the violet prints of his hands. While blood drips from the sockets of her punched-out teeth, she wonders how much new ones will cost, because they don't have any money at the moment – they never have any money. She eats soup, porridge. She doesn't smile. It becomes more and more difficult for her to lie down next to him at night – she doesn't want him to touch her, but what can she say? She has to fulfill her duties.

Her wifely duties, that's what she says to this day.

It's hard for her to remember how it would begin. It was always over something small, something insignificant that she hadn't even thought to worry about.

Her mother-in-law asks her to cook in a big, deep pan, but she tells her another pot would be better, and the older woman complains to him; it's her fault for insisting, why make a big deal over a stupid pan . . .

She's late coming home from work – a goat is having a tough birth and she has to go find its owner in the village – she gets back at eight o'clock, only to be met with their raging and ranting: she must have been out sleeping with another man, what will people say; surely they are right, what would it have cost her to send someone to tell her husband, since she knows he is insanely jealous . . .

His mother doesn't like her food, doesn't approve of the way she raises the children, thinks the apartment is too cramped, doesn't want them to move to the city. Who cares if there is no work in the village and no school for the kids . . .

It grows harder and harder for her to summon the guilt within herself, but she knows it's there somewhere.

Her mother-in-law wants them to pool their salaries and buy her a house, but my grandma refuses: after all, they have two kids and their own family to take care of . . .

He never acts this way when they are alone. If my grandma doesn't reply, but keeps quiet instead; if she hides, she sometimes manages to avoid the worst; it's easier to let the old woman have her say, and afterward the two of them can talk it over together, on their own. The old woman is constantly comparing her sons, comparing their wives, their children. Each is always better than his brother.

One day their little boy has a bad fall in the yard. All three of them – him, her and her mother-in-law – are at home. Eva runs to comfort him and hug him, to talk to him.

That youngin' won't never amount to nothing, her mother-in-law says in her heavy dialect. *You'll make him into a little sissy.* And she keeps harping on about it until she drives him berserk. That same night Ignat tells Eva how he fell in the yard as a child, right under the big terrace, almost in the same spot where little Pavel had fallen, and he had cried for his mother, begged her to come down and help him, but she had laughed at him from the veranda with his little brother in her arms and the baby had looked down on him, silent and stunned, while her laughter shook the tears from his eyes until finally his father had heard the commotion from somewhere and had come to pick him up. His leg was broken. He recalled how when he was only four or five, they had tied him to a tree in the middle of a field along with the dog, because there was nobody to look after him – everyone was working the land.

'And now he treats those dogs like kings, those damn dogs,' she huffs into the phone.

'She treated the child she carried under her heart for nine months and in her arms for another two years that way, and here I was expecting her to be kind to me,' she tells me.

After my uncle was born, my mother came along next, both breech, both difficult labors, after which she had to recover quickly, because she had to work. They moved back to my grandmother's hometown and they had to pay off their apartment, to furnish it, plus the kids meant endless expenses. Construction on the apartment building was behind schedule: the workers hadn't understood the blueprints and by the time the architect arrived from the neighboring city, they had already poured the foundations backward – the bedrooms faced the big boulevard, while the kitchens and living rooms overlooked the quiet back courtyard. They had to live somewhere – my grandmother's old house had been torn down to make room for the new concrete colossus; even though her father's house had been bigger than the apartment, they still had to buy space in the new block, which wasn't even half-built when my mother started first grade. They were paying for a home they didn't live in, and the glue of that debt held their marriage together.

* * *

They live at the vet clinic where they work. The two other families that they share the house with pretend not to hear anything.

They don't ask Eva why her face is bruised; they don't ask why she can't hold the microscope in her right hand.

They don't ask where her teeth are.

They don't ask why both kids stutter. Their father makes fun of them in the evening at the dinner table, he pulls faces, but when the nurse from Lily's kindergarten comes by to check why the child stutters to the point of choking, my grandmother says nothing. Ignat often goes around to the village co-ops to castrate pigs, to help cows and sheep give birth, to vaccinate the livestock. Rumors reach her about other women, but she pays no heed. One day, while looking at samples from the laboratory, she overhears the doctor talking to their other co-workers. The only things she catches is:

'Ignat wants to sow his oats with all the women in the county, but still wants Eva under his thumb.'

So the others know, too. The words sting the back of her neck like a slap, she does not raise her eyes from the microscope, she pretends she hasn't heard, she writes down the results in the book she has open, takes the next sample, changes the slides. That day she works late. She finishes other people's jobs, cleans the laboratory twice, she checks the signatures that she had already double-checked, waits in hope of some last-minute patient, something urgent that can't be delayed. Her mother-in-law comes several times and pounds on the door, screaming and cursing; they can surely hear her in the next neighbourhood over, but Eva ignores her, pretends not to be there. Finally, it gets to eight o'clock and there is nothing more to be done. She shuts the door behind her and composes her excuses before stepping into the two little rooms they call home. She is still hanging up her white lab coat by the door when she is grabbed from behind and hurled into the living room.

* * *

My mother is six and a half when she got her ear pulled at kindergarten for the first time because she didn't want to eat her toast, since there was a fly writhing in the jam. The comrade-teacher walked her home, because her mother didn't come to get her on time, and she was afraid her mother had died, that she would have to live alone with her father. She was bawling the whole afternoon despite her father's and grandmother's coaxing, which quickly turned into slaps. Finally, they shut her in the bathroom to teach her a lesson.

But she doesn't stop, she does not give in, not even alone in the dark, her backside burning from wetting herself – she keeps on praying. She hears her grandmother going in and out, surely looking for her mother. She hears the words the older woman calls her mother – *No-good whore, I hope she goes to 'ell, running wild on the streets again.* What is a *whore*? She'll ask her mother, if only she would come home – *Please, Mama, come home.* Her father is smoking in the kitchen, her brother doesn't dare come out of the bedroom, her grandmother looks in on him from time to time to tell him if it wasn't for her and his father, he would never amount to anything with such a loose woman in the house.

My mother's howl has died down to hoarse spasms and sobs when she hears the front door unlocking and recognizes her mother's footsteps. A sense of relief overtakes her fear, and she darts toward the door – her eyes have adjusted to the darkness, and she quickly finds the handle, opens it and runs into the hallway. She sees her father's feet, but suddenly something comes crashing down and knocks her to the ground, the rug slides from beneath her knees and she can feel her trousers rubbing against the bare concrete of the floor – the stinging pain of torn skin overpowers the itching between her legs. She realizes from her mother's scent that she is beneath the woman's body.

'Are you OK, sweetie?' Eva asks her quickly, and the little girl only nods before two big hands jerk her mother toward the ceiling.

'Mama, Mama, Mama, Mama!' the child screams.

'Mother, get this bawling brat out of here.' her father shouts. 'Where the hell do you think you're going? Where're you going, now I'm really going to mess you up!'

My mother fights her grandmother – she doesn't give in. The old woman is enormous, she has strong arms, yet the little girl manages to land a kick to her belly and to escape from her grasp. She darts back to her mother.

'Daddy. Please. I. Beg. You. Please. I. Beg.'

The pleas are mixed with sobs. Her father's hand meets her face – the mother sees how the child flies to the side. Before she can reach her little girl, the hands grab her once again and drag her toward the bedroom. The last thing she sees is little Lily sitting up, looking around for her.

The muted blows are interwoven with a dull growling and cursing. Time stands still. The little girl scratches at the door, pleading with her father, calling to her mother. Her grandmother is singing folk songs to little Pavel and bouncing him on her knee. Mute tears run down his face.

They are interrupted by a pounding on the door. When her father goes to open it, his hands are covered in blood. The little girl does not even wait to see who is knocking, she rushes into the room to look for her mother and finds her curled up in a ball in the corner, behind the armchair.

'Mama, lower your hands, Mama, lower them . . .'

They wrestle – her mother is hiding her face in her hands, only half-conscious, her daughter's voice is like a distant echo. She doesn't want the child to see her – if she dies, is this how she will remember her? Strangers enter the room. Eva lowers her hands – her face is now an unrecognizable mask: the little girl is reminded of the steaks her father pounds with a hammer. She starts bawling even louder. Where her mother's lips had been just a short while earlier, there is now a dark-red abyss, her eyes are puffy, a thick liquid trickles from them, drying into a crust in the corners; blood gushes from both her nostrils. Her mother staggers to her feet and the monstrous face disappears, an unpleasant scent wafting toward them – her dark work trousers are stained, something yellowish drips from a trouser-leg.

'Comrade Spassova, can you hear us?' My mother turns her head in the direction of the voice and recognizes the dark-blue cloth, the black leather of the boots and grabs onto the trouser-leg, clinging to it.

'Please, please, please.'

The police officer shakes his leg. He looks toward her father.

'Mother!' he yells. 'Take this child or else I'll . . .'

'Comrade! Now you just calm down . . .' one of the uniformed officers shouts in response.

Her grandmother tries to pull her away, but she refuses to let go. She knows they won't dare do anything to her in front of other people. To her surprise, however, the police officer grabs her by the collar, lifts her straight into the air and hands her to her grandmother, who catches her, but can't get her out of the room. Their battle continues silently, but not particularly fiercely – the old woman doesn't want to leave the room either.

'Comrade, what is the meaning of this?' the other policeman starts in. 'It's eleven o'clock at night, and we can hear you all the way from the street.'

'Everyone's got problems, but they can be solved quietly and peacefully, without waking up the whole neighborhood,' the first cop adds.

'And what about you, Comrade?' The policeman turns to her mother. 'Do you have anything to say?'

'Comrade, shall we call an ambulance?'

Her mother shakes her head, staggers over and reaches for the arm of the chair. The policemen trade glances, and one turns to her father:

'Where is the phone?'

'Come on now, there's no need for an ambulance, what ambulance,' her grandmother shouts into her ear.

No one pays attention to her. The little girl answers: 'By the sewing machine in the living room.'

Her grandmother squeezes her shoulder with terrible force. The little girl keeps quiet; she has decided she will not scream anymore.

The ambulance takes her mother away. The little girl begs the police to let her go with her mother, to not leave her at home – look, she's not crying, she's behaving like a big girl – but no one listens to her. Her father sends both children into the bedroom – if he hears so much as a peep, he'll beat the shit out of them.

A silence that is painfully familiar overtakes the house. The children lie awake in the big bed, listening to their grandmother's snoring. The police have warned them all not to let this happen again and if they do have problems, not to involve the whole neighborhood and not to disturb the neighbors. Afterward, they wish them a good night.

Yana

'He got a ticket for driving without a seat belt and now he's stressed out.'

'So what if he's stressed out, can't he go out for a run, do some work and take a load off his mind that way, does he have to drink?'

'We're not going to yell and hit each other like you and Dad used to!' the mother tells the grandmother.

The older woman throws up her hands, gets up from the sofa and stands in the doorway.

'So now what, I can't go into the kitchen just to potter around?'

'Later, when he goes to bed,' her daughter whispers. 'Leave him alone, let him sit quietly by himself in there for now. I'll go and talk to him in a bit. Yana, have you done your maths homework?'

The girl has been drawing pot-bellied flowers in the margins of her maths workbook, spirals swirling in their stamens.

'I will in a second,' the girl answers weakly.

'Let me see!' The mother wrests the workbook from under the child's elbow and the petal of the last flower unravels in a line along the edge of the page.

'What is it? What do you think you're doing, child?'

Her mother smacks her on the head with the workbook.

'Mama, it's hard, I'm sleepy, I'll finish it tomorrow, the homework isn't due until Friday anyway . . .'

'But doodling's not hard! Do you know how much these workbooks cost? Just look at the scribbled mess inside! Here, let your grandma take a look as well. How many times have I told you not to cross stuff out and to use a pencil, just look at these problems! How am I supposed to sell these books when you are finished with them? And you, instead of just shuffling around in the doorway like a dummy, shut the damn door and sit down!' the younger woman says with a sniff.

The grandmother heads toward the armchair, whose pattern peeks out from beneath the rumpled sheets covering the furniture.

'Look here, young lady' – the mother's fingers dig into the little girl's wrist – 'I'm exhausted, you have absolutely no idea what I'm going through. So do as you're told, or God help me, I don't know what'll happen to you. Do you understand what I'm telling you?'

'Mama, you're hurting me.'

'Do you understand me?'

'Mama . . .'

'Answer the question, you little shit.'

'Yes.'

'You ungrateful little . . .'

'Hey, hey now! Stop that, honey!' The elderly woman rises from her seat. The light in the hallway goes on – a tall silhouette appears in the beveled glass partition, and it opens.

'Good evening!'

When he drinks, he turns into a different person. At least that's what they say. Sometimes he hears them. But he doesn't mind – he's always wanted to be someone else.

'Well now! What, are you crying? Why are you crying?' The father starts toward the little girl, but on the way, he stumbles over one of the footstools and roars, slurring heavily: 'Piece of fuckin' shit! Aaah, now you better lis'n to me hard, get these stools and chairs outta here, 'cause I'm 'bout to go crazy and I'mma get rid of every last one of you, I swear to God! This place was a helluva lot better empty, a man can't breathe in here now, you, you just spend money on shit . . .'

He staggers and tries to catch himself on the table. Their eyes watch his hand look for support, instead finding a full glass of water, knocking it over – the water spills over the maths workbook, over the edge of the table and right into the mother's lap.

'Whoopsie!' His drunken laughter echoes in the glass of the chandelier. The little girl quickly jumps up to make room for him – he collapses onto the couch, throwing his arm heavily around the girl's shoulders.

'So what's up? Why are you crying, huh, little girl? What's going on? Tell Daddy now.'

'She's not crying, she's just—' the mother starts to say.

'Keep quiet, you!' he roars. 'Let the girl speak. There's no need for you to interfere!' His index finger is pointing straight at the younger woman's face. Only the quick twitch of her eyelids betrays fear.

'You know what happened to your daddy today? Mr Policeman slapped him with a nice little fine. 'Cause he was driving drunk, 'cause he was driving without a seat belt. But you tell me, do you think your daddy's a good driver?'

'Yes.'

'Heh, heh. Yes, but actually, no!' The other hand, clenched into a fist, pounds the table and everyone jumps. 'Your father is a loser. Just ask your mother.'

'I never . . .'

'Didn' I just tell you to shut up, you dirty, lying bitch! Hey! I'll kill you all!' He stops for a moment, lost in thought, as if remembering something. 'Yes, your father is a loser. I want you to say it.'

Outside, the tram crosses the rail junction with quick, distinct beats. A horn sounds.

The little girl thinks about the changing traffic lights. All day people draw on the junction with their footsteps – to her they look like the round notes on the musical staff of the tracks, the traffic lanes and the pavements. What does the melody of their everyday motion sound like?

'Yana, can you hear me, my girl?' Her father's hand tugs at her. 'I want you to say to me, "My father is a loser. Daddy is a loser."'

'Leave the child alone, Mitko' – her mother's gentle voice

contains a tremor of falsity – 'please, go back to the kitchen and let's not fight.'

Her palm startles him. He has never struck her, even though she has provoked him when he is drinking and she has grabbed him, calling him all sorts of names, cursing him, shoving him and wanting him to shove her too; she has gathered up her things, bawling, threatening to leave, performatively piling all sorts of random things by the door, and they have screamed at each other for hours until they both finally collapse.

'Who're you to tell me where I can go in my own home? Don't ever touch me again.'

'No, I'm going to touch you and tell you to leave the kid alone. The kid you don't give a shit about in any case . . . The thing you just spilled water all over was her maths workbook, which is important . . .'

'No, don't ever touch me again,' he repeats.

'Honey, since he doesn't want you to touch him, then don't, leave him be, don't antagonize . . .' the grandmother chimes in.

'Shut up, Mom.'

'Mama, please, leave Daddy alone,' the little girl interjects almost in a whisper.

'I won't have you touching me with those hands, who knows where they've been . . . And since you touched me now, you'll tell your daughter and your mother where those hands of yours have been, those hands that you then touched' – he hiccups – 'your husband with.'

His eyes narrow as he tries to glare at her. The room stinks of alcohol and cigarettes.

'Tell them, goddammit!' His hand suddenly shoots toward the woman's hair, their bodies press against the child. The elderly woman lets out a soft scream. The little girl feels the warm urine running between her legs and soaking into the couch before dripping onto the hardwood floor.

Lily

Surely he must've worked in the emergency room with my mother. Surely their shifts must have not overlapped at first – he was on the night shift; she was on the day shift. Perhaps I saw him after that, during one of the many times when there was no one to look after me so I would go to work with my mother, first in the ambulance riding around the city, responding to emergencies, then locked up by myself in some hospital room, with a book or if I got lucky, in front of the hospital computer. My childhood smelled of illness and death.

The head of my mother's department makes passes at her; the old doctors drop dirty hints to her. They're all married. She has nothing – no specialization, no apartment, just a child that she doesn't know how to take care of. She's afraid that if she says the wrong thing, she'll lose her job and will have to go back to the provinces. Everyone is connected to and dependent on each other. So she takes it all as a joke. But one of her male colleagues is shy, quiet. He's not like the others. He's a hard worker. A few times she catches him looking at her in the break room. She returns his gaze. Perhaps this will be her revenge. Perhaps someone will finally save her.

In May 1999, she and my father cross paths at home a total of three times. I am already at the village with my other grandparents. A month later my father finishes his residency, and they go out to dinner with his parents. My grandmother and my mother count my father's cups.

'Why don't you keep a closer eye on him?' her mother-in-law asks.

'I'm not his mother,' she replies spitefully.

On 15 August, they scrape together the last of their money to buy me a Barbie for my birthday – two days later my mother comes to the countryside to give it to me. I cry and beg her to take me back to Sofia with her. My grandma tells her I have a hard time falling asleep alone. My mother ignores this, asks her for money – my grandma gives it to her without asking why. My mother sneaks away on the early train at five in the morning, so I won't cause a scene.

When I'm not there, they manage to save a little more, but they can never quite make ends meet. That summer my mother takes another leave of absence from her residency so she can work full-time and make more money. She'll restart it the following year. She's constantly reading the pharmaceutical dictionary – that puts her to sleep faster than anything.

She gets up early for work – she likes being the first one there, before the start of the shift. The sink in the kitchen reeks of piss more and more often – that's what he does when he's drunk. She scrubs it with a Brillo pad and soap; she makes a big pot of coffee and reads about cardiac conditions. She'll restart her residency this winter, once things stabilize a bit and my grandma comes to live with us to look after me.

At seven thirty she is already standing in front of a swastika spray-painted on the back door of the A&E department. The lines creep across the dark-red stucco that is covered with a layer of brown Sofia dust. All around her empty symbols are repeated – hammers and sickles, crosses, stars and moons. And of course, the seal of the most supreme religion – the cock. Dicks drawn everywhere: in lifts, on the walls, in toilets, someone has even painted a huge prick on the pavement in waterproof paint, with three thick, greasy hairs coming from each testicle. A crude attempt to fertilize the daily grind.

The mornings are still cool. Her co-workers, just like most of Sofia's inhabitants, are still on holiday. During the summer, no one gets sick, there are no phantom aches and pains or high blood pressure. She goes down to the first floor, where the heat is more bearable, to write up the medical histories. She is on the same shift as him for the first time. He is writing as well. They spend the morning like that, without exchanging a word. She can feel his gaze upon her; she permits herself to glance back at him several times. He's handsome, even though he is clearly starting to show his age. Or perhaps he simply seems handsome to her.

During the lunch break she gets up; he gets up as well. The staff lounge overlooks the internal courtyard. The curtains are old, the color of vomit. They pull them shut and the air splinters into a million glittering dust motes. He locks the door. While he takes off her clothes and licks her nipples, she tells herself that everything's still OK, that no line has been crossed, that there is still time to turn back. But then she thinks about that fucking kitchen sink. She sees the grinning face in front of hers, hears him telling her how it's more ecological that way. Because she'll wash the dishes afterward in any case, that's what he tells her. As she senses the other man for the first time, the canine loyalty she feels towards a life that will never materialize dies – the deeper he penetrates her, the faster the future melts away. She is glad he doesn't speak, that would ruin everything. He quietly groans at the end. She waits for him, checks whether the phone to the ground floor is working – there's a dial tone. He goes to touch her between her legs, but she pushes his hand away. She's ashamed. Someone's slippers squeak in the hallway – they both stay silent until the shadow passes in front of the crack under the door.

The telephone rings, he picks it up, he's hard again.

'A patient's arrived, I'll do the intake,' he tells her, then gets dressed quickly and carefully opens the door.

She is left alone.

11

There's not a single living soul on the beach, only hundreds of giant seashells and conches scattered on the sand, discarded by the storms. For a long time, I was angry at my grandmother and my mother for never asking about my story. But even if they had asked, I wouldn't have known what to tell them. They are my story.

I remember the first time I realized my mother was a separate human being, that her name was not 'Mom', that she had a name of her own, with its own history. I remember that early pain, childlike in its rawness, of the realization that my mother had a life before me. And that despite me, she probably continued to inhabit the secret world of adults.

The seagulls scream over the waves. It's getting colder. Summer's leaving. The phone vibrates again:

*You know, I've never had an o****m*

After I quell the childish desire to pull away, I ask:

Never? Even on your own?

Now it's too late, my life's almost over, she replies.

I don't respond.

When you were born, I felt happiness for the first time and saw everything that was good in the world, she writes.

I think I'll live until you graduate university, reads the last message.

I start typing several times, then delete what I've written. I grab a conch shell, examine the blue-gray surface. I run my finger over the rough exterior, then over the smooth, pink interior. I raise it to my ear and listen to the ocean whispering. The conch absorbs the warmth of my palm. We are powerless to be anything else for each other, so I resign myself to this powerlessness – I wish to calmly cross the incidental, unfathomable harmony of the world. I take a swing and, with all the force I am capable of, throw the conch into the ocean.

night

Resignation syndrome. The illness appears in Sweden among refugees from the former Soviet and Yugoslav republics. Hundreds were diagnosed in the nineties, children of immigrants facing deportation – four hundred and twenty-four cases between 2003 and 2005 alone. They develop symptoms of depression, become isolated, stop speaking or moving. Scientists say it's a reaction to the stress of moving, mostly to the lack of hope. The worst cases were tube-fed for years. They recover only as the family regains hope, they say.

So it is a thing, I mutter as I exit Wikipedia. I put my phone away and return to the night.

I thought about resignation syndrome when Tim told me about the Dutch famine in the winter of 1944 – that was when his wife's parents ran away to the States – thousands died of starvation and years later scientists discovered traces in the genes of the grown-up children. Horror marks the alleles of an entire generation. No one will ask what slumbers inside the bodies of the Transition children, the children who lived in the Eastern Europe of the nineties, somewhere between Communism and capitalism. Our history will barely be allotted two or three sentences in a textbook full of myths and legends. We grew up and became statistics, both those who left and those who remained.

Resignation syndrome. It just got stuck in my head! I told you, it's this resignation I can't stand . . .

Do you hate them? Your mother? Your grandmother? Your father?

I don't know . . . I don't love them.

Your mother also ran away . . .

She did . . .

. . . because she hated them . . .

Give me a cigarette, please.

I don't believe you when you say you don't love them.

Yana

'I had a terrible dream,' the elderly woman tells her daughter at breakfast. They are drinking coffee with milk from the farmer's market – greasy bubbles and yellowish chunks of foam float on the surface. They pour a splash of coffee with lots of milk for the little girl, so she won't feel left out.

'Your grandma,' she continues, then turns to the little girl, 'my mother . . . Anyway, she was sitting on the veranda, there was no railing, and she was right on the very edge and her legs were hanging down and in her lap she had a big ball of yarn, green and all tangled up. So I open the door from the bedroom onto the balcony, see her back and ask: "Mom, what are you doing?" but she doesn't answer me. And I'm just about to step out onto the balcony when it suddenly breaks off and falls straight down, but my mother just keeps sitting there, untangling and untangling the yarn. And then I woke up.'

'Yana, did you do your homework? You two need to leave soon.'

'Yes.'

'Well, go and get ready, have a wash and then you two need to head out.'

'Mom, can't I go by myself now . . . ? You've already let me a few times . . . And the other kids all walk to school on their own, it's close . . .'

'What, so some stranger in a car can snatch you up and we never see you again? Get a move on 'cause I'm starting to get annoyed.'

Could she have forgotten?

'Oh, and Yana, I talked to your teacher, tonight your grandma will pick you up early, before your last class, for the recital. So make sure not to dawdle!'

The more she wishes time would slow down, the faster the day goes, but the little girl does not remember the faces or the words, only the anxiety. She and her grandmother cross the entire city and arrive at the Academy – the small chamber auditorium is in the basement. Tired evening light filters in through the windows. It's full of parents and even some distant relatives who have been strong-armed into coming. The little girl is there with only her grandmother and her mother. She hates recitals. She hates the audience, hates the conversations between parents who chit-chat as if their kids aren't there at all, as if they don't understand what is being said about them. She hates that she is not like the others – she doesn't go to a nice school, doesn't have nice clothes, doesn't have brothers and sisters. She doesn't even have a dad to stand next to her mother, like the other fathers stand next to the other mothers, even the divorced ones. She is friends with only one of the other kids – Asya, whose dad ran off with a younger woman, so now she is being raised by her mom and her grandma. This is the only thing she and Asya have in common, otherwise Asya plays better than all the others, she goes to competitions, and her mother looks at the other mothers with a thin little smile, which curves into a giant arc and almost slips into her mouth. This thin little smile reveals that this success is not her daughter's but rather her own, it's personal – the girl's glittering future is entirely her doing. All the mothers are constantly talking about all the sacrifices they have made for one thing or another and the little girl wonders why they had kids at all, since taking care of them is so awful. Her mother complains the loudest, always in front of the largest crowd, who all nod with the most enormous sympathy.

She's sure of one thing – that her mother is disappointed, even ashamed of her, because the little girl is not the best, she doesn't even come second or third, and that is a failure that is just as personal as the other mothers' successes with their children. This guilt weighs on her chest, squeezes her lungs, gets entangled in her larynx. She has already understood that she will never impress her mother: that would mean having to rip her mind out of her body, to squash it like a firebug on the hot asphalt, and afterward to find somebody else's essence – one her mother could love – and to stuff it inside of her, without it being rejected like an incompatible organ. The little girl has said that she doesn't like playing the piano, but every time she does her mother reminds her of how, when she was five, she had pointed at the TV when there was a concert playing and said that she wanted to play, too. You can't just go changing your mind day in and day out, her mother tells her. You need to have discipline.

At the entrance exam before first grade, she is the only one out of all the children who can read fluently, with no mistakes, and the teacher praises her. For the first time. Her mother replies that this is because she just lounges around all day reading comic books instead of doing something productive like practicing her piano. The little girl can no longer read fluently, she doesn't know when this happened, she is afraid to talk. When she opens her mouth, what comes out is not words but syllables that get tangled up on their way to the sentence and scatter nonsensically into the constituent sounds. She manages to fake being ill for only one recital. After that, her mother catches on to her and does not hide her disappointment, because of *all the sacrifices she has made*, so that the little girl could have the chance to play in front of so many people. The worst part isn't that she comes out on stage and can't even say her name. No, far worse are the condescending, pitying looks of the parents, in which she can read gratitude that this is not their child.

She is most afraid of peeing herself in front of the audience. So for hours before the recital, she doesn't drink water or eat, which makes her dizzy. She doesn't understand why her body betrays her like this, why she doesn't have control over anything, not even her own self. The teacher picks out the pieces in advance – the ones the child has played the best throughout the year. Her pieces always start with horrifying letters, which loom over her like evil giants that she has to overcome, but there's not a single airy vowel for her to grasp onto, to lift her up.

'Preludes by Schumann' – the tall gate of the P, which she has no key to; the wrought-iron bars of the M, a gilded cage from which there is no escape. A Waltz by Czerny, with that W whose vibrato refuses to transition into 'a'; or that CZ, whose pointy edges snag along the way to the end of the word and so has to be pulled along until her tongue nearly bursts at the seams. The worst of all is Camille Saint-Saëns with his carnival, that insurmountable C and the hissing 's' – every time you start sliding down it, the sharp ending sends you straight back to the start and spits you right out into the beak of the next sound. She likes 'Le Cygne' – 'The Swan' – best of all, plus it's so easy to slide right across that L – it's over before you know it . . . But they never let her play what she likes, and she's too afraid to ask in any case – her mother has taught her that she has to do as she is told, otherwise people will think she's badly brought up. So for that reason she has to go out and say in front of everyone that she will play 'Hens and Roosters'.

The day becomes an endless repetition – *hensandroosters, hensandroosters, hensandroosters* – she watches her lips in the mirror, whispers it to herself on the tram – she can say it now, so why can't she also say it in front of people?

She nervously counts how many kids are left before it's her turn to get up on stage. She's calm – there are six whole performances to go.

Then five, then four . . .

The familiar twinge appears in her stomach.

Three.

A sharp pain in her lower abdomen. She always runs out after her performance – not only because she is ashamed and crying, but also because she gets painful diarrhea and has no choice but to squat in the Academy's decrepit bathrooms that reek of people and bleach, until her legs go numb.

Two.

Asya's mother has fiery red hair and her eyebrows have been plucked and afterward thinly drawn back on, making her always look slightly surprised. She has a mole on her left cheek, her skin looks soft, she smells of perfume, she dresses elegantly and beautifully, her outfits are always well put together. She works at the National Radio, she's an artistic type, with a normal job, not a doctor wiping old people's asses for a pittance, her mother says. That's why she's beautiful. Only people who don't have other worries can afford to be beautiful, her mother thinks.

One.

The professor's son has been accepted to law school in England. The teacher's eldest students will also start going abroad to study, because their parents have money and because the borders are open, her grandma adds, not like it was back in her day, when they grew up like wild beasts trapped on a reserve. Anthony, who will play 'The Lion', is seventeen – his father is filming him with a video camera as he walks out on stage. Good thing we don't have money for a camera, the little girl thinks. Or a father to hold it.

Zero.

The thick caramel of the words boils over in her red-hot stomach, climbs up the ladder of her throat, cools down; her lips stick together, her tongue grows heavy, the words get tangled in her uvula, they're stuck – the agitation condenses into tears.

Her whole body is shaking. Her mouth is full of roosters and hens flocking between her teeth, nesting in her molars. That H grows, towering higher and higher, she reaches her little hands out toward it, but it keeps stretching up and up and up, smashing through the roof of the Academy and heading for the clouds, hiding the sun – surely it is visible from outer space.

'Yana will play "Hens and Roosters!"' She hears the professor's voice. 'Come on, Yana darling, we can't wait to hear it!'

She doesn't want to turn her eyes toward the audience, she doesn't want to see the knowing glances that accompany the dull applause. She sits down, places her shaking hands on the keyboard and hopes that everyone is too far away to see her tears.

Lily

'I want to study in Mihaylovgrad. At the German High School. I don't care what Dad says, I've signed up for the entrance exams,' my mother announces to her mother with the confidence of a fourteen-year-old.

They are picking corn. As long as Lily can remember, they've spent the summers in the field picking corn. Afterward they dry it, and she and her mother spend whole days stripping the kernels from the cobs into a giant wooden chest. Half of it goes to her uncle and aunt.

'Victoria told me that this summer they're going to the seaside in Sinemorets, then skiing in the winter' – she passes on her cousin's news – 'while we're sitting here husking corn.'

Her mother doesn't say anything. That's what she always does – when she hears something she doesn't like, she keeps silent and doesn't say anything.

'Are you going to talk to him? About Mihaylovgrad. Comrade Petrova says it would be a crime not to send me there. I'm the best in the class. There's nothing left for me to do here.'

'There's plenty for you to do. Who will help me around the house?'

'What about Pavel?'

Her brother roams the streets, goes swimming in the river with his friends and does Lord knows what else, then afterward, when he deigns to come home, she has to serve him dinner and wash his dirty underwear.

'Mom, please. Isn't school the most important thing? The German High School is really good. I won't let you down, I promise.'

'This town has started growing, you'll see, just give it a few years and it'll be much better . . .'

'Mom, please.'

Her mother sighs. 'Of course I'll talk to him, sweetie. You just take your exams, everything else will be a breeze.'

'Thanks, Mom. Thanks so much, Mama,' she says.

Thanks, Mom, and I'm sorry about everything that I can't tell you, my mother thinks.

I can't live with the two of you anymore.

I can't wipe up any more blood.

I can't clean, cook and do the laundry anymore while you lie in the bedroom. I can't bend over you to check whether you're still breathing.

I can't beg you to leave him, convince you that we'll figure something out.

I want to go where you are not.

I can't forgive your resignation. I'm afraid that if I stay here, I'll end up exactly like you.

My guilt for hating you is killing me.

But who are you to teach me what kind of woman to be?

Mom, I want to be like the other girls, I want you to be like the other women; I want us to be beautiful and to laugh together, to get bouquets of flowers, to go and eat cakes on Sunday, to lazily look through photos from summer vacations during the holidays curled up on the couch, both of us laughing, did I tell you that already, for us both to laugh and laugh . . .

Mom, I'm sick of us crying.

I feel guilty for leaving you alone, Mama. Forgive me, because I'll never be able to forgive myself . . .

*   *   *

Her hands ache from stripping corn off the cobs. She looks down at them – they seem fat, her fingers are like sausages, every bit as clumsy as her body. She eavesdrops at the living room door, being careful not to let them see her through the glass pane. On the other side, her father, mother and grandmother are sketching out her future.

'She'll go to Mihaylovgrad and run wild,' she hears the old woman's dried-up voice.

'I'm not going to raise a whore,' her father's voice chimes in.

'Ignat, I want us to discuss this without your mother in the room,' her mother snaps, undaunted. Since they've been keeping the older woman at arm's length, the two of them haven't been fighting as fiercely as before. But even their infrequent arguments are more than enough – her father's temper has worsened with the years.

'Fourteen years old, just a snot-nosed kid, how could you think to send her off alone? Who'll keep an eye on her?' The old woman does not let up.

'Mom, please leave us be, afterward I'll come to you, and we'll talk it over,' Ignat says.

'Mother Ivanka, please leave us,' her mother echoes.

My mother darts into her room before the old woman goes to the bedroom across the hall, muttering under her breath.

She passes her exams with excellent results, just like all the exams before.

* * *

On the final warm September evening before they send her to the high school, her mother watches the girl standing shoulder to shoulder with her father and thinks to herself, in this child – starting with the stubbornness, through the glimmers of a harsh sense of humor, and the disdain for everyone around her, all the way to the clipped movements while eating – in this child, there is far more of him than there is of her.

*   *   *

My mother's true youth smells of old paper and ink. The envelopes are slightly rough to the touch, covered with the fine dust of time. The once tidy letters have blurred with age. A stamp with a lion standing proudly on hind legs, the ears of wheat that surround it like a laurel wreath, and the five-pointed red star – a world that no longer exists. Even the towns and streets have new names. I wonder if my mother ever imagined that these letters would cross the ocean, that they would be taken from her mother's drawers just before I left for America.

The light bulb on the porch gives off dim light, but it's enough to read by. My skin is sticky from sweat and humidity, but a cool breeze arrives with the darkness. I light a cigarette; the ocean's salt mixes with the tobacco. The folded sheets of paper crackle as I open them.

21 September 1982, from her mother

... Today we went to see your dad in the hospital. I don't know what to tell you, he isn't doing terribly, but he's also not doing well... he's got to make a firm decision to stick to his diet and no alcohol at all... Your brother is working on the brigade. Things are really quiet here at home. Your grandma mostly keeps to her room. Last night after reading your letter, she said that you

shouldn't have gone to study at that high school, that things were better here, that you wouldn't be having such a hard time (or else she's just sorry about the money). Chin up and show everyone why you chose that school.

I went out to the vineyard and filled 7 jars of tomato sauce, your brother and I picked almonds, although there's not much on the tree this year . . . Granny Docha's whole family says hello, as does Granny Petra, your uncle and aunt and your cousins, as well as your dad . . .

13 October 1982, from her mother
. . . I was a little worried when I came back from Mihaylovgrad the other day, because you were sad when I left. Lily, sweetheart, don't let yourself get down, I'm with you in spirit every day and every night. On Saturday we harvested half the vines, there's still a few rows by the house that we need to do. On Sunday we cooked up a pan of marmalade, so you'll have that to eat. I'll make more, too . . . Your brother was at school for a few days, then since Monday he's been back at the work brigade, picking grapes. Emil gave him a record with some really interesting music on it, something foreign and Western, he can tell you what group it is. Last night your cousins were over here and they couldn't get enough of that record . . .

1 November 1982, from her mother
. . . Your brother was chosen as class secretary, he was grumbling

about it, but I was happy, hopefully this will make him study more . . . All the grannies here are fine. Grandpa Georgi is in the hospital, he's got a lump on his neck, yesterday your brother went to see him . . .

29 March 1983, from her mother
. . . Yesterday (Monday) your brother washed up the cutlery from lunch for the first time. And he even made soup . . .

Tuesday, 13 January 1987, 4.30 p.m., from a girlfriend
Hi, Lily, I know you might be cross with me, 'cause I haven't written to you in so long

. . .

There're so many things I want to tell you but I don't know where to start. So: I got a cat, a black tomcat with white spots his name is Chocho and he's nine months old, civilized and well-trained my mom didn't used to like cats but now she's so attached to him that she treats him like a prince and I love him like a little brother too.

now what, my grades have really gone down on the one hand it's my fault but on the other Mom and Dad almost got divorced he was shooting at us with a rifle he's a hunter right so he has a gun and was chasing us around the room. A couple of times we slept at other people's houses for me this was a total tragedy I was really upset and got to be so touchy that I couldn't even stand myself the last time it was a while ago now he hurled himself at her and I tried to defend her but he took the belt out of his trousers and started hitting me with it until I fell to the ground unconscious. When I took off my jeans my mom screamed everything was already over I was covered in blood and for two weeks I had to go to school with gauze on my backside. Now they've made up but I will never forget what my dad did to me I don't love him anymore . . .

I'm telling you this in confidence 'cause I don't have anyone else, I had another girlfriend we were friends for years but I found out too late that she was not my friend at all Grandma and Grandpa don't know my mom and I aren't gonna tell them

. . .

I hope I'm not bothering you with this letter drop me a line I hope to see you soon maybe during the holidays maybe I can come visit if you're not going somewhere of course

. . .

Sending you 1001 kisses.

10 February 1987, from her mother

. . . I don't know how to respond to those final questions, as I've never been to an exhibition.

XOXO, Mom

Postmarked 3 September 1987, to her mother

. . . Like Misho told us, some girl in Berkovitsa happened to

talk to somebody from the brigade headquarters at the Economics Institute and he promised to fix us up with a 'good' brigade. And most likely our names are on the list right next to this other girl from Mihaylovgrad. So we're working in the village of Bohot, it's on the road to Lovech about ten minutes away by bus, at a poultry farm. The work is nice, because we're inside, not out hoeing the fields, and we can even hope for 20 leva as pay . . .

Postmarked 21 September 1987, to the whole family
. . . We went to Tsarevets and Sveta Gora with Victoria and Uncle Georgi, there's a Ferris wheel there and the guy running it must've forgotten about us, so even though all or almost all of the gondolas were empty, he put us in number 6, turned it on and then we went around and around until Grandma Ivanka felt so sick that she finally yelled at him to stop the ride . . .

Postmarked 1 December 1987, to her mother
. . . What else can I say you definitely find yourselves at least a little Christmas tree, because it sets the tone for the holidays otherwise it's just a nice meal for no reason. My days are so monotonous that I want us all to be in an incredible mood for Christmas and to have a really good time . . . Write to me or call if you happen to find a convenient phone and let me know how you all are . . .

Postmarked 17 December 1987, to her mother
Dearly beloved!

On the eve of 8 December, I got your telegram wishing me a Happy Students' Holiday – thank you so much for the good wishes . . . On the evening of the 8th we had a really great time and I came home bright-eyed and bushy-tailed at around midnight . . . The food was really good and there was a non-stop video concert with Celentano, Madonna and so on. Everything was exactly as it should be . . . we drank a bit of champagne, but nobody was drunk, nobody made a scene or a fool of themselves. After we ate, we danced for three and a half hours straight. The funniest part was one of the girls who's usually super shy got a bit tipsy and busted out some dance moves that absolutely blew our minds . . .

1988 – empty pages and bad student poetry. A blank sheet of paper, almost translucent from the years.

Pleven, 5 November 1988, to the whole family
. . . Don't forget if you come out this way or if you send me something slip in some cockroach poison, because this place is full of them and I'm always afraid one is going to crawl on me.

5 June 1989, to her father
Dear Dad! For the first time in a long time – or perhaps for the

first time ever – I have received such a warm, lovely letter.

You are right that I am careless and despite the fact that I think about home quite often, as there really is no place like home, I rarely think to write, but I believe I'll have lots of time in the future to write you long letters.

. . .

Dad, when I start writing quickly my handwriting looks almost exactly like yours. A few days ago I was thinking that when I sit down at the table to study, it's more comfortable for me to sit sideways – just like you always sit – your torso is parallel to the table but your legs are crossed to the side.

I really miss you and Mom and being home in general.

8 December 1989, from her father

. . . The weather here is downright nasty. It's really cold. The sun is out, but it's nippy as hell . . . At the moment I'm listening to the radio programme for university students as I'm writing. It's fine, but some of them have absurd demands. I think they're asking too much – wasn't getting rid of the Communists a month ago enough? Our country, given the shape it's in now, will have a hard time living up to these 'ideals'. I don't have anything else to report. I'm going out to look for an iron and a sink for the bathroom . . .

12 December 1989, from her father

. . . Call if you need anything. We may be poor, but we're here

for you . . . We're keeping up with the reforms . . .

. . . Try to distance yourself a bit from the hotheads, 'cause in times like these you don't know how long they'll last and what's going to happen to who today or tomorrow. Be careful!

14 December 1989

Hello everyone!

I was really happy to get Dad's letter on Sunday. Don't worry about my political activities. Medicine is one of those academic fields where if you choose to study it, there's no time for strikes, demonstrations and all the rest of the stuff shaking up the whole country at the moment.

. . .

I'm fine, and I've been discussing the political situation with my landlady. I'll come visit at New Year!

Undated

. . . Now for some bad news. Thanks to a curriculum reform from the new university administration, I'm being forced to take a leave of absence. I would never in a million years have thought that something like this could happen and I feel awful about it, because everyone is going to think I'm a fool. I'll have the right to take my final exams during January. And then I only have the state exams left.

I can't imagine you really want to see me, which is why I don't dare to come home. I'm looking for a job so I won't be a burden on you like I have been until now. There's a chance I could get hired as a cleaner or a cook (I went and asked). The people from the unemployment office didn't believe that I would want to work as a cleaner, but frankly it's all the same to me.

To be honest, I feel ashamed to tell you that I had to stop my studies, but on the other hand I really don't care. I'm studying English, reading newspapers and feeling down about everything, but when I start work I'm sure I'll be fine . . .

There's so much I don't know about my mother's life. Maybe if she had told me, I wouldn't feel so guilty about not understanding why we lived the way we did. Maybe we wouldn't be strangers, trapped only by the obligation of blood.

12

'What the hell do you remember from that time . . . You don't remember shit.'

'Yeah, I do! It was nice back then. I don't have bad memories, I even miss it. Some things were better, there was more order and discipline . . . You remember how they lined us up?'

Sylvia and Dancho were born around fifteen years after my mother, if my calculations are correct – sometime during the 1980s.

Hurricane season starts earlier than usual this year – mid-September. The gusts reach up to seventy miles per hour, the beaches are closed, barely any cars are on the roads. The wind plays with the traffic lights hanging on thin cables above the roadways, street signs roll on the sidewalk and the highway, trash flies all over the place.

'The nineties when we grew up were so piss poor and miserable. Yana, you might not remember at all, we were just hitting our teens. There wasn't any toilet paper to wipe your ass with . . . My balls were black from newspaper ink.' Dancho gesticulates wildly. 'Now the students, coming here, I've seen them, they start complaining – oh, it's so dirty, oh, there's too many people in the same house, oh this, oh that . . . You have no idea what it means to be piss poor.'

We're sheltered from the wind on the porch, sitting around the table, smoking and drinking. Sylvia chimes in: 'We felt so cool, when we found out we could come here. Do you know what brigada meant for our parents? Brigada meant working for the Communists, going to preserve vegetables or pick fruit every summer, for no money, to meet the quotas, shit like that, forced labor, you couldn't say a word. While our brigada was in America!'

'I don't even know if anybody else calls it brigada. I think only we Bulgarians call it brigada,' says Emo.

'You can't even imagine what it was like to leave Bulgaria – when was it, 2002 was the first time, right?' Sylvia nods in confirmation to Dancho. 'And not from Sofia, but from the countryside, Jesus fucking Christ, what poverty . . . When we came here, we couldn't believe it. Now you know that these houses aren't anything special and it's all bought on credit that you then spend your whole life paying back, you become a slave to stuff you can't afford . . . Whatever . . . We came and we saw – huge cars, dirt-cheap gas, cheap all-you-can-eat food, you go into the store and you don't know where to look first . . . I didn't even know the names for certain foods, what they were, what they were made from . . . I got fat as a pig. The first summer when I went back I brought some cheap crap for my friends, fifty-cent chocolate bars, and they looked at me like I was from outer space—'

'And not only the food,' Sylvia interrupts. 'The clothes, too! The make-up, the lotions, no . . . Everything, everything! You could tell when somebody went abroad and came back, he'd just carry himself differently, they called us 'the Americans' in Karnobat, everyone was jealous . . .'

'I got clued in to where the real money is from my very first brigada,' says Emo. 'I started buying phones, MP3 players, the first iPod had just come out, they went crazy for it over here, no one had heard of it in Bulgaria . . . And I bought ten, fifteen probably, spent almost all my money from the summer, then I went back to Bulgaria and doubled, tripled it.'

The storm slams into the house, then calms down, then roars again. I watch the rain beating at the facades of the houses across the way.

'Remember Sava, that guy from Pernik, or was it Pleven, Pazardzhik, I don't remember anymore . . .'

'He was from Pazardzhik,' says Dancho. 'Crazy sonuvabitch.'

'Yeeeah, Sava . . . He was hell-bent on saving up, there were these competitions about who'd make the most money . . . He survived all summer on hot dogs and ramen. No joke, I swear. I'll never forget him at this one party, stuffing himself, everyone else was making out, dancing, he's eating. He worked so hard he didn't gain a pound, he even lost some weight. And he returned home with thirty thousand for just three months of work!'

'A legend.'

'Why can't I remember that guy?'

'What about Mia?'

'Now *her* I remember!' Sylvia yells over the storm. 'Wasn't that the girl who worked at four different places?'

'The very same.' Emo opens another beer. 'The one who studied at the American University in Blagoevgrad and paid her tuition by bartending.'

'What did she study?'

'Uh, I don't know, Dancho. Economics, politics, something stupid like that.'

'This chick was an absolute ma-chine.' Dancho is enthralled. 'She had three or four gigs as a waitress, made four hundred bucks or more a day in tips and was on her feet for eighteen hours a day. I think she had one day off a week, something like that.'

'She paid her tuition off and graduated.'

'So what?' Dancho snorts. 'She still works there, we went to Ocean City last month and she's still there. Nine years, she says. And she loves it. She serves booze to the old farts and they drool over her rack.'

'I didn't even graduate,' Sylvia says. 'My English will never be that good, even after so many years here, as you can see. So I'll never find a job that uses my degree – I studied accounting, if you can believe it.' She shakes her head and stares off into space. 'Once you've been to America, you start measuring everything in dollars and hours, you know?'

'OK, Dancho, how long has it been now since you've been home, if you're . . .'

'2007 . . . so eight, nine years.' Dancho crushes his cigarette butt into the ashtray.

I wait for him to go on, but he doesn't.

'When I go home, I go and see his parents, show them

pictures, we chat [illegible]' Sylvia says. 'Of course they miss him. But everyone understands that it's better this way – our old classmates, those who stayed behind, hang around the pubs all day or play cards on their front stoops. Most are unemployed. Still living with their parents.'

She stops for a moment, as if she is wondering whether to continue or not. 'They're just glad we send them money. Otherwise, how would they survive? With their two hundred leva a month pensions. A hundred bucks.'

'No one stays here because they want to,' Emo says. 'Foreign place, foreign people . . . Look at Nelly, saving up to get married. What's your knee-jerk reaction? To say "that fucking slut" . . . That's what one guy said a few days ago. But last year' – Emo lowers his voice – 'her father . . . he . . . he hung himself on the basketball hoop in the neighborhood schoolyard. Her mother gets a widow's pension. What're you gonna do?' He lights up a new cigarette. 'And besides – it's not like we're thieves? Aren't we busting our asses? How would these shitty resorts stay in business without us? Tell me, these assholes looking for entertainment, not that they're to blame, their lives are just as fucked as ours, tell me, what would they stuff themselves with if it wasn't for us?'

'Yeah, and there's poverty here too, just look at the black people, and the whites too, with these junkies . . .'

'Fuck it, Dancho, at least here I can choose whether or not I'm poor. It's not like back there, where your destiny is shit, and if you open your mouth to call it shit – you swallow even more shit.'

‘That’s because people haven’t learned. Here, people have different habits, it’s—’

‘What habits and what are they learning? You’re talking pure bullshit. People are the same everywhere, the difference is that the dumber you are in Bulgaria, the more successful you are, because idiots are harmless and you feel good, being smarter, you’re not as screwed as they are. The idiot is grateful to you for feeding him, you can turn and laugh at him, curse at him over the table and feel better about yourself.’

‘Come on, boys, don’t be so negative—’ Sylvia starts in.

Dancho interrupts her: ‘I’ve said it once, I’ll say it again, we got the short end of the stick . . . We’re not to blame for the shit that happens to us. Shit breeds shit.’

‘I think in our parents’ time it wasn’t as shitty. There were plenty of bad things, but there was also order, and people were disciplined, life was different.’ Sylvia is defeated and has apparently decided that if she can’t stop the conversation, she’ll join it.

Emo doesn’t need much more than that: ‘All that bullshit about order and discipline, how many times have I told you? How is it possible that back in the day everything was so orderly and disciplined and once the People’s Republic became a democratic republic, all that order suddenly disappeared? Complete and utter horseshit. You know what that was? A scam. And a swindle. Because those at the top were hard-asses, the scamming and swindling happened behind the scenes. The only difference between then and now is that the invisible has become visible. That’s all. The rest is bullshit.’

Emo gasps for air, the argument has tired him out but there's a glint in his eye – he's ready for the next adversary. He grabs Dancho's cigarettes again.

'Go get more beer,' Dancho snaps at Sylvia and she gets up, slides the veranda door open and sinks into the dark interior of the house. 'You may be right, but you may be wrong.'

'You bet I'm right,' Emo continues. 'There's only one difference between Americans and Bulgarians. You wanna know what it is? You want me to tell you?'

Dancho nods and waves his hand in resignation, his cigarette smoke drawing gray arches.

'The difference is that Bulgarians reject the world, because, as you say, they've always gotten the short end of the stick and then they bow their heads and just let the shit wash over them, waiting for it to pass on its own, over and over again . . . Until the shit piled so high it reached your ears . . . And when people here get the short end of the stick, they look at what everyone else got and say: we're going to do it like them. That's the fucking difference. The Bulgarian looks at the other guys and says, "The world is shit, full of shitheads, why the hell should I play by the rules," while the American says, "This guy's a shithead, which means I have to be good enough for two people." And while we're whining, the world goes on. Even if it's two steps forward, one step back.'

'Total bullshit,' Dancho says.

All of a sudden, the wind turns and the rain hits us in the face. The pack of cigarettes is soaked in seconds, the ashtray fills with water and the butts float on top like tiny orange-white boats. Wet hands reach from all directions grabbing bottles, lighters, plates, jackets and phones. I hear the door sliding open and shut behind my back. I start walking in no particular direction – there's so much water that I'm already wading through a small pool. The rain envelops me in a thick cocoon.

I finally make it inside, the lights are on – we can't see one another in broad daylight – everyone is laughing and swearing and a wet trail leads to the kitchen island where we leave our drenched possessions. I feel the pockets of my shorts to see if my phone is wet. The screen lights up: three unread messages from my mother. As I tell Sylvia that no, I don't need a towel, I'm not that wet, the words leave the screen, crawl up my hands and soak through my skin – I go numb.

5.20 Are you there?
5.53 Text me back
5.59 Your grandmother isn't doing well

Lily and Eva

'Let's see what this *city boy from Sofia*' – he emphasizes – 'has to say about our little Podunk neck of the woods, huh, Eva?' The old man chuckles.

She sets the warm pumpkin pastry down next to the pot of stewed chicken, beside which a large pan of pork and cabbage is cooling. The bread is wrapped in a white cloth with yellowish stains. They've splurged on some sweets as well; Ignat bought the last ones at the store – cookies with peach jam and meringues – two full trays are shoved in the corner right next to the wall. How long has it been since these kids have had a square meal, Lord only knows how students live in the dorms in times like this. Another thought is also running through her mind – who on earth is Lily bringing home to them, who is this 'classmate' she told them about over the phone? Forks and knives rattle in the other room – Ignat himself has volunteered to set the table; she grabs glasses for soft drinks and goes to help him.

'You've got to pick out a wine, too,' she tells him, and he heads back toward the kitchen. Thirty years of marriage shows in their everyday gestures. He shops; she cooks. He goes to the vineyard; she takes care of the housework. He watches TV; she reads. He fixes things; she cleans.

With the passing of the years, the mistakes don't sting as badly – here and there they ache like old wounds before a storm – at worst, she might dream about something that has happened, but just like a dream the feeling quickly fades and disappears in the fog of time.

She finds him digging through the highest cupboard, where they keep the plastic and glass bottles of homemade alcohol. They are dithering over what exactly to choose when the dilapidated doorbell buzzes weakly three times and muted laughter floats in from the other side of the door.

'Goodness gracious, they're here!' Eva jumps up, smooths

down her hair, heads toward the door but then realizes she still has her apron on, so she turns back.

'Go and open it, for Christ's sake,' Ignat mutters.

'Hush you, I just need to take this off, it's dirty,' she replies.

She hangs the apron on a nail and almost trips on her way out of the kitchen as she rushes to the front door. The bell buzzes again.

'Coming!' Lily hears her mother's forced laughter through the rotting wooden door.

Eva turns the first, second and third locks, and the door sags slightly in the frame – we need to replace the hinges, she thinks – then turns the knob and opens with a flourish. First, she sees her daughter – smiling, a bit heavier, so she has been eating. Then her gaze stops to rest on the tall man next to her. It's the middle of January, shortly after New Year, but he is wearing a thin leather jacket with a shirt, perhaps even just a T-shirt, under it. Her eyes drop to his faded joggers and torn, muddy trainers. His face is handsome but tired, it looks yellow under the dim light of the staircase, his eyes are bulging somehow, as if he is too thin.

'Mom? Can we come in?' The voice tears her away from the young man.

She hadn't realized that she was blocking the door with her body.

'Oh yes, yes, of course, come right on in.' She steps back onto the linoleum in the hallway and stands back by the wall to let them pass. 'I'm Eva, nice to meet you.'

'Dimitar.' He gives her his frozen hand.

Ignat comes out of the kitchen, kisses his daughter, then looks at Dimitar, and Eva knows that he sees the same thing she does. But he is a good host – if for no other reason than that he has always seen guests as an opportunity to show off – bewilderment flits across his face for a moment, only she can read it, before the older man pulls the younger one to him and leads him into the living room. Eva stays behind to line up their shoes. When she picks his up, flakes of dirt fall from the soles.

They scurry around the table; in unspoken agreement they place the young man next to the stove, Lily rushes to help her mother, but not before whispering to her father not to fill the young man's glass too much – he can't hold his drink. In the kitchen mother and daughter hug again, this time for longer. Eva strokes Lily's black hair and tucks it behind her ear, breathing in the familiar scent, happy to see her.

'His parents have an apartment in central Sofia,' Lily tells her while hunting in a cupboard for napkins.

'That's great, sweetie.' Eva points to the pot with the chicken, picks up the cabbage and the two of them head toward the living room.

'They also have two houses, one in the mountains and one on the sea. His mom's a doctor, his dad was a ship's captain, but now he's retired,' Lily continues.

'Bring the bread, will you, Eva!' a voice shouts from the living room.

She startles, grabs the wrapped loaf and turns toward her daughter: 'Lily, honey, be a good girl and open that cupboard, won't you, and take out the sliced bread.'

They open and close the doors – it's cold in the kitchen. Their apartment, like all apartments in the concrete panel-blocks, is a home with several climates, as they can't afford to heat all the rooms – frugalness, cultivated over the years. They go back for the pumpkin pastry and sweets.

'He's a year older, he'll start his surgery specialization next year. His parents are part of the intelligentsia . . .'

'That's great, sweetie.' Eva almost drops the pan of pumpkin pastry, but steadies it on her knee and heads back toward the living room.

It's a quiet dinner. She steals glances at them: Lily eats like her father, dunking her food straight in the salt dish. The young man eats as if he were starving. Eva constantly refills his plate, getting up to bring things over, she even offers to wrap him in a blanket and Lily kicks her under the table. He is quiet and polite, putting up with Ignat in good humor, but without saying much. Eva tries to delve inside that silence, to examine it. Is this good-natured silence that of a patient man or of a person who is hiding something – she can't say. She prefers quiet people, but something about this young man makes her feel ill at ease. She gets angry with herself, scolds herself silently – after all, they are the children of this miserable Transition, is it their fault that they're ragged and hungry?

She questions him – where is he from, who is he, what is he. He answers politely, without saying much.

'Was your dad a commie, tell me the truth now,' Ignat cuts in. They've forgotten to keep an eye on his glass. Eva and Lily shush him at the same time, and he chuckles. The young man laughs as well.

He tells them how his grandfather on his mother's side was an engineer before the Red Army coup in 1944, how he'd graduated in the same class as the famous poet and martyr Nikola Vaptsarov, how during the post-revolutionary purges he'd survived by hiding in a classmate's cellar. He had then sat around unemployed for a few years, until things really went south at a local factory and some acquaintance who had since risen through the Party ranks thought to call him in. He saved the factory, so they gave him a steady job, albeit a low-ranking one, since he refused to join the Party. He was such a talented engineer that he climbed the ladder over the years, but he never did become a Party member, though he won all sorts of recognition and awards, nevertheless.

Ignat fills up the young man's glass again, then refills his own, despite Lily's whispers. This story strikes Eva as fishy – she doesn't believe the Party would just forgive someone like that. Surely this is what the grandfather told his young grandson to plant memories of a dignified man. Eva can't blame him. In these undignified times there are no dignified people, she thinks. How will she tell her story to her own grandchildren? The memory of how Pavel was refused entry into the Military Academy burns in her heart. She remembers how he told her with tears in his eyes that it was her fault since she was the daughter of fascists. She glances at her own daughter, who is proud of these unknown people, her future in-laws with their Sofia apartment, and once again reproaches herself for the stubborn heaviness in her chest.

The four of them drift into the drowsiness caused by a full stomach, and Lily tells her mother that she'll go and show him where they'll sleep, she'll turn on the heater to warm up the room and make up the bed. Eva glances at Ignat, who is about to say something, but he catches her eye and stops. *These are grown-up people, you can't act like a medieval bey*, she has told him. Instead, he comes over to her when the young couple leaves the room and says:

'Tomorrow we've got to go get this youngster some new clothes, we've got to take him to Uncle Kiro to sew him a couple of pairs of trousers, from that woolen cloth, remember, the stuff we bought last autumn.'

'Come on now, just how am I going to tell him . . .'

'Listen here, woman, you tell Lily to tell him, 'cause just look how disheveled he is, what'll everyone in the neighborhood say – Ignat and Eva's girl brought home a tramp . . .'

The young couple comes back and the older couple instantly falls silent. They ask them whether they're still hungry, no, they're not, do they want tea, coffee, more wine, anything else, her father pulls out some chocolates, the younger couple sits down again, they haven't had chocolate since who knows when, laughter. Ignat pours himself another glass of wine and launches into his usual sermon about how you need to pile your table with the best for your guests, how they have a little farm out by the vineyard, which is why they always have a bit of meat, a little something to add to the cabbage. They're poor folk, but generous as poor folk always are, 'cause they know what it means to have nothing, and on and on . . .

The two women clear the table, their movements equally hurried. Now and again Lily playfully pinches her mother and the two of them giggle.

Despite her best efforts, Eva remembers her own mother and father – the worst thoughts always come in the evening.

She recalls when her own mother, may she rest in peace, found out about the beatings and the broken bones, about the horrific headaches and the fear, about her mother-in-law; she remembers her mother pounding her thighs and asking her over and over,

Oh, my poor dear girl, how did you survive, my poor dear girl, how did you survive . . .

Yes, no matter what is eating away at her on the inside, it will be hers alone and she will carry it within her, hidden in silence. When they bring the last dishes back to the kitchen, the mother hugs the daughter the way parents hug their children before leaving them forever, and asks her simply:

'Are you sure, honey?'

For a split second, the time it takes to blink, the smile disappears from Lily's face. Then she hugs her mother and whispers into her warm neck, which smells of her mama: 'Yes.'

night

The horizon lights up gently, as if the ocean itself is glowing. There are exactly six cigarettes left in the pack. Someone is always working in America, there's a well-stocked store even at the edge of the continent, the edge of the night. Scarcity is unknown – this country is perpetual satiation, endlessly satisfying the human drive, 24/7. But we're not ready to turn back to the world yet, we don't want to admit that the best night is ending.

The American tells his story. This is the first time I actually listen without my thoughts galloping alongside the other person's words. About children playing in the suburbs – the fortresses of white America. About a father who worked for the same company his whole life and a mother who raised four boys without a single complaint – breakfast, lunch and dinner; hockey, football, baseball; the clothes always clean, the house always clean; homework done . . .

My father always laughs, embraces my mother and says – Hey, Jen, you're a lucky woman, thank goodness you never had to work.

I see the house, the red shutters and the graying clapboard, the flowers in the yard, the toys scattered across the lawn.

One salary was enough for a house, a car and four children, can you imagine that today . . .

Of course not, one salary isn't even enough to break your leg.

Sometimes I wonder where this America went, who stole it from the hands of people like my father, the people who built it. Lucky bastards – being born in a country that had triumphed over the world . . .

Not where I come from, I say, their generation was the saddest in the world, being the same age as the dictatorship, growing up and maturing with it – the older you get, the more it grows, you go to school together, the regime attends your wedding, it's your colleague at work, it sits at the table at night and sticks its fingers down your throat, it takes the best pieces of everything.

You know what they say at home? They say, 'We'll catch up.' That someday we'll finally have the freedom, the money, all of it. My grandmother and my grandfather are waiting for what your mother and father had. The clean streets. The nice cashiers. Just the sound of the phrase, waiting to catch up with something . . . And the more we wait, the more the world recedes into the distance.

What did the victors do to the world . . .

They gnawed it to the bone. Excuse my French, but I piss on the world if that's the end result of the greatest era in history.

You know, he tells me, *when I think 'ten years ago', I always think of the nineties. And it's been almost thirty years.*

The night recedes toward the resort. It's 4.25 a.m.

You know, I never ended up telling her why I didn't want to play. My mother. Why I hated the piano. It wasn't just the recitals or the students, nor the books.

I haven't told a single soul.

She often worked night shifts, and he and I would be left home alone, I must have been seven or eight, he would get drunk and make me play, I would sit on the bench, having pissed myself from fear, my underwear stuck to my ass, he would stand behind me and I'd hear him swallow, I would keep playing the same melody again and again. I was afraid, and at some point in the night he'd just leave the room but I'd continue playing because I was too scared to turn around.

I don't know why I didn't tell her, probably because she told me that she lived only for me, that she was going to kill herself if I kept up my ingratitude, that she had sacrificed everything, her life, her happiness for me. I didn't allow myself any fear, any tears, I didn't want to say a word. She had enough pain already. I didn't want to be another burden for her.

He extends an arm toward me. There are four cigarettes left in the pack.

Yana

The January frost fiercely bites their cheeks and tangles in their hair. On the news they're constantly saying that this is the coldest winter in decades. Even the smog-blackened slush has frozen into solid mounds. The windows of the tram are covered in lacy crystals of frost – she tries to wipe the window with the sleeve of her jacket and her grandma scolds her, saying it's dirty. The elderly woman isn't constantly trying to edify her like her mother does – on the contrary, in the evenings, instead of reading books or watching television, her grandma tells her about her life. She learns that her grandmother has also fallen in love, only not with her grandfather, but she has learned to respect him, and according to Grandma, respect is more important than love in a marriage.

'Getting married is like being given a bag full of snakes. You root around inside hoping to pull out a garter snake. Harmless. But you've pulled out a viper!' Her grandma laughs.

The girl does not join in with her laughter.

Her grandma tells her other things as well, things that make her feel ashamed, but she keeps quiet and listens, somehow understanding that these words have been ripening in her for a whole lifetime: she is repeatedly told that the physical aspects of marriage are a spousal obligation, nothing more, that she never experienced any pleasure and for her all this talk about sex is just a perversion, that's why the girl should be careful, she should be very careful with men, so she doesn't get taken in by foolish talk. The girl wonders whether these stories remained unheard because to her mother, her grandfather, her uncle – in short for everyone else – her grandma was a mother, a wife, a daughter-in-law, a daughter, but never Eva, never simply Eva . . .

Night after night, while her father drinks in the kitchen and the girl lies in her bed with her grandma, unable to fall asleep, she listens to the stories and makes promises to herself. She will never listen to her mother like her grandma listened to her own mother; she will never keep quiet like her grandma kept quiet, *even way back when I could sense that something was off about your father, but I kept quiet . . .*

They are participants in their own unhappiness, they have no right to stuff her full of their advice – their advice only ever finds them curled up in terror in the girl's bedroom.

They change to another tram; the orange street lights are reflected in the snow. Cars belch out burned-up fumes from beneath their snowy caps; smog irritates throats. When they reach the entrance of their apartment building and see that the kitchen windows are dark, the girl's stomach clenches. Her grandma squeezes her hand lightly, as if trying to convince herself that everything is all right, that there is nothing to be afraid of. The lights in the living room are on, that means her mother is home. The girl has school the next day, so there are – she does the maths in her head – only eleven hours left until she has to get up. They go inside quietly, without making much noise – he hates noise while he's drinking – they line up their shoes and tiptoe toward the living room, and she sneaks a glance at the kitchen door. It's closed. In the living room, her mother is sitting on the piano stool, which is raised almost as high as it will go, writing out medical case histories on the ironing board.

'Come and help me,' her mother says in lieu of a greeting.

The girl really has to go to the bathroom, but she'll hold it. On the worst occasions, when he's really drunk, the three women pee into a ten-litre plastic jug that's been sawed in half on the balcony. They might get lucky and he might go to bed early that night, in which case the three of them will slip out of the living room silently, brush their teeth and quickly do their business, then lock themselves in the girl's room, sliding the latch on the door. Her grandma will sleep in the armchair, she and her mother will cuddle on the bed, and that's how they will spend the night. The girl doesn't like lying next to her mother – she hates how the woman clutches her greedily. On the whole there is something perverse in the two women's refusal to respect the girl's pleas not to touch her, as if she is some appendage to their bodies instead of a separate person.

The two of them sit down and each pick up one thin folded sheet of paper stuffed full of other documents, photos, longish electrocardiograms. The girl copies from the case histories that have already been filled out – she can perfectly imitate her mother's handwriting and that of all her colleagues.

Either we do this or they'll fire me and we'll be out on the street, her mother tells her when the girl asks for the first time why they make her invent all these illnesses – part of a widespread scheme to drain the National Health Insurance fund. Her mother gets the most twenty-four-hour shifts of anyone and writes the most case histories because she is a GP – she doesn't have a speciality.

Because she didn't think when she was young, the grandmother shakes her head, clicking her tongue.

Why don't you complain to someone and say that it's wrong to lie, the little girl asks her mother, and her mother replies that the person she would have to complain to is the same person who ordered her to write them in the first place.

The door to the living room suddenly opens and her father's head pokes through – his eyes are red slits, he has a hard time focusing his gaze.

'So you got home, huh?' He stares straight at the girl.

'We got home, we got home,' the grandma replies, her voice full of forced cheerfulness.

He stares at them, then slowly closes the door and through the glass they watch his silhouette disappear toward the kitchen.

'You didn't do something to set him off?' The grandma turns to the mother, but she has not even raised her eyes from the case history she's filling out, and the girl immediately knows that her mother has been shouting again, threatening and insulting him, that she went to antagonize him for no reason, looking for meaning where there is only painful madness.

The grandma sighs noisily, the mother shoots her a look, but they keep writing. The only sounds are the whisper of the paper and the grandma's sighs. The girl glances at the clock – eight, eight thirty, nine, nine thirty – she gets hungry, but she knows she can only eat after her father goes to bed, which will surely be after midnight. She is cross with herself for turning down her grandma's offer of banitsa. The greasy, doughy snack makes her want to puke, but if she had eaten, her stomach wouldn't be so empty now. Finally, she can't bear it anymore and goes out on the balcony to pee – the cold pinches her skin, the snow around the base of the jug melts, steam rises into the air. She goes back inside, her grandma is lying in the armchair dozing, her mother turns out the lights, leaving only the nightlight on the ironing board. The girl curls up on the couch and tries to sleep, tries not to think about food, not to think about food, *nottothinkabout* . . .

The silence shatters. She opens her eyes. The floor beneath her feet sparkles like the snow outside.

The second explosion sends a volley of glass dust into her face – she runs her hand over her cheek and feels the tiny shards digging into her soft skin. She hears her father's roar, followed by the third volley: 'Now this is our marriage!'

The doorway resembles a monstrous maw; one of the glass icicles falls and breaks.

'Mama!' she cries, and with relief feels her mother next to her – she has come over to stand beside them. He crosses the living room, knocks over the ironing board and goes toward the balcony.

One, two, three glass explosions.

An icy wind bursts into the room.

'Now this, this is our marriage,' he keeps bellowing.

Four,

five,

six.

The last window is now broken. Outside, the snow covers the city in a layer of peace, time has gone still, bearing witness from the balcony, from the rooftops, from the clouds the color of *café au lait*. She sees several snowflakes falling onto the glass, melting into glittering droplets.

He walks back across the room, squats down and slips through the empty pane in the door – the glass teeth shred his T-shirt and stains appear on his back. Her mother starts to stand up, to go over to him, but the girl clings to her wrists, looking at her grandma in desperation, who also grabs the mother by the shoulders. The two of them whisper quietly:

Please stay here, please stay here, and the younger woman gives in.

A crash comes from the glassed-in kitchen balcony, the wind barges freely into the apartment, raging around, blowing in from the kitchen, rushing down the hallway, finding openings and exiting through the living room balcony, then doubling back in a crazy loop. It's getting colder and colder, but the three of them do not feel the cold, only the fear: her mother is thinking about adrenaline, about the fight-or-flight response, $C_9H_{13}NO_3$; the grandma juggles various things in her mind: where are the knives, where is the paperweight, something heavy they could use to defend themselves; the girl simply doesn't want her mother to die, she's afraid that her mother will die, she imagines her mother's body sprawled in the middle of the room, on top of the glass, she hears in her head all the things her mother has told her about what would happen if she died – the orphanage, where you get raped and drugged, or going back to her grandma's small town to live with them, amid the cornfields and the past, or worse yet, she could be given to her father, good God, please let her mother not die . . . if only her mother wouldn't die . . .

Schlocky Macedonian music blares from the kitchen. The

light in the hallway comes on, and he is standing before them in his shredded T-shirt, red rivulets creeping down his arms and dripping onto the floor with a quiet glassy clink. The room smells of ice and blood.

'You.' He points at the girl – a dark drop falls from his index finger and soaks into a page of the case history. Her father can hardly speak. 'Go and play. Your mother wants you to play more. To practice.'

'Now's not the time, it's almost twelve o'clock,' her mother says, but he doesn't hear her, his finger stays pointed like a weapon.

She'll play the whole night through, as long as it keeps her mother alive.

She digs the piano stool out from under the piles of paper and goes into the room next door where the piano is. Her grandmother follows close behind her, not letting her out of her sight, her father also goes into the room, her mother stays on the couch. The little girl goes to sit down, but he knocks her aside and sits down at the keyboard.

'First, I've gotta show you how it's done, like this, right . . . I've gotta show you,' he slurs.

The cold and the alcohol have frozen his long fingers, fingers that can sew life back into a body with utter precision. He pounds away mercilessly, the piano howls in pain, dark blood drips from its black-and-white keys, trickling into the cracks and soaking into the wood. The girl imagines red caterpillars crawling over the strings and reaching all the way to the hammers, burrowing into the notes themselves. He finally stops, grabs her by the shoulders and sits her down on the stool.

Her hands don't belong to her body, she doesn't feel the contact with the ivory of the keys. Whatever is left of her sense of her own self has curled up above her stomach, frozen into icicles along her ribs, stabbing her with every breath. With effort, he drags over the footstool and sits down on her left. The girl plays from memory, she is afraid to reach for the sheet music, the back of her head burns, her fingers beg the keys not to budge, to stay where they belong, for just a little bit longer while she plays. This will all be over at some point. She is sure that if she stops playing, her father will kill her mother. She curses herself for not having practiced for days.

'No, no, no! It's no good!' His hands, those strange frightening hands that she vaguely remembers are her father's, open like the talons of a bird of prey and rapaciously sink into the low notes. The piano shudders. 'Now this is how you've gotta play! Now that's music!'

He soon tires, waves his hand and points at her to start playing again.

She obeys.

His right hand starts sliding up and down her back, pressing on her shoulders,

playing with her hair,

dropping down to her waist,

it stops lazily,

then again heads for the curve of her neck.

'You'll make a pretty little whore, too,' he tells her, 'just like all the rest of them, you too, you'll make such a pretty little whore . . .'

She swallows back her tears, she's afraid to cry, the picture blurs, she vaguely senses her mother and grandmother jumping up at once, but the doorbell interrupts them, it rings very clearly, then a second time, loud pounding on the door,

once

twice,

three heavy knocks.

A thick male voice floats in from the staircase. The father jumps up and leaves the room, the kitchen door slams. The mother rushes to answer the door, the grandmother hugs the girl and starts murmuring something into her hair.

'Leave me alone,' she hisses, pushing her grandmother away.

The doorbell startles time awake, and when it starts moving again, it has sped up. Suddenly the girl is terribly cold, she's shaking, the grandmother shuts the door to the room and slides across the latch, she wraps the girl in a blanket and sets her near the radiator that is only half-working.

Stay here, stay here and get warm, you need to warm up now, she hears her grandmother like a distant echo.

Mama, Mama, Grandma . . . Mama, please, go and see if she's . . . please, don't go out, please bring back my mom, Mama! Mama!

Shhh, hush now, hush, I've got to go and find your mother now, haven't I, just sit here really quiet, just sit quietly and wait, the echo replies and her grandmother leaves the room.

The girl is left alone with the piano, from whose mouth drips dark drool.

The girl gets up, dragging the blanket after her and, as she crosses the living room, the glass sticks to the cloth and scrapes against yet more glass, crunching under her feet. Shards of glass fall from the door when she opens it. A glassy, icy world.

She stands in the dark and listens. She can't figure out who on earth would have come at this hour, why they've come, because she knows when they ask the neighbors if they hear what happens at home they say:

No, no, we didn't hear anything, because the TV was on,
because we were out,
because that's your private business
and surely it can't be so bad, since we didn't hear anything,
no, we're elderly folks, we're hard of hearing as it is.

Then they meet her on the stairs and tell her how much she's grown:

We've known your father since he was yay big, and just like you he played in the park and would disappear all day down the paths, he liked to court trouble always roaming around all alone, and would you look at him now, a doctor, knock on wood that you grow up big and strong like him, too . . .

The light in the hallway is on and she finds herself face-to-face with a man as tall as her father. He looks at her questioningly. She suddenly realizes she is barefoot – she feels the pain and cold in her feet, standing there in a little puddle of blood.

'Is this the kid?' he says toward the kitchen.

'Come on now, tell me, how could a big girl like you wet herself?' He smiles, and the girl looks down at her jeans and sees the familiar dark line around her crotch that trickles all the way down to her ankles.

She looks through the door frame into the kitchen. Her father is sitting in the plastic chair near the wall, bloodied, staring at the floor, while two men are standing over him: one tall and the other short and fat, the latter scribbling something in a little notebook.

'Just what do you think you're doing, scaring the neighbors like that, huh?' the fat one says jokingly as he writes. 'And now that you've made this mess, you're all going to freeze to death, you're quite the big shot, huh, a really manly thing to do, no question about it.'

Her mother is standing near the cupboards facing the police but not saying anything. The girl can't see her grandmother.

'Look here, my boy, this is your warning. If we need to come here again, we'll take you away with us,' the fat cop goes on. 'Although now that I think about it, given how cold it is here, you might just prefer being in hot water.'

'And you, ma'am, do you and the child here have anywhere to sleep? Do you want us to drive you somewhere?'

'We don't have anywhere to go, besides I need to be at work in a few hours, couldn't you—'

'Fiiine,' the fat cop cuts her off, 'so look, listen here, you two' – he turns to the mother and the father – 'when you two are having a spat, you need to figure it out quietly, and call somebody tomorrow to board up these windows, 'cause you're gonna freeze your asses off. And that kid . . .'

The girl doesn't want to listen to them anymore, the other cop keeps staring at her with that look they give her at recitals, but with something else as well: mockery, ridicule. *How could a big girl like you wet herself . . .*

'Mom, you'll come to my room after, right?' she asks her mother. 'Promise?' Her mother nods and that's enough for her to turn around and make her way back through the glass, to shut the door to her bedroom and to slide the latch into place until the two women come back to join her.

The three of them lie huddled together for warmth, under four blankets – the girl is in the middle, squeezed into the prison of their two bodies; she can hear soft music from her father's room. She just wants to escape from the vice of their scents, from their heavy warmth. The wind howls on the other side of the door, raging in the living room. The case histories are drying on the radiator in their room, the dry papers gathered in a pile by the wall. Half-asleep, the girl listens to the women's whispers, struggling to follow their conversation, but she only catches fragments, which drop into her consciousness like broken glass.

She was little and doesn't remember, *but the neighbor lady from his mother's apartment block, who lived on the top floor, a very nice little old lady with round glasses, her son was a drunk and killed her, raped her and they arrested him an hour later, drinking brandy at the cafe of the National Palace of Culture. It was all over the newspapers . . .*

Whispers, whispers, whispers and glass.

You remember Angel, a nice kid, a classmate of Dimitar's, he drank himself to death last year at the age of thirty-three, left behind a four-year-old daughter . . .

Glass, glass, glass and whispers.

I stayed with your father, because I didn't have any money, there was nowhere for us to go, but you have no reason to stay here, run away, live your life, there's no point, there's no point . . .

Footsteps, whispers and glass.

I didn't tell you, it was years ago, but I woke up and he was standing by the bed with the iron in his hand, and I asked him why, and he said that Yana had surely taken it out, and I fell back to sleep, it never even crossed my mind, but maybe even back then he wanted to kill me, he wanted to kill us . . .

Her mother gets ready for work, the girl watches her gathering up her things in the dark – the white coat from the wardrobe, the pile of case histories – even in the dark she can see her skin prickling from the cold. It's quiet outside, the trams aren't even running yet, the snowflakes look black and enormous as they dance ethereally in the brown sky like the feathers that sometimes fall from her pillow. The girl is about to stop her mother – *Mama, can't you just not go* – but then she realizes that the danger is at home, that out in the world nothing will happen to her, nothing can catch up with them out there, and she remembers how when she was little she would cling to her mother's leg, refusing to let her go to work, bawling ugly tears until she was blue in the face – *Please, Mama, please, don't go* – but now she feels like chasing her out of the apartment as fast as she can – *Go, before he wakes up, run, Mama. Run!*

Just like every other morning, her mother leans down and kisses her goodbye, they hug, her mother tells her when she'll be home, covers her up and tells her how much she'll miss her.

Her grandma snores softly, the girl pulls the covers up to her nose and drifts off, but beyond her eyelids the color of the light changes and she instinctively opens her eyes. The orange chandelier in the living room is on, and through the door she sees a dark shadow. The little girl pushes aside the covers, being careful not to wake up her grandma, opens the door a crack, then quickly shuts it behind her.

The fear that your father will kill you.

The fear that your father will kill your mother.

He has hidden his face in his palms, his hands are bloody and muddy. He is sitting on top of a pile of wet paper and glass. Grief washes over her. She wants to hug him, to help him, to make him love her, love her mother, love himself. She doesn't want to stand frozen with fear in front of that shadow – a memory from the past, or perhaps it was the other way around: her father was a shadow of a person in the present . . . He raises his head to look at her with sad, drunk eyes, his face is dirty – he has clearly gone outside.

'Come here,' he says in a voice hoarse from shouting, cigarettes and alcohol. 'Come here.'

She glances back, the bedroom door is closed, her grandma is fast asleep. She sits down carefully next to him. He pats his pockets, digs around inside them, takes out a pack of cigarettes – those same white Victorys he's smoked for as long as she can remember – and his red lighter. He lights up, holds out the pack to her – she shakes her head.

'It's good you don't smoke. It's harmful,' he tells her.

They sit like that for some time. He smokes and plays with the lighter, first bringing it close to his eyes, then down to the carpet.

'Dad?'

'What?'

'You're not going to light the carpet on fire, are you?'

He startles, fixes his gaze on her, then shakes his head.

'No . . . no. Of course I won't. How could you think such a thing?' He hugs her, squeezing her tightly; she lets her head rest against his chest. Somewhere deep inside, beyond the stale scent of vomit and cigarettes, he smells like her dad.

'When I was young, I killed a man,' he tells her.

She feels a burning in the back of her head that starts crawling down her back.

'On the Greek border, they'd sent us there, the harshest border, 'cause it was with the West. They told us to shoot. Just to shoot. At the runaways. You can't know, but someday you'll understand. And so I shot. Then I went to find him, why I did that, even I don't know. He died in my arms.'

He curls his thumbs and index fingers together into circles and looks through the circles with his right eye, the left is closed – he's aiming somewhere at the bookcase.

'I shot. And he just . . . He died in my arms.'

He lets her go. His cigarette has gone out in the wind, and he struggles to relight it. 'And I shouldn't have.'

He shudders. The ash falls on the carpet.

'They gave me a new suit and tickets to the movies. Later they moved me, 'cause of other stuff, I couldn't handle it . . . Your father is a loser, Yana. A loser.'

'Why are your hands dirty?' she asks him.

He looks at his hands in surprise, as if he is only now seeing them. He sniffs the tips of his fingers. There's a thick layer of fresh dirt under the nails, there are muddy streaks on his white T-shirt – he's wiped his hands on it. Suddenly he smiles, as if he has only now thought of something.

'Because I buried him in the park,' he replied. 'I buried him in the little garden across the way, the boy with the straw-blond hair, who tried to run away . . .'

'Daddy?'

'Yeah . . .'

'Are you going to kill me and Mama?'

The smoking cigarette juts out between his fingers. Now he takes aim at her. She looks him straight in the eye, without blinking, without crying – such things are pointless, her mother and grandmother cry, they are constantly crying and whining. And what comes of it?

He drops his hands, his head droops, and he starts to cry. He sobs like a child, shaking his head, the tears leaving light tracks on his dirty face.

The child hugs her father; the girl hugs the man. The two of them stay like that a long time – he cries, she is silent, watching the snow pile up on the city's rusty wounds.

Eva and Yana

To: The superintendent of the Third Police Precinct, Sofia
From: Eva Spassova Ivanova, XX St., Entr. A, Apt. 71, city X
FORMAL COMPLAINT

Dear Sir,

Since 4 December 1994 my daughter Lilia X has been married to Dimitar X . . . until the Christmas of 2001 she presented things in the best light to me as her mother. But he began coming home late, not returning at night with the excuse that there had been an emergency – he graduated from medical school and has been working at the central Pirogov Hospital for four years – in the trauma room in A&E. Since the spring of 2002, he has been systematically absent from home, he has spent money without providing an explanation, he has started openly bringing alcohol home and drinking there. After yet another request on the part of my daughter as to why he is behaving this way, he stated that he has a girlfriend, a life of his own, his own friends and that she and the child – they have a daughter in first grade – are of no interest to him. She took it very hard, being neglected because of another woman, we as parents have as well. Our family accepted him like a son because he's our son's age. Because my daughter was very worried and my granddaughter was starting first grade, I came back to Sofia, with the idea of helping their relationship and taking the granddaughter to school. That same afternoon he came home, the child was happy that he was going to come to her first day at school, but he left the house with a bag on his shoulder and, to the child's question as to whether he was going to be at the ceremony, he answered, that if he couldn't make it she shouldn't be upset with him, that he was not a normal father!!!!! And in fact, he did not show up on 16 September 2002, it was just myself, my daughter and his mother, who is constantly telling me that my daughter is incapable of dialogue, not with her or with him. But she don't say nothing about him not returning home for days on end, drinking, spending money like crazy, that in 1995 after the child was born he slipped into the same condition, that at my daughter's insistence he underwent treatment. Her fault, she should have left him instead of acting like a replacement for his mother and raising him for nine years. But last year he refused to go to treatment, he grew resentful toward her and the child. He thinks they want to take his apartment. His disappearances kept happening, until on 25 January 2003 he came home at 9 a.m., got drunk on wine in the afternoon, my granddaughter and I were at the cinema, during which time he was rude to my daughter and ordered us to leave the apartment and threatened to kill us, and after we returned he exploded in such a rage that he broke the windows with his bare hands and shouted horrible threats. I hope there are details in the report from the police officers who were called by the neighbors. While the police officers were present he was docile, after they left we spent the night terrified until six in the morning on 26 January 2003. I reckon that since March he hasn't had very much money, so he's started lingering around the apartment, becoming more cynical and threatening to kill someone, constantly saying that he has murdered a man and buried him. When he's blackout drunk he claims he will divorce her, kick us out and murder us. When he's sober, we're going to live here and he's leaving to go abroad, starting with Germany, England, Switzerland, Libya.

Another nightmare came on Monday, 28 April 2003 – at 9 p.m. he came in to me and my granddaughter and asked where my daughter was, she was on a night shift, he wanted to remind her that one month had passed since his warning during the holidays, and he gave her two months to move out with the child. After making sure my daughter wasn't there, he began tormenting the child, she plays piano at the Conservatory, in the beginner's class, he made her play the piano for him and from 9 p.m. to 10 p.m. it was a nightmare – she was playing, he was cursing and insulting me. Suddenly he started touching her on the back, on the neck and hair, and mentioned offhandedly that she has become quite a 'nice piece of ass', I apologize profusely for this vulgar language. Afterward I found her underwear soaking wet.

On 23 April 2003, after I took my granddaughter to play in the park, he went out, came home with cut-up, dirty hands and said that he had killed someone and that he was going to kill my daughter in the same way. He then went out and didn't come home all night. Today, 1 May 2003, he came home at 5.50 a.m., slammed the lift door and tried to force the child to play for him. She refused and he grabbed her, but her grandfather had arrived for Easter and he intervened. We invited him to lunch, he didn't eat anything, spewing curses left and right at all of us, he exposed himself several times and started to provoke my husband. I was worried for my granddaughter and my daughter that he was going to lose control and that's when I called the police – the gentleman who answered turned out to be one of the officers who came during the events of 25 January 2003. They talked to him, he slept for an hour or two, during which time my granddaughter refused to sleep in the apartment and left with her mother for her night shift. The police came a second time and took him away with them, and he came home at 8 p.m.

We haven't complained in writing because my daughter is ashamed and feels guilty that she does not drink with him, that she loves her daughter so much, that she bought a piano which was an unnecessary expense, that she wanted to renovate the apartment, that she allowed him to complete his specialization, that she wanted to have a husband with good standing and dignity. He is currently aggressive, threatens murder and repeatedly says he has killed a man and buried him and that this will happen to us, too. Other times, like today, 1 May 2003, he cries, he cries but doesn't say why.

My request is that you declare this man legally insane and thus separate him by law from my daughter and my granddaughter.

Respectfully:

Eva Ivanova,

2 May 2003

Sofia

I find the complaint tucked away between my mother's letters.

They never sent it.

night

As a child you're told that now is the time to enjoy life, to be happy. As if later on you won't have the right. Being a child, they say, is the best thing in the world, once it's over you'll miss it your whole life. And I couldn't understand what was so good about it.

It took time to forget – his hands sliding down my back, crawling over my shoulders, the warmth between my legs, on the nape of my neck, as if someone had stuck an iron to the back of my head, choking on the words – *Daddy, stop* – that tangled around my tongue both wet and dry, twice as large as my mouth. Was this what my mother and grandmother feared? Were they preparing for this moment their whole lives with their horror scenarios? I thought monsters lived out in the world, not at home . . .

The more time passed, the less I thought of him. But my mother always needed to remind me that he didn't call on my birthdays, at Christmas, for the start of the school year. On Christmas Eve, there was always an even number of dishes on the table, breaking Bulgarian custom and making the holiday into a funeral – stuffed vine leaves, the *pitka* bread, dried fruit, and my mother's tears. In times of celebration, we grieved.

He didn't live with us, but she never let him go.

She'd tell me, *Everyone will keep an eye on you, now that you're the child of divorced parents;*

You piece of shit,

Ingrate,

Loafer,

Parasite,

Moron,

Fool,

Cretin,

You'll be sweeping the streets if you don't study,

Idiot,

Trash,

You little piece of shit, don't talk back to me, I'll . . .

I'll give you to foster care, let them deal with you,

Freak,

Sitting on your lazy ass all day,

Just like your father,

Nothing good will come of you,

Nothing good will come of you,

Nothing.

Nothing.

Nothing.

You have to think of your mother, of the hard life she's had, my grandmother would say after yet another round of vitriol, *she's having a hard time coping with the divorce and you need to be understanding, that's why she talks to you like that. She has your grandfather's ways, look, they both treat me the same way. He blows off steam the same way, half an hour later he's forgotten everything and it's all sunshine and roses, and you're the one who's sad . . . Don't take it to heart . . . We have to spare your mother.*

There wasn't room for two victims at home.

I was born three times. Once from her, then when my father left, and finally – when she left.

In time it all faded away.

In time you manage to convince yourself that such things only happen to other people.

13

Tim and I follow the bay toward Philadelphia. The landscape is so flat it hurts – the eye longs for a hint of a curve on the empty horizon. A sequence of billboards creates a fence around the highway, their colorful fonts screaming into the emptiness.

Our secret is happiness. What's yours?

The perfect bathroom at the perfect price

Got diamonds? The proposal she'll never forget!

Floors and more . . .

The American highway is a microcosm, a latitude with its own climate and natural laws. The European traveler, comfortably seated on their high-speed train or curled up in the compromise of a low-cost airline, cannot imagine the American road until he experiences it – with all its raw and unbridled freedom, with its shameless capitalism.

The road feeds, sells, shelters, warns, beckons, preaches. Explosions of marketing jargon alternate with mirror-like salt lakes, small forests, endless fields of corn and rapeseed. We pass dilapidated single-story houses with pick-up trucks parked in their tiny yards, and I wonder what it feels like to step out the door and directly onto the road, to live with the road, on the road, surrounded at once by everything and nothing.

We go to one such rotting house with a broken window – someone has put cardboard behind it with something written on it: you can see the 'C', 'L', 'O', 'S' and half of an 'E'. Only the first-floor windows are clean, the upstairs is boarded up. A scruffy chair sits on a dirty turquoise veranda, a radio buzzing next to it. We follow the arrows on the skewed electric pole: 'Stop here', 'Peaches', 'Plums', 'Dogs Welcome Here', 'Entrance', 'Do not block the alley' . . . We head toward a small addition on the right where several cases of peaches, tomatoes and melons are arranged. A large man in overalls is hammering something to the facade – a cut-out sign in the shape of a jar, painted red, with a 'JAM' label on it.

'My wife makes 'em. She's in the backyard now, paintin' the melon,' the man says with a slight accent. 'Youse good? I have a mean strawberry jam, just made it, haven't even called the restaurants.'

There are countless restaurants in the resort, their head chefs in eternal competition with one another. One of the best things about the job, our chef Tom has told me, are the hours spent looking for the best ingredients around the state. Everything that grows on trees and is cared for by a human hand is considered a luxury. The good farmers are scattered across the flatlands, their surviving heritage farms besieged by the corporate land surrounding us. What would my grandmother say if she knew that the canned vegetables they prepare every summer according to old Socialist custom – because there was never enough food in the stores and people were torn from their land prematurely, so everybody kept a garden – could have brought them a fortune, had they been born in the right place? As kids we didn't give a damn about granny's *lyutenitsa*, that delicious red bell pepper and tomato spread, we begged our parents to buy us ketchup, like they had in McDonald's. Maybe someday American children will beg their parents for lyutenitsa.

'Not on business, we're going to Philly,' Tim says. 'But because I know you have nice stuff, I thought we'd grab something for the road. OK, maybe I'll swipe a jar or two of that jam.'

'Swipe away, 's long as you pay for it.' The man smiles. 'Holler if you need help.'

We enter the wooden addition, the smell of melons, peaches and dirt in the air. Memories flood my mind: the hubbub of the oriental Women's Market or the Dimitar Petkov Market in Sofia, or the market next to the St Sedmochislenitsi church downtown, where the aromas change like the seasons. I've been prone to nostalgia lately, which annoys me. We fill a basket with pears. Tim feels the melons and wonders which one he should pick.

'Don't you know how to pick a melon?' I approach him.

'How?' He laughs.

I leave the basket on the ground and start gently knocking on the melons. My grandfather would spend hours at the markets, picking the best things, knocking on melons and watermelons in search of the right sound or arguing with the butcher over the best piece of meat, always convinced someone was trying to cheat him – *Do you know how many pigs*

I've slaughtered in my days, you motherf . . . On the way out, he'd point to this or that person, telling me that they were a Communist.

'The sound has to be slightly hollow and you have to smell them. It's not a rule, more of a feel.'

We pay, he exchanges a few more words with the owner, we promise that we'll spread the word about the jam, we say goodbye three times, toss everything in the trunk and start the car.

'I wish I'd learned how to preserve stuff,' I tell him as we wait for the cars to pass so we can enter traffic. 'I hated it so much as a kid. Now I understand it's a dying art. Soon preserving produce will be a dead language.'

'Maybe one day, when the apocalypse comes.'

'My grandmother probably keeps the recipes somewhere . . .'

I swallow my guilt. I'm looking at yet another curve in the road. We drive under an overpass, the American flag hanging over the road. Immediately after, a green sign tells us that there's food nearby – McDonald's, KFC, Chick-fil-A.

'My grandmother wasn't feeling well a while ago,' I blurt out into the silence.

'What do you mean? How come?'

'She couldn't speak for a few minutes, made only sounds, her eyesight went bad, but by the time they made it to the ER all was well.'

After the relief comes the reproach.

'Why didn't you say anything?'

'I didn't want to talk about it. And everything sorted itself out quickly, so it didn't make any sense.'

'Were you worried?'

'No. Maybe a bit. I don't know. At the same time . . . Maybe because I'm away, I have the feeling that it isn't happening to me. As if they're other people. Voices on the telephone. Friends of friends.'

'Do you want to go home?'

'No. You know that if I go home, I can't come back.'

'What if something happens to her?'

'I don't know. But nothing's happened, that's what matters.'

Another overpass, another flag.

'Besides, my grandmother always told me that the young can't live for the old.' It sounds like an excuse.

'No one is saying you have to live for them, nor stay there. Just figure your situation out, so that you're not separated from them like this. After all, they're family. You can't choose your blood, but you have to learn to live with it.'

Only a thin strip of land separates us from the ocean – I can taste the salt in the air.

'You didn't stay just for him, did you?' Tim asks me. It makes me uncomfortable that he knows, but I realize it's hard to hide these things, sooner or later everyone finds out.

'No. I stayed because I have no idea where to go.'

We slow down, enter a town, rolling slowly past a Liberty gas station, with its white-blue font against a red striped background.

'You can't live like . . .'

'Like what?'

'You know like what. You don't fit in.'

'I didn't fit in there, either.'

'No one's saying you should stay there. And it's not a question of going back now, maybe someday.'

'Someday. I want . . .'

I don't know what I want. I want to live without the constant pressure to provide an explanation. Why I am, where I am. I thought we were free to choose? Or we just transferred the dangerous borders into our minds.

We join the expressway and pass a sign in honor of veterans, small flags flapping in the wind.

Overcome dizziness without medication

The best of Philly, bachelor parties and exclusive offers, club Risk

'How can I explain it? You can't even breathe right with these people.'

'And yet they call, seek you out, they probably miss you.'

'Bullshit. I'm just somewhere their unwanted opinion can't reach.'

'You need to grow up.'

'Excuse me?'

'Grow up. Understand them, as adults . . . You're grown now, you can let it all go in one ear, out the other, no one can force anything on you . . . What's more, maybe they used to be like that, but that doesn't mean they're still that way. How long have you been living on your own?'

'Since I was sixteen.'

'Don't you think they've changed at least a bit during this time?'

'Tim, don't be offended, but you're too normal to understand.' I'm annoyed. 'Plus, I don't have a place to go home to.'

'What do you mean?'

'I don't have a home in my hometown. My mother and I had the right to live in my dad's apartment until I turned eighteen. That's that. So stop nagging me.'

Tim is probably the same age as my grandparents, but his mind is fresh, springy. It's the first time an older person has spoken to me like an equal, has listened to what I have to say. I have fun with him, I didn't expect him to fulfill the promise he's been making since last year, to take me to his hometown, Philly. I'd prefer to go there than to Las Vegas or a trip organized by the Russians, crammed with ten more people into a squeaking van, two hours per place; the idea of such a road trip is unbearable – rushing around, a race to check places off, selfies, tags, six nights, ten different places, ten states in ten days . . . Fast travel, fast food, fast news, fast fucks, everything fast. The road is not a road unless you immerse yourself in the local life, sit at somebody else's table, laugh with them, get lost, miss the last train somewhere. I am hungry for the large and small history from which everything is made.

We enter a storm, and the surrounding cars melt away in clouds of white vapor, tires hissing, rain falling on hot concrete, instantly turning into mist. We slow down and drive with the traffic, obeying the elements. The lights are reflected on signs pointing toward unknown places where strangers live, each person lost in their own small life, ignorant of the world. Tim indicates right and takes the lane toward New Jersey.

'Don't let it go to your head when I say you're not like the others. I don't mean you're special.' He waves his hand. 'It's almost an insult, everyone is so fucking special nowadays, it's an act of heroism to be ordinary . . . I will be the last person to tell you there's shameful work. But whatever it may be, don't convince yourself you're only good for cleaning.'

We sit in silence, let it soak into our skin, all the way to the bone. Decent people can share silence. The storm ends abruptly, and the sun shines on a new sign:

Del. Mem. Br. 2
Atlantic City 76
New York City 135

'Have you been to New York?'

'No. Only the airport. Diana went.'

'And?'

'I don't know. She said they went shopping.'

'Where?'

'Same stores that we have, only bigger, she said. Before I came here, I spent a whole summer in Berlin. I've been to Vienna and France, too, on school trips . . . Same stores everywhere. And our teachers always took us shopping. Main streets are the same everywhere – McDonald's, Starbucks, clothes . . . You buy a keychain from Vienna, from Paris, from Berlin – it all says *Made in China*. What do I need New York for?'

Tim smiles.

'I want to go somewhere you can buy something made by real people. Where real people live. Not . . . tourists and suits.'

Tim thinks.

'I miss the black-and-white of youth. Life's such a blunt statement when you're young.'

I roll my eyes. 'It's not fair to tell me I'm wrong just because I'm young . . . It all seems the same to me.'

'New York is New York, Paris is Paris . . .'

'Sure, but you go for what they used to be. Now they're mall cities.'

'It's too early for you to be cynical and say it's all the same.'

Tim lets out a smile that says *you're not old enough*, I respond with a *your age has made you smug* look, the sun grows stronger and we don sunglasses at the same time, I-295 joins Jersey. The road forks into various exits and ramps, crawls and bends into over- or underpasses. We pass a yellow bus full of children. Some wave at me – I wave back. An orange sign warns us: 'Last Exit Before the Bridge!'

The marshy green-yellow coast ends abruptly, water glistening like broken glass. Tim joins the right lane of the bridge. If I extended my arm and threw a pebble, it would land in water. I make waves with my hand, then roll the window down all the way and stick my head out, the wind blowing through my hair like in a stupid Hollywood movie, but this is my movie. I lean into the cliché – I'm happy.

'Did you know where they were sending you, before you came?'

'No. They offer you the job, you say yes or no. Sometimes they tell you what's nearby, attractions, things like that.'

'There are no accidents. Don't listen to what they say about lower, slower Delaware,' Tim says. 'This river nursed America.'

And he begins to weave his own stories. Of the first European settlers who used the water as a way in, to the heart of the new land; of the Lenape tribes who observed the newcomers from the riverbanks, which they called 'rapid river' or 'great river' in their long-lost tongue. There is nothing more worthy of grief than dead languages, in which a whole other world lies buried. They were a matrilineal society, the Lenape, he goes on – inheritance was passed down on the maternal side, the family lived closer to the wife's parents, there were up to four generations in one house. The wife's brother was more important for the children than their own father, because he was related to the mother by blood. The father was technically from a different clan.

'Are any of them left today? The Lenape, I mean,' I ask.

'Everything is watered down. Whatever's left is different, a mix of tribes and traditions. But it's something. It's survival.'

Survival. One of the most Bulgarian of words. My other grandfather appears in my mind, talking about his own river, the Iskar river gorge with its prehistoric sea and the fossils in the rocks, fragments of frozen time. Of my paternal many-times-great-grandfather's flight – he came from somewhere near Turnovo, his story almost like a legend, a fairy tale passed down through generations. He killed two Ottoman Turks who raped his wife Katina, who then hanged herself . . . But my great-grandfather never spoke of it, and the rest of the family could only wonder. He crossed the Balkans with a bag of clothes, his five children and a handful of gold coins in his pocket as he looked for a place to build a new house, finally deciding to settle on a mountain slope under the shadow of Grohoten, which owes its name to the river's murmur and the frequent storms that resonate at its peak. He built a house up there, at that height. The children grew up, got married, the city below them expanded, my great-grandmothers were born, each inheriting one of the gold coins that are still passed down from generation to generation, along with the story . . . The memory of the coin is almost like a dream, huge in my infant hand. Such a distant recollection that I'm not sure whether it wasn't actually a dream. The story of ancestors I've never seen, not even in photos, a seemingly small story but actually big-H History, human, as Bulgarian as it is Turkish and Native and American . . . The story of the weak fleeing the strong; of those who rule over others in the unbearable anarchy of faith from which only beautiful words such as justice, memory, honor provide shelter – all the human fictions that help us to survive the raw truth. From the Balkans to Delaware Bay, dirt keeps the bones of the defeated and the forgotten warm.

'Lift up your feet!' Tim interrupts my thoughts. 'Every time you cross a state border, you have to lift up your feet.'

We gently lift our feet from the car floor. We enter New Jersey. Tim laughs.

'Welcome to the asshole of America.'

Yana

The heat is crushing. The days are scorching, at night the vicious Danube mosquitoes reign.

Fat lot of good the Danube does us, all that water, but it's still hotter than blue blazes, her grandma says.

Her grandfather adds that *all European shit reaches Bulgaria, the ass of Europe, downstream.*

Ever since her father left, the mother sends the girl to her grandparents, to the countryside in the summer, as soon as school is out. The girl goes to the vineyard, where they pick peas, cherries, apricots and peaches. It's either that or she has to sit locked up in the apartment in the sweltering provincial town. On the way to the lozé, she and her grandfather buy sacks of sugar from the place they call 'Commerce', which is full of cheap Chinese crap and bargain foods, since everything comes directly from the port. Afterward at the vineyard, they pick, slice and pit the fruit, her grandma tosses the chunks into enormous cast-iron pans and runs water over them to force the worms out.

Summer has rouged the fat cherries' cheeks. Sparkles of

sunlight frolic in the dappled shade and wind, playing tag on the water. The girl lies in the dust with her head resting on her interlaced fingers, staring over the edge of the pan. So this is how insects see the world.

The ants and firebugs sidle up to the water, sense the danger and back away. The worms, driven from their flooded homes, writhe and twist on the tin bottom of the pan. So many tiny tragedies in an otherwise perfectly pleasant afternoon.

You can eat your fill of the cherries from the pan, without needing to pick out the worms by hand like you have to when you eat them straight from the tree.

'You're gonna give yourself a belly ache,' her grandfather says.

He has a knack for turning joy to sorrow.

Read a book?

You'll tire your eyes out and have to get glasses before your time, he tells her. *You won't find a husband, 'cause nobody wants a girl like that, with Coke bottles on her eyes.*

Ride a bike?

Some drunk driver'll come flying around the corner, he'll run her right over and drive off. And then how would they bury her? *Goddammit all*, she never spares a thought for how tough things are for them.

Play with the boys?

Her grandfather will be sure to pass by and give them a murderous look, he'll raise his black hand with its knotty fingers and bring his thumb and middle finger together three times, like scissors. So they will know what's coming to them if they mess with her.

'Let her eat if she wants,' her grandmother replies.

'I feel bad for the worms. Just look how they're writhing around,' the girl says.

'They've 'ad a good life, they've eaten their fill and now it's our turn.'

Her grandmother builds pyramids of preserving jars, huffing and puffing in the heat. The girl remembers how her mother said that her grandma was the only person on earth who could stand her grandfather.

He glances at them sulkily from under his black brows. She recalls how when she was little, she told him he looked like a Gypsy, and he was furious, but she didn't understand why – after all, he was very dark-skinned, just like the Gypsies are. Now he is sitting in the shade, hunched over a wooden cable reel, his knees almost touching his ears, smoothing out the edges of old lids for the canning jars. Once she asked him why he didn't just buy new lids and that made him angry. Everything made him angry. She reaches out and picks up several lids. She likes running her fingernail along the pink rubber ring inside, which smells like last year's preserves.

Soon her grandma will toss out the worms' corpses. Then she'll pour two packages of sugar over the fruit, she'll cover it with water, she'll take out her big ladle (almost twice as big as a soup spoon) and she'll fill up the jars, which her grandfather will seal with the smoothed-out lids. They'll line up the jars in the big black cauldron, the old man will light a fire beneath it, and her grandma will huff and puff even more loudly around it, for two or three hours, in the worst heat of the day. This is how her favorite cherry preserves are born. They will eat them throughout the winter, when there is nothing else for dessert.

The girl gets up and heads toward the cherry tree, whose branches embrace the yard, creeping along the fence, forking above the neighbor's roof and filling his gutters with pits. The house next door, Grandpa Georgi's, is new, white and beautiful, complete with terracotta; not like theirs, whose bare bricks her grandfather had promised to plaster and whitewash thirty years ago. From the top of the tree she can see the village, the silvery capillaries of the little river, then the border, and past it the thick Romanian forest and the eternally squawking jackdaws. Her grandfather's old radio picks up more Romanian stations than Bulgarian.

'When are we going back into town?' she asks them.

'We might not go back tonight at all, dearie,' her grandma replies. 'We've got lots of work to do.'

There are no other kids around the vineyard, there are no mothers and fathers, only old people. Some of the neighbors live there year-round, others come only in the spring and summer, just long enough to plant and harvest the crops. There's no water, nor any TV. This year her grandfather has decided to plant watermelons, so he and her grandma carry buckets of water from the well to the field and back, bucket by bucket, until everything is watered. It takes them two or – on the drier days – even three hours. When she tells her mother on the phone, she replies, *Only your grandfather could be enough of a stubborn idiot to plant watermelons in the desert*. There isn't even a toilet – the outhouse is in the yard, full of spiders and centipedes, while the echo of buzzing flies fills the pit. A sandy dirt road leads to the house, but not many cars go by.

'But I want to go back to town,' the girl replies. 'I can go by myself on my bike, I know the way, you could just give me the key . . .'

'We can't let you go by yourself, sweetie, you're too young still' – the answer is ready, before she has even asked.

'I'm not a little kid, I'm almost fourteen already! I've been going to school on my own in Sofia for a whole year now!' she pushes back.

'I'm sorry, sweetie, but you can't. Come on, be a little more patient, go play upstairs, read a book or a magazine of your uncle's and the time will pass before you know it . . .'

'But I don't want to sit up there anymore, I want to be in town with the other kids, I'll stay there and wait for you to get back . . .'

The slap comes from behind and lands on her left ear. She hears her grandma's muffled voice. Her grandfather lifts her off the ground by the straps of her vest top, carries her to the second floor, tosses her into the room and slams the metal door. From the other side all she can hear is his enormous ring of keys jangling. She stands up in the semi-darkness of the room.

She takes off her wet trousers and underwear and puts on

clean ones, leaves the dirty clothes in the corner to be washed in accordance with her unspoken agreement with her grandma. She paces around the room a bit, opens and closes the wardrobe doors, and sits down on the one free bed of the two – on the other, tufts of St John's wort are drying. She lies down and quietly cries herself into an exhausted sleep.

She decides that she will never set foot in the vineyard again. But she won't stay in the apartment either, where the cockroaches come out even in the daytime, where her friends' shouts beneath her window are intolerable, and the cable television is intolerable as well – she has learned all the songs on MTV and VH1 by heart already. She uses her solitude to craft her plan to perfection. She feels something new, something heavy on her chest that suffocates her in the night; she carries a constant worry inside her, she startles at the smallest thing, once she almost swallowed her tongue in her sleep, but her grandma saved her.

For the first time in her life, she feels hatred. She hates her mother, who is constantly telling her how much she despises her parents, yet despite everything she still sends the girl to them summer after summer. She hates her grandma and grandpa for their stupid rules and for the fact that they don't seem to hear what she tells them. She hates how they are constantly accusing her of things she hasn't done or hasn't even thought to do. She hates their fears of non-existent dangers and gossip – nobody gives a rip about anyone else, everyone is too concerned with themselves. She has never lied, but because they are all liars – they see themselves in her. She never does anything bad, but because they never admit their own mistakes – she has to shoulder their guilt.

Engrossed in their melon patch, they think they can make her into a preserve as well – that they can seal her up with a seventh-hand lid, boil her in the cauldron and she'll come out exactly as they want her to be, and afterward they'll put her in the pantry with all the others waiting for their turn to get eaten.

First, she gathers up the money. Ten leva and eighty cents – the cost of a train ticket to Sofia with her student pass – she deftly sneaks it out of her grandma's purse one day. She asks for money every couple of days – for chocolate, for gum, for a magazine. Fifty cents here, a lev there, once even two leva. In the meantime, she has been secretly taking her clothes out of the closet, one or two things a day, and folding them into her duffel bag. She buys a ticket six days in advance, for the earliest train, at 4.25 in the morning. That's the only time the keys are in the door, plus at night the old folks are asleep – her grandpa gets up to pee ten times a night, but otherwise is deaf as a doornail. Besides, early in the morning there is no danger of a nosy neighbor seeing her and questioning her, one of those do-gooders ready to either spread rumors or look the other way, depending on the circumstances. She timidly goes up to the woman at the ticket window, afraid that she'll ask where she thinks she's going as a young girl on her own. But the cashier doesn't even pay attention, she's busy talking on the phone, just looks annoyed at all the coins. The girl tucks the ticket into her wallet, which she then slips into the waistband of her skirt. Her secret digs into her under her clothes.

Five days.

Her grandma leaves her at home and the girl manages to go out, but she has to come home before the old man gets back, so he doesn't see her outside. She and her grandma have a hundred complicated agreements about what they can and can't tell him. She hates weaving this web of lies, it's as if she is doing something wrong. She and the neighborhood kids sit on the steps in front of the apartment building and watch the grayish-black clouds pile up in the west. The air grows still, the bugs disappear. Right when it becomes intolerable and they can't breathe from the heat, the sky opens up and rain pours down on the town, and then turns to hail. The whole evening her grandma moans over the fruit and vegetables they didn't manage to pick.

Four days.

Her grandma is at home again, because the rain watered the gardens so there's nothing to do at the villa. The girl manages to wheedle her permission to go down to the river with the other kids; they won't tell her grandfather, who refuses to let her go in case she drowns. The boys know the river well – every day they find salvation from the heat in its cool, shallow waters, while she suffocates in the hot concrete panel-block apartment.

They pass the dike and go down to the lazy river. A crafty river, her grandma has told her, it's flowing fast thanks to the rains in the mountains, that's why they won't let her swim in it. All the other kids throw down their bags and towels near a deepish pool, then climb back up to the dike. One by one, they take running starts from the other end of the dike and hurl themselves into the pool, swimming out and splashing around in the shallows, the water reaching their knees. The boys' bodies are sunburned, sinewy, eternally in motion. Of all the girls, she is the chubbiest, and the old terry-cloth swimsuit her grandma dug out of somewhere sags around her body.

Suddenly she gets scared. She thinks about the kids swept away by the current one day many years ago, about all the old folks' other warnings. The bobbing heads call to her from the water, cajoling her, saying the pool is a meter and a half deep, two at most. But what if it has rained in the mountains and the water suddenly comes rushing down? The biggest show-off dives down and picks up a rock from the bottom, which he displays to her triumphantly. She takes a deep breath and closes her eyes. She takes a few steps back over the hot sandy soil, the dry grass entwining around the soles of her feet. She counts to three – one, two, three – takes a running start and feels herself freeze in the air for what feels like an eternity, before she hits the cold water. Her feet smash into the muck on the bottom, creating a brownish cloud, and her head cuts through the surface, where the other kids' laughter and shouts are floating and where she can hear her own as well. She jumps in more times than she can count. She moves like she never has before – she jostles and laughs with the others, joining in the chasing and teasing. Everyone has brought something to eat, some things have been carefully wrapped up by their mother or grandmother, while those who lied about where they were going have pinched something from the cupboards or spent their last coins at the store. They gather up the towels and lay out the egg-and-cheese sandwiches, banitsa, chips, ice-cold juice, gummy bears. They eat, wash their greasy hands in the river and again jump into the pool. Exhaustion makes the food even more delicious – the girl quickly gets full, she doesn't just stuff herself out of boredom and this true hunger is much nicer, it's as if she is tasting for the first time the cool salt of feta cheese, the softness of the bread and the juiciness of the tomatoes. She lies on her towel and watches the pearls of water that shimmer on her skin.

Three days.

Locked up again. She flips through the channels – there's nothing interesting on. She runs her finger over the spines of the books, mainly dull Bulgarian classics: *Under the Yoke, Uncles, One Hundred Great Bulgarians, Advice for the Good Farmer* . . . Zero. Zilch. Nada. She rereads a few colorful magazines, eats without tasting the food. Around three o'clock in the afternoon she gives in to the heat and lies down in the bedroom. She tosses and turns, restless. The clock moves terribly slowly. It's hot. She takes her clothes off. She feels guilty doing so, but she is alone and can't stand it anymore. What she wouldn't give just to talk to somebody.

Two days.

Polly's mom found her wet swimsuit in the washing machine and punished her by cutting off her long, shiny hair, shaving her head almost bald, like a boy. They munch on sunflower seeds in front of the apartment building and talk about how much they hate all parents. The girl is tempted to tell her about her plan, but then decides against it. She doesn't trust anyone.

One day.

Her grandma is being so understanding with her that she hesitates. It makes her feel guilty: how can she run away when she knows it'll hurt them? But why should she think about them, since they don't think about her? They tell her they love her, but they don't love her, rather they love their own outdated rules and fears. For them, caring is a key, a lid. You can't love somebody you know nothing about.

Less than twelve hours.

He snores open-mouthed in front of the TV. His dentures have fallen out of his upper gums and it's as if he has two mouths. Her grandma clears the table, shakes the tablecloth over the balcony railing, lines up the dirty dishes in the kitchen – in the morning she'll mop up the grease with a chunk of bread that she will then soak in water for the dogs. She tells the girl it's time to go to bed. The old couple sleep in separate rooms. They brush their teeth. The girl looks under the bed, where her duffel bag of clothes is hidden. The tomcat rubs against her and goes out onto the balcony. The cat! She hides his food and water so he doesn't eat before the trip.

The screen on her phone lights up, the bluish glow showing 3.25. Her grandma's hands and feet twitch slightly, she lets out a snore from time to time. She can also hear the old man's snoring through the wall. Now or never. Her hands shake as she feels around for her clothes in the dark, quickly gets dressed, quietly grabs her bag and slips out of the room. She takes the cat carrier from the hallway. In the kitchen she taps the food bowl softly and the cat immediately appears. Suddenly the light in the hallway goes on. At the last possible moment, the girl grabs the cat and darts toward the far end of the kitchen. The cat squirms in her arms, its eyes fixed on its food. She hears the flapping of her grandfather's giant feet in his ancient slippers. His shadow creeps across the linoleum of the kitchen.

3.37.

Sighs and soft curses float from the toilet. The girl struggles to thrust the mutinous tomcat into the carrier. She only hopes he doesn't start meowing. In desperation she shoves the food bowl in with him and he starts munching on the food, all purrs. It'll take her about half an hour to get to the station. She should already be on her way.

'Goddammit, goddammit.' After the curses she hears the toilet flush. More sighs, getting up, the light switch snaps off and the old man heads back toward his room.

'Here, kithy, kithy, kithy,' his voice can be heard. When he's not wearing his dentures, he lisps. The cat lifts its head from the dish.

'Here, kithy, kithy, kithy,' again.

The girl's heart is beating so hard that it surely can be heard from the hallway.

'Nyah.' Something between a lip smack and a grunt, the door to the living room rattles, then the door to his room, the creaking of bedsprings.

3.42.

She'll wait two more minutes to make sure he doesn't get up again. Sometimes he goes two or three times in a short amount of time, then the next morning he'll complain and curse that he couldn't take a piss.

3.44.

The bag with her clothes and the cat weighs more than she expected. She turns the key slowly, to avoid it clicking noisily. She carries the bag out, then the cat carrier, and carefully closes the door. She can't lock it, she can only hope that the draft won't blow it open – over the years the rotted-out wood has become very light. She won't take the lift so as not to make noise – she heads down the stairs. The cat shifts from one end of the carrier to the other. What a porker he is, they've stuffed him for the whole summer. She tosses the bag over her shoulder so she can grab the cage with both hands. She goes down the stairs: fifth floor, fourth, third, second, first.

The nocturnal freshness pleasantly caresses her face. There are no cars. She is most afraid of running into a Gypsy or a man. The stars are this bright only right before dawn. The handle of the Big Dipper stretches all the way down the main street, as if showing her the way. Corona Borealis glints in the distance, nearby Hercules bravely conquers the Cosmos, frozen in an eternal eleventh labor, battling the soon-to-be-slain Dragon. She loves the stars, mementos of the gods' eternal machinations.

3.59.

She turns around constantly – she has the feeling she can hear footsteps behind her. Have they woken up? What if her grandpa jumps on his bike and sets out looking for her? Would it really take him that long to catch up? She decides to turn onto one of the side streets, to go down a little street that runs parallel to the main road. There are no street lights there, and she is even more scared, but here there is less chance of getting caught. From the yards she can hear a drowsy clucking. She reaches the big boulevard that leads to the train station. Relieved, she catches sight of the train.

She imagines train stations like hearts, while the rails are the veins of an enormous organism, just like in her mother's anatomy textbooks. The little town has two train stations: one is the old 'royal station', that's what her grandma calls it – her heart sinks a bit when she thinks of her grandma – the royal station resembles the beautiful Viennese-style houses downtown, all of them gnawed at by time. The other station is connected to it, it was built later, during Communism – a square, crude structure of black metal and gray marble. They look like stepsisters forced to live together. The royal station has long since ceased to function, only the other one works now and that was where she bought her ticket several days ago. The clock on the facade shows 4.10 – fifteen minutes until the train leaves.

She heads directly for the platform, but suddenly freezes.

What if her grandfather is waiting for her there? What if when she steps into the train carriage, his lanky, hunched body suddenly jumps out, his strong arms grab her and pull her back? She looks around, but there is no one there – besides two retirees saying their goodbyes and a younger woman finishing her cigarette. The girl dashes toward the closest door in relief. First she puts the cat carrier on the floor of the carriage and pushes it inside, then takes the duffel bag from her shoulders. The cat meows again, this time more loudly, as if asking her where they are going.

'Shhh,' she whispers to him breathlessly.

The metal steps of the old train carriages are terribly steep. This is what she was most afraid of, that she wouldn't be able to get in on her own, that she would fall and get stuck between the stairs and the rails. But she is astonished to realize that there is not as much space between the first step and the gravel of the tracks as she remembered. She easily climbs the steps, her anxiety transforming into elation, even courage. She settles into an empty, well-lit compartment. She pulls across the curtain, upon which the logo of the railway alternates with greasy stains of various size and color. That way she can see the platform yet remain invisible to passers-by.

The station fills up with people – travelers and their well-wishers smoke and drink coffee from small plastic cups or exchange bags of homemade sandwiches, candy bars and bottles of soft drinks. The cat meows a few more times, so she takes her jacket out of the bag and covers the carrier with it, and he quiets down. All that is left in the minutes before it sets off is the calming ringing of the train. The only thing she took was water – she didn't want anything from her grandmother and grandfather, not even food. The thought of her grandma slices through her again, but she chases it away. The cat stirs in his carrier. She refuses to allow guilt to darken her mood. She takes out her phone and pushes the middle button.

The time is 4.24.

night

What do you miss most?

Nothing.
Everything.

I don't know how to explain it . . . I don't miss the place, I miss a certain time. I miss the person I was back then.

At that age, between twelve and sixteen, when I didn't know anything but thought I knew everything. Everything inside me was raw and unruly. The end of the world came every day, and afterward we'd laugh until we couldn't breathe.

I was sure I'd marry my first love. I thought I'd wait . . . you know . . . until we were eighteen . . . I was so in love. We'd spend hours on the phone, sometimes the whole night, and now I can't remember what the hell we had to say to each other.

I miss the parks between the panel-blocks. The benches, the gazebos, the abandoned playgrounds where we'd gather to eat sunflower seeds, flicking the shells on the ground, drinking beer. We'd return home after dark to get yelled at for being slackers, and then we'd sit in front of the computer or we'd grab the phone and go right back to our conversations. You're right, what the hell *did* we have to talk about?

I miss the scents of the neighborhood at twilight. All these mothers and grandmothers cooking all these . . . *mandji*. I miss the word 'mandja'.

What's mandja?

Some things are untranslatable.

I miss the smell of roasted peppers, of stuffed cabbage leaves, of red stew with potatoes, of chicken kasha, of freshly baked bread – you know what, bakeries are among the few things to survive in a world where everything has become the same, bread smells different in every country, I swear – what was I saying, oh yeah . . . I miss my mother or my grandmother calling me home from the balcony – come on, come up, dinner's getting cold. As a child all you want is for them to leave you alone, and then you spend your whole life waiting for someone to come out on the balcony and call you home.

I miss picking a peach straight off the tree, cleaning the cobwebs from its stinging skin, biting into it and feeling the tingle on my tongue for hours. I miss running barefoot in the cooling dust after a hot day, I miss the crickets. I miss that one time lying on the tin roof of a bus stop, stargazing with this boy who liked me and whom I was too embarrassed to kiss. I miss my childhood awkwardness.

Do you gaze at the stars with all the boys? Let me know if you're still embarrassed.

I miss the aimless roaming. After a certain age you can't just roam anymore, you start walking with a purpose, you're constantly thinking about going somewhere else, right? When you're at home you think about the world outside; when you're out in the world you yearn for home. But back then we had perfected the art of roaming. And we were always right where we were. I miss those carefree streets, boulevards, parks and malls. It must have been . . . 2008, 2009? The world was falling apart, and we had no idea. Not. A. Clue. We were bored to death at school by the same things our mothers and grandmothers had been bored by, waiting for that obligation to end so we could shamelessly retreat into our own worlds. Now I know why people long for their youth – you only live in the present when you're young. Afterward you either remain in the past or you crave a future that never comes.

I miss leaving for school at 6.30 a.m. Early mornings are beautiful in every season. In autumn they're fragrant with fallen leaves and rain; in wintertime only the crunch of your footsteps disrupts the quiet of the streets; the whirling snowflakes turn into plum blossoms, in spring birds sing from three or four in the morning until summertime, but in Sofia you can only hear them before dawn, while everything else is still asleep.

I miss the time after school, too, leaving a trail of gossip with my best friends, scattered beads of laughter. Or with the boy I liked – we'd take all the side streets where we'd kiss, then I'd walk him home, then he'd walk me home, and so on. I miss the tickle of this secret that my mother would try to pry from me with her questions about why I was so late.

I miss skipping school and pooling our pennies for fries and ice cream at McDonald's, sitting for hours around the brightly colored tables and talking about the same nonsense we had left behind on the benches in the summer.

Don't laugh about McDonald's, I tell him. McDonald's is the only thing we understood of our parents' free world dreams. Everything else had stayed the same.

14

The tollbooth tower is like a lighthouse in an asphalt ocean. We fly between two of the columns separating the lanes, the device records the toll and beeps. We're surrounded by trucks, tankers, eighteen-wheelers. The road pumps life into the hulking torso of America. The radio is off, we pass through thick forests and the silence is complete, not even a single billboard. Heavy white clouds are draped across the horizon. The grass along the road has been clipped, the trees have been trimmed, nature has been tamed. I read somewhere that you can't talk about wilderness anymore – man has interfered everywhere, cutting, scything, weeding and blazing trails. I also read that it's no coincidence that both world wars happened after the end of colonization, because we finally realized we are prisoners of this world, there is nowhere to run from ourselves, and it has driven us insane.

After an eternity we deviate from the straight line via yet another interchange and we take another highway. Tim doesn't use GPS, he knows the way. Suddenly we are back in the noise of life. The green around us turns to gray, New Jersey vomits cisterns and smoking towers, factories and pipes, metal scaffolding, wires and enormous chimneys, thousands of square miles of concrete and steel.

'Probably what hell looks like,' Tim mutters.

The billboards are getting ever louder, hinting that we're getting closer to the city. I spot skyscrapers in the distance.

'Have you ever seen an ad for anything . . . useful?' I ask. He doesn't respond, lost in some thought of his own.

There is almost no traffic; we cross the bridge, the border between Jersey and Pennsylvania, our feet in the air – and we descend toward the heart of Philadelphia.

We crawl into the caravan of cars, and I let the AC fight the hot breath of the city. A homeless man walks between the lanes, waving his arms and talking to himself, looking up at the sky. For him, this busy road is a desert, for the drivers he's a mirage.

The skyscrapers glisten in the sun. I think about those Western European cities with lofty cathedrals and turreted castles – they were the first thing a distant traveler would see on their way in. I wonder if this sight hasn't been imprinted somewhere in the collective subconscious through the thousands of eyes that have found solace from the loneliness of the road for centuries, and this is why now New York, Philadelphia and Boston look like steel and glass variations of medieval fortresses, their skyscrapers cathedrals of a new world religion.

The highway cuts into the flesh of the city, the stream of cars doesn't stop, Tim looks for an exit so we can enter the Philadelphia grid. Tall concrete walls separate us from the world, insulating us from the noise – those on the move have no right to intrude on the lives of those who stay put, they must pass through the body of the city as quickly as possible. We finally manage to break away from the traffic and leave the car to walk toward Center City.

'I need to stretch my legs a bit, I'm sick of driving.'

On Race Street we pass rushing students, late for lectures. 'Did you go to college?' I ask Tim.

'Yeah. I did two years of philosophy, you know. I was a child of the sixties, the Vietnam protests, I was so into all of it, the whole Eastern thing. My father, may he rest in peace, was old-school – son of a miner, Welsh immigrants – and when I started he told me he couldn't wait for me to find a job at the philosophers' factory.' He laughs and shakes his head. 'I gave up and switched during my third year. Accounting. I worked as an accountant for many years, then got sick of it. Life happened.'

'I told my mom I was going to college in the States. I was too ashamed to tell her I just didn't want to go home. I'm ashamed to tell my friends back home that I clean or wait tables. No offense.'

'None taken. Why don't you go to school?'

'Honestly?' I ask, and Tim nods.

'I'm too scared of making the wrong choice. For my whole life my mother was always complaining about how tired she was, from her patients, from being broke . . .'

'Hm.'

'And this whole thing with college, there's something . . . I don't know. I feel like the world around me' – Tim raises his eyebrows as he does every time I generalize, so I course-correct 'fine, I feel like my parents are frozen in their own time and think graduating from college is some kind of big deal . . .'

'No one's saying college will make you a genius, it just gives you some role in the larger machine. Knowledge only holds meaning for a minority of people. For the rest it's just a means to an end, nothing wrong with that.'

'Sure, but it's something else, too. It's different. They believe that it's a really big deal. Education, education, education . . . But in reality, you graduate and you work at a customer service center for a Western company, or you find some other job with shit pay, or you escape abroad.'

'Cut us some slack . . . The world is changing so fast, and I don't know if you know, but your brain starts dying at twenty-five . . . It won't be long before you find out what it's like for us old fools.'

I see two white towers in the distance, one is a clock while the other is a cathedral, which look out of place amid the modern architecture.

'I wouldn't want to be twenty years old today for anything in the world.' Tim sighs. 'It was simpler back then. Or at least that's the way I see it. You didn't need much to live with dignity. With a college degree.' He smiles at me. 'Or at least here in the States. But now . . . I don't know. I don't know where we got all tangled up, but sometimes I feel like I blinked and ended up in a different place. Or maybe I'm just getting old and that's why it feels that way . . . We definitely had better music,' Tim says.

I give an apologetic shrug.

From the intersection of Arch and Broad he points out where the first Presbyterian church once stood, founded a few years after William Penn came to the city. The settlers had left under the pretense of building a new world, but they just brought Europe over with them.

'When you look back and see how things turned out, everything becomes clear,' Tim continues as we make our way toward City Hall through the sea of tourists. 'I've got more than half a century of life under my belt, the luxury of time allows me to draw some conclusions. We thought we were a generation of rebels, that being "normal" meant being boring; we thought we'd defeated racism and war. Only later did we realize we'd ignored something terrifying that was trickling into the foundations of everything we had done after '45, and so the rot spread until it all collapsed. That's where we're at.' He waves his hand in the air.

'Do you really believe that?'

'What?'

'That the past was good, and then suddenly everything fell apart.'

He raises his arms and his eyebrows at the same time, his eyes bluer than ever, pupils contracted from the bright light: 'I'm just describing what I see around me. I feel like we fought harder back then. We knew we were dependent on one another. Now everybody seems too self-obsessed.'

'Well, I feel like the past seems simpler precisely because it's the past. Like you say, it gives you some perspective. If you ask my grandparents, it's all the Communists' fault. There's a portrait of the royal family at home, only that painting and the portrait of my great-grandfather are clean, everything else hanging on the walls is covered in dust.'

Tim laughs.

'And I believed it, too, when I was younger. I had to grow up and read to understand that the cruelty of one side becomes the cruelty of the other once the power changes hands. Anyway . . .'

We cross JFK Boulevard, and Tim leads me along the white walls of City Hall. From the top of the tower William Penn keeps an eye on his Philadelphia, arm outstretched just above my head. There's music coming from inside the building. Tim tugs me – I follow him through the dark passageway toward the courtyard. The music grows clearer, a cello or maybe a viola, the sound echoing in the enclosed space, looking for a way out to the city, climbing the facade higher and higher, coiling like a snake around the high tower and dissolving into the sky.

From inside the courtyard, City Hall looks even more like a fairy-tale castle, with its white walls and gray roof, towers with pointy hats, arched windows and Greek columns. A small crowd has gathered around the cellist. Tim joins them. The rest of the courtyard is empty, and I start walking along the walls, touching their rough surface. I like to do this with old buildings, to imagine the hands that touched them before me, the way we leave invisible traces on the stone. I recognize the Nocturne in D minor, Tchaikovsky, the notes swirling like soap bubbles in the air. Tim reaches into his back pocket and pulls his phone out. The gesture is barely conscious, a reflex – everyone is always taking a video, every recording a small theft from the present. Suddenly I wish it were impossible, that we could just listen here and now, without tearing off a piece for tomorrow or for someone else.

I stand in the middle of the courtyard, in the center of a large compass with a ring of golden zodiac signs around it on the ground. The faces of two women are pictured in the middle, perhaps a mother and a daughter, surrounded by something that looks like barbed wire, with ERES MI TODO written above. I step to the side, onto the golden Libra scales, so I'm standing at the bottom of the artwork.

'You coming?' I hear Tim's voice behind me. I reluctantly look away from their faces. We head down Market Street toward Old City – the road looks exactly like Friedrichstrasse in Berlin, and I feel as if we're just about to reach Checkpoint Charlie, the same tall, shiny buildings, the same rushing passers-by, the same bags from the same stores. Nothing changes except for the phonetics, and the dead people who have given their names to the streets and the tapestry of the subway maps, as well as the greetings, the emergency numbers; but only the outer shell of the world shifts, everything else remains the same: humanity peeks out at me through the shopping sprees, the gossip, the embraces, the phone calls, *do I need to pick up anything from the store on my way home.*

We turn onto 6th and a wave of tourists crashes into us, drowning us in noise and laughter, sightseeing double-deckers, bucket hats and shutter clicks, Velcro sandals, whining children.

We quickly pass a few teenagers taking a selfie with the Liberty Bell.

'Did you know there's no proof that the bell rang on Independence Day? I read a while back that someone wrote that story much later, about the bell ringing, I mean, and then some historian just copied it in his book without checking,' Tim says.

A middle-aged blonde woman clearly overhears him and stares daggers at him.

'Isn't it better this way?' I say absent-mindedly, still looking at the woman who passes her phone to her son and stands next to the bell. She sticks her hand inside her bag and pulls out a small American flag.

'Which way?'

'With fairy tales. That way at least you have something to believe in.'

'Hmm, you believe in bullshit and made-up stories,' Tim keeps grumbling.

I shrug and nudge him to keep moving, away from the blonde woman and her ever-fiercer glowers.

'I come from a place where people don't believe in anything,' I say. 'No one remembers anything or worse – everyone remembers things as it suits them . . .'

'You think it's any different here?' He scoffs. We start walking around the park.

'I have this horrible thought,' Tim says.

‘What?’

‘I don’t even know if I can say it.’

‘Oh, come on.’

‘Oof . . . I don’t know if you’d understand. I’m from a different generation . . .’

‘Tim, please, don’t give me that crap. I hate when someone takes me for—’

‘It’s not that,’ he interrupts. ‘It’s not. My father was a World War Two veteran. He remembered the Depression, from when he was a kid. My mother, too, God rest her soul. They met in ’38, my sister was just born when they shipped him off to Europe. Then we grew up. We turned against our parents, we didn’t understand why they held on to their goddamn security and stability so tight. Now I’m older I get it, it was out of fear . . . Only later in life did I realize what kind of people my mother and my father were, the dignity they carried themselves with and that they demanded in turn from their mayor, their sheriff, their world. And this horrible thought comes to mind: that constant suffering is necessary to keep people in line, to teach us compassion for others. That there is no great truth without great suffering. My father had seen what man is capable of and he never forgot it.’

We’re quiet for a long time after that. We get ice cream and sit in the park. On the bench next to us an old man watches the young people, seeing his past. Then we continue our tour, we look without seeing, we read and forget what we’ve read. There is something comical about the bronze Founding Fathers, sitting around the table or frozen around the room in eternal conversation. The plaques tell the stories of great men, so distant in their perfection. Suddenly I wish I could read a pamphlet from that time or a dirty joke or a love letter or hear some gossip from the Great Men's maids, so as to find out who these 'We the People' are – who the hell are these people anyway – I want to hear what was said on the streets of Philadelphia during those early days of July. Did history happen then the way it does now – by the by, only appearing as news or when a headline accidentally clings to the eye. What were the rumors and what were the cartoons, where does the independence fit in the American housewife's 1776 calendar?

'Did you like it?' Tim asks, having read my thoughts. I nod and shrug and he understands. 'Let's go up north. There's no better place to see the end of history than the place where it started.'

Yana

The train crawls through the Danube Plain, stopping at empty stations inhabited only by stray dogs and memories. Amid the ruins, some bent old man might appear like a phantom and rush in little steps toward the doors, afraid that the train will leave without him. She is tired, but she can't fall asleep.

The glow of dawn bursts across the fields. The train tracks divide day and night – on her left the rows of sunflowers bathe in the morning light, while beyond the doors of the compartment the world is still veiled in purple. And she is split between freedom and guilt, over the fact that her freedom means someone else's pain. The passengers doze, the cat twitches in his sleep, the faint scent of cigarette smoke wafts in the air. The sunflowers alternate with swathes of plowed land, wheat, alfalfa. The electrical wires trace a constant musical staff on the sky, while the swallows alight there to compose their melodies. Only the silhouettes of the abandoned factories hint that there used to be people in these places. When they wake up, the elderly folks on the train will start knitting together in their stories everything that time long ago unraveled. Full of sorrow, time and guilt, their words will fill the holes in the crumbling facades and will sprout up fresh in the deserted fields; from their disappointment with the present they will build the bright future they missed out on.

She is leaving behind her childhood: the scent of the village house and games of hide-and-seek until four in the morning; the taste of cherry preserves on toast with homemade butter; the helpless childhood of parental commands; a distracted childhood spent longing for grown-up conversations . . . With every clacking turn of the train's wheels, the past piles up, warm and sickly sweet. Will she ever go back? Surely, someday, but never like that again – coddled and condemned.

'Times were different back then . . .'

'No, nowadays . . .'

For a moment, the two voices prevail over the clacking

of the wheels. The later the hour, the thicker the human swarms on the platforms, passengers quickly finishing their cigarettes and tossing the butts on the rails before they get on. From one of the neighboring compartments, she hears a transistor radio that flickers between singing and the white noise of the mountains.

'Tickets and cards . . . Oh, hey, Yana! What are you doing here?' The compartment door has opened suddenly, and Charlie Chaplin is standing on the threshold.

Charlie Chaplin is short, slightly pudgy and smells of goats. She doesn't know his real name, only that he's from the north-western villages and everyone calls him by the name of the famous actor he so resembles. The girl freezes. It feels like the noise echoing in the compartment isn't the rhythm of the train, but the beating of her heart.

'Mom called to tell me to come home, but Grandma couldn't take me because they have a lot to do out at the vineyard,' she says, astonished at her own cold-blooded quick thinking.

'I seeee,' Charlie says, raising his eyebrows. 'And did your grandma buy you a ticket?'

'Yes,' she replied, searching for her wallet in a panic, until she remembers that the ticket is in her pocket. 'But they already punched it . . .'

'We check a second time after Mezdra. Come on, hand it over now, or else I will send you back home with the train!' Smiling, Charlie reaches out his hand, his fingers twitching in anticipation.

The girl takes out the crumpled paper, unfolds it, smooths it out on her knee and hands it to him. Charlie snatches the ticket and examines it for several beats, bringing it close to his face, turning it over, rereading it. Finally, he punches it with his perforator and holds it out to her. Then he snatches his hand away.

'What about your student card?'

The girl tries to dig calmly through the contents of each of her pockets, looking for the yellow laminated student card. She notices her hands are shaking, but she hopes that he doesn't see. She hands him the card. He glances at the photo and gives it back to her, along with the ticket.

'Just so you know, I'm going to ask your grandma about you tonight!' he tells her.

She smiles, he shuts the door and waves at her through the glass, she turns around and watches with relief as he disappears down the train carriage. She doesn't worry about him asking her grandma, because she knows that her grandma will lie, just like she lies about everything else, because for her what's important isn't what her life is really like, but what other people think.

Around the train, the Lakatnik cliffs bare their teeth, perforated by caves. She is closer to home than to what she has left behind. She checks on the dozing cat and finally drifts into a deep sleep that is interrupted by the brakes screeching at the Sofia platform.

The girl listens to a conversation between two elderly women, who are jostling in front of her in the narrow corridor to get off the train. They are speaking so loudly that they can surely be heard at the far end of the carriage.

'In this country, the only functioning institution is the grandmother . . . But what else do I have to do, what, should I let them shuttle me around to the seaside or to Rila Monastery with other old bags like me . . . No thanks, have fun, but I'd rather watch my grandkids, besides that way I can keep up with my soaps every day, I've got a full schedule . . .'

The women melt into the crowd that drains down into the underpass. The clamor of the city scares and excites her at the same time; it both repels and attracts her. The cat meows in alarm as they pass a stray dog. A few Gypsy women sweep the pavement lazily, chatting in a mix of their language and Bulgarian. Through the windows of the tram, she gazes at the crowded streets, at the mothers with pushchairs and children, at the cars and buses – everything seems so colorful, big and noisy to her, and she realizes that this is why they have always called her 'the Sofianite' in the village and asked her what it was like to ride the tram and the metro. Finally, they turn down Tsar Simeon – she's back, she's coming home to her own room, to her own books, to Mount Vitosha in the window, to the freedom of quiet afternoons when her mother is at work and she is alone. Her mother will surely be angry with her, but what of it? Her mother's anger passes much faster and hurts far less than her grandfather's. And in any case, someone is always angry with her for something, let there at least be a good reason for it. The lift stops, she slides aside the gate and pushes open the door. *We're almost home*, she tells the cat and knocks on the door three times. Suddenly she realizes that her mother could be at work, but so what? She'll call her best friend, they'll get ice cream and wait in the park. From the other side of the door she hears her mother's footsteps, a quiet rustling at the spyhole, the turning of the key.

'Mom! I . . .' the girl begins . . .

The woman in the door frame is much thinner than she was two months ago, the last time she saw her. Dark circles ring her eyes, her hair has gone gray at the roots, her gaze is resigned. The girl rushes forward and hugs her mother, thirstily drinking in her maternal scent. Suddenly the fear – of getting caught, of getting sent back, of getting beaten – bursts free. The humiliation grabs her by the throat, explodes out in sobs, rage runs from her eyes and soaks into her mother's blouse. They stand hugging on the threshold, the cat looks at the inside of the apartment and meows impatiently. The mother leans down, wipes the tears from the girl's cheeks and says:

'When you hate me, just remember that I didn't have anywhere else to come home to.'

dawn

The day breaks in soft iridescence. The beach resembles flowing silk, the ocean glows pastel green. We walk toward his house and talk, stop, listen to the waves, watch the seagulls who have awoken to search for food.

After they separated, she changed the wallpaper all by herself, renovated the house entirely. There was no trace of him left, just this one spot in his room . . . You can probably still see the blood spatters on the wall from that one night, down in the corner. Then the same old mold took over the new wallpaper. The cockroaches crawled over the freshly painted walls. The stray dogs still slept in the entrance. You know, sometimes I dream about my childhood room – it's always raining outside and the water pours through the windows, over the walls and the wallpaper with bears and balloons, the one she picked, it peels and falls down, black mold underneath, yellowing plaster, rotting wood . . .

What about him? Did you miss him?

No. I just felt bad for him when I imagined him all by himself on Christmas. Or on his birthday. I thought: at least my mother has me, while he has nothing. Later on, I found out he was never alone. I've seen pictures.

There isn't a single photo of my mother and me together after I turned twelve.

But other than that, it was no big deal. In the same way other people naturally had fathers, I just as naturally did not.

Yana

'I'll call you tonight,' the mother says from the doorway. 'There's food in the fridge, ring if you need anything.'

The girl just nods, not lifting her head up from her book.

'I love you.'

'Love you too.'

A sigh, the door slamming, the lift. Only then does the girl breathe easily, close the book and stare into nothingness. Her mother's twenty-four-hour shifts are her favorite time: she's alone, no more going to the hospital with its stench of death and disinfectant, no more eating hospital cheese sandwiches on white bread or chicken with cabbage, no more peeing in the bushes behind the abandoned building site because the toilet is covered with the shit and puke of sick old people.

She enjoys the summer days and nights spent strolling the streets with friends or at home in the apartment. How much fits into one summer, into one year, into one city, her capital of firsts:

first kiss;

first clumsy but intense orgasm from someone else's hand;

first beer bought on her own;

first time getting drunk with friends;

first cigarette;

first fight with a boy and first make-up;

then the first heartbreak;

first bad poem;

first lie to herself about being in love with someone else, to get back at the first;

first out-of-town trip with a friend;

first lie;

first theft from her mother's purse;

first thong;

first F at school;

first piano lesson skipped without telling her mother . . .

She looks out the window – a bird soars high in the sky. Clouds gather over Vitosha, the fierce heat promising storms. Five o'clock in the afternoon, August. Somewhere other mothers are going home to their children. All her friends have gone away somewhere. She and her mother don't go on holiday, except for the one September when she was a little girl and her mother took her to a doctors' convention. She remembered the buffet – she'd never seen so much delicious food in one place and ate herself sick – she also remembered how tired her mother was, how she'd go to bed after dinner at seven thirty in the evening and the girl would watch Turkish soap operas on TV or wander around the resort alone. These summer days are unbearable – she feels abandoned, as if the center of the world has shifted elsewhere and she has been forgotten. Somewhere far away, her friends are making memories without her. She has not seen the sea for a long time. She's pissed off that no one misses her. She gets dressed, shoves the books in the bookcase aside to get some money, grabs her keys, phone and jacket, and leaves the empty apartment. Sometimes she hears echoes of the past in the pipes and swears she can even smell it.

Near St Nicholas Church on Pirotska Street, she skirts the drug addicts and drunks finishing yet another two-liter bottle for the day; others are going in and out of the dingy cafe, hiding in the surrounding ruins like lizards. She heads downtown, where women with enormous lips, breasts and crimped hair drink tiny coffees and smoke slim cigarettes, while the men with shaved heads beside them stare angrily at passers-by from behind large sunglasses. The prettiest girls in her school shop in the new stores here. Maybe for her next birthday she'll ask not for presents but for money to buy clothes like that, too. The park around the National Palace of Culture has been taken over by skaters who whiz past the pensioners, treating them like particularly interesting obstacles. She heads back down Patriarch, all the way to the Priest and the Odeon Cinema, past the dropped blinds of the bars. New restaurants have popped up in the crooked streets between Patriarch and Graf Ignatiev – they are different from the pubs she knows with their sticky wooden tables and the greasy smell of grilled meat – and her eyes slide over the taped-up menus, the shiny cutlery, not understanding what she reads. The university peeks out from the other end of the boulevard, which seems to end right at its facade. Turning back along Graf Ignatiev, more new stores, bakeries, 'squat shops' that sell cigarettes and alcohol from basements, and full shop windows, people carrying all sorts of bags and boxes full of fleeting happiness; people smoking, drinking and laughing; people calling to one another... So much life buzzing and pollinating time. She comes up on the market at Sedmochislenitsi, catches a whiff of rotting fruit and sauerkraut and boiled corn, hears the warning bell of the tram as the Number 10 zips past her. She follows the tracks and reaches the florists at the junction with Rakovska, flowers and smog, then come the magical labyrinths of the book market on Slaveykov Square with vendors who dazzle, recommend, rummage through piles of books, haggle, shrug and point to a colleague right over there, just a little ways down, the last table.

Slaveykov smells of McDonald's fries, the scent merges with the square and a memory is born, the most generic aroma in the world will always awaken an appetite in her for the books, carefully wrapped in cellophane, with an orange price tag and handwriting that varies with each seller. She walks down Solunska Street, past the pet store, puppies and kittens scratching at the window; across the street their stray brethren bask in the afternoon sun, ragged and hungry, but at least free. In the small cobbled park there are the homeless and some pensioners who have retrained as antique dealers and now sell all sorts of the junk that old people's cellars are filled with: Communist-era pins, ugly beige porcelain plates with even uglier flowers, jewelry and harmonicas, calendars, notebooks, sheet music. Damp and yellowed books from publishers that are all 'the people's' something or other – she picks one up, opens it, it's full of big, fat words, full of nonsense, does she need anything, an old man with a yellow beard asks, no thanks, she continues on, back to Vitoshka and Stamboliyski, back home.

She loves the gray city, with its hundreds of stray dogs and cats; an urban palimpsest of a chaotic past; with dog shit on the pavement and overflowing dustbins; with the asthmatic coughing of old second-, third-, fifth-hand Western cars; with its cracked pavements where women break their cheap heels on their way home and men curse the day they were born, the same pavements where the homeless and drunk sleep in the saddest of all worlds; where the shiny black SUVs are parked, caked in Sofia mud. She loves the nasty brown dust that filters in everywhere; she loves Vitosha Mountain, which presses poison down like a lid over the city, as if trying to kill them all, like a mother horrified by her children; she loves even the pickpockets who roam through the trams and streets like shadows, in the old trams and buses; even the faces made vicious by misery, who criss-cross the city like mutts bitten and beaten down by life, ready to snarl and bite back. She loves the city the way you love something broken, out of spite, out of pity, but also unconditionally, the way you can only love something in which you can see yourself reflected.

She doesn't feel like going home. She is drawn to the light of the non-stop shop. She goes inside, buys herself whatever she wants; she also buys menthol cigarettes – they don't ask for ID. She stays in the park until dark, watching from afar the faces of high school classmates she recognizes but who wouldn't recognize her, wouldn't invite her to join them. She knows how this day will end, with the TV and the lights on in the small hours of the night, because she is afraid of the dark and the silence and can't fall asleep. In the morning, her mother will come home, stare at something – the girl always manages to be in the wrong – and will say that no one loves her, that she can't rely on anyone, no one but her ever takes care of anything; that the girl is an ingrate; that she can't understand the exhaustion of a person who works two jobs to support her and pay off their loans; that she doesn't study hard enough, that she's not enough, that there's always something not enough to make her mother happy; that her mother at her age was more everything: smarter, more responsible, she took better care of her mother; that she was too noisy during the day when her mother was trying to sleep, that she purposely slammed the door loudly when she went to the bathroom, why was she talking to her friends on the phone . . . Then the insults will come, always the same: *You're just like your father.*

And she will leave the apartment yet again, swallowing back her tears, and wander down the same streets, asking herself how she could possibly be just like someone she doesn't even know.

15

We're back in the car, crawling through the labyrinth. There is no escaping the city's grip; there's city, city and more city – everywhere. We head north on Broad. My eyes skim the chessboard of facades: white and old, black and new. The walls of glass and concrete come to an end as we leave Center City, and I can once again see the sky; open parking lots and low buildings alternate on both sides of the road.

'Will it annoy you if I tell you a bit about myself?' Tim asks.

'Nah, not at all . . .' I hesitate. 'I'd rather you told me. If you want to.'

He smiles. 'When you get old, you start babbling about yourself, always the same stories. You'll have to forgive me.'

He asks for a cigarette.

'My mother was a botanist and I used to go with her to gather flowers to press. I felt so bad, we'd pick these gorgeous flowers and shut them between the pages of books to dry. Yet at the same time I was happy, because I got to spend time with her. Flowers with my mother and fishing with my father. The best days of my life.'

The car slows down. Something catches my gaze on Tim's side – one, two, three pairs of children's eyes, painted on the side of a building like T. J. Eckleburg's, peering at the traffic on Broad.

'My daughter used to go here.' Tim nods in the direction.

'You have a daughter?'

'Had.'

The only sound in the car comes from the turn signal. 'Tim, I'm sorry . . .'

'No, no. This is exactly what I wanted to talk about. It's been a while since I talked to someone the way I do with you.' He shakes his head. 'I like it.'

We smoke and wait at the traffic lights.

'I spent my life in Philly. I was born and raised here, fell in love here, married here . . . did everything here. We vacationed down south, at the beaches. Three hours by car. Until ten years ago this was the longest trip I had ever taken . . . I'd never talked to a foreigner so much before I met you. At work, with the guys – you know how it is, we mess around, but to be honest I feel sorry for them. That they needed to move somewhere else, because something was missing at home.'

We crawl down tiny streets between square two-story houses that look as if they've been crammed together with great force.

'You've made fun of that kind of customer a few times, but I spent a long time thinking that America was the greatest country in the world,' Tim continues.

We pass a small intersection and enter a new quadrant of narrow streets and houses. Two men are chatting on the corner, and they stop and stare at Tim. Then they notice me – one elbows the other and they start laughing. I guess at what they must think and I feel gross. Tim doesn't even notice. He slows down the car even more, I now understand that he's giving me a tour of the neighborhood, and I start paying more attention, trying to understand what he's trying to show me. I see the squalor through the open doors, the houses nothing at all like the huge mansions I clean on the coast. Kids and adults sit on plastic chairs or on the steps outside.

'My daughter graduated with honors from Penn State and started a good job, she was wonderful, I was proud to have raised such a great kid.'

Tim carefully drives around a child's abandoned bicycle.

'They called me in 2012, she had been in a small car accident, nothing serious, of course as a parent you always worry. I immediately went to the hospital, broken leg, but otherwise minor injuries. She had insurance, no problem, they told us she'd be good to go in a month or two. She was in a lot of pain, so the doctor gave her something really strong, she didn't suffer, they discharged her in a few days and she came back home with us.'

A child in an orange shirt squats next to the front steps of one of the houses, searching for something underneath the steps.

'She recovered at home and returned to work, and then went back to her own place – she was still living with her boyfriend. A few months later we found out they had split up, but we didn't pay much attention, we didn't ask, things like that happen and it was none of our business.'

We drive past shut garages. There are piles of trash and dry leaves in front of some of them. The setting sun gives the air a golden tint.

'Little by little Sarah stopped calling. She used to call more often, her mother complained to me about it, but I didn't give it much thought. I told her she's a big girl and has things to do, maybe she's dating someone new, we can't keep tabs on her. One day my wife couldn't stand it anymore and got in the car. She came home after midnight.'

Tim takes a right, then another left – a new labyrinth.

'"Sarah's apartment is almost empty," she told me. "Sarah's lost a lot of weight." I got a bit worried, but not too much. I chose to think that Sue was exaggerating. I don't know if it's ever happened to you, but if not, it probably will someday – sometimes the truth is so hard that you make up a different story. I went to see her as well, I saw what my wife saw, I talked to Sarah and chose to believe her out of stubbornness. That she had too much stress at work, she had gotten into minimalism, things like that. She asked for money. I told her – if there's ever anything she needs, give us a call. And I left. I'd like to think it was because I trusted her and so on, but in reality, I just didn't want to look at her.'

We cross yet another intersection, past Martinez's grocery store, the landscape blurs, every street resembles the previous one, every house is the same as the next one.

'Then she started calling again, this time it was me she

called more. She'd briefly ask how we were, what was new, and then she would demand money. She'd quit her job, said there was some sort of an issue with her co-workers, she started looking for something new, but then she didn't like the new company, she needed time to decide what to do. Every time Sue would invite her home, to come stay with us until she figured her life out, but she would refuse, she didn't want to be a burden, she just needed a hundred bucks to make it through the week. Sue begged me to reconsider, to stop just giving her money, but that is your purpose as a parent, to help out, that's how I'd shut her down. Sue started writing down the calls and next to the date how much money we had given her. I found that out later and went ballistic. I told her . . .' his voice trembles and he takes a sharp inhale, 'I told her that she was betraying the trust of our only child.'

'Tim . . .' I feel like I have to say something. How do you listen to a story like that?

Tim waves his hand. 'The first time they called us from the hospital was about a year and a half later.'

We park the car between a rusty pick-up truck and an overflowing garbage can. He doesn't kill the engine so the air conditioning stays on, but I can still feel the heat coming from outside.

'Overdose, luckily the ambulance got there in time.' Tim is fidgeting with his hands. 'There was no insurance anymore, nothing. So the bills were huge. We paid everything, no questions asked. Then Sue went in to see her, I waited outside the room. I could barely listen to what the doctor was telling me. What I gathered was that after the fracture they gave her OxyContin. She kept taking it for a while after that. But because it got harder and harder to find, "people like Sarah", that's how he said it, chose cheaper alternatives – heroin, fentanyl. "People like Sarah . . ." "What do you mean, like Sarah?" I asked him, and he started hemming and hawing, trying to "Sir, Sir" me. The only thing I said to him was that people like him fucked my child up and now they have to fix her . . .'

I can't imagine Tim ever being rude.

'I was furious. I don't remember leaving, I just remember Sue and I drove home without saying a word to each other.'

'Sue said Sarah needed treatment. I told her she shouldn't listen to bullshit from quacks who are just looking for something to sell so that they can pocket the money. Can you believe it, I asked her, that our child could be . . . a junkie, see' – he tries to smile, but grimaces instead – 'I still have a hard time saying it . . . "Aren't these the same people who offered Sarah those fucking pills," I told her, "and you're ready to jump on the next bandwagon for treatment and whatever else they tell us to do." We took her home. She promised she'd get better, as long as we didn't send her away. Sue stopped talking to me, she just cooked meals and made the beds. Sarah was doing better, she went out, told me she'd been going to job interviews. One day Sue asked me where her gold earrings were, I didn't even pay any attention, she was always losing things. She just gave me this look . . . We'd started fighting more, those fights that have no resolution, you hold your ground and the other person holds theirs and with time you become enemy territories. But other things started disappearing, too. I kept refusing to admit it until I finally broke, then Sue and I sat down with Sarah for a talk. Then she lost it. She told us she couldn't believe her own parents were accusing her of theft, that we had made her feel guilty her whole life, that she couldn't live this way anymore. The next day she moved out without saying another word. Sue was going to these meetings, for "parents like us", and sometimes she invited me to come along, but it made me sick just hearing her talk about it. Two weeks later Sarah called me to ask for money, begged me not to tell her mother. I gave her the money. But we had a joint account and Sue saw the transactions. One morning I woke up and she was gone.'

Tim gulps. I decide to look at him and see he's crying. I return my gaze to the dashboard.

Why is he telling me all this?

'"I can't be your enemy anymore, I can't sit here while you kill our child," she'd written. A month or two later they found Sarah in that house over there, next to the garbage. That's it. I won't burden you with any more of it.'

For a while there's silence, Tim breathes a bit heavier than usual, I stare at the trash container in the rearview mirror. A pigeon tries to hump another pigeon, some wrappers fall from the overflowing dumpster. I imagine Sarah was like the girl from the intersection, but with Tim's crystal-blue eyes, staring into nothingness. He finally speaks: 'I know I've probably ruined your Philadelphia trip . . .'

'You haven't ruined it.'

'. . . I'm just telling you, because . . . You remind me of her, I think every young girl will remind me of her in some way. It's my own problem. But what I wanted to tell you most of all, and you won't get it until you live it, I'm sorry, it's a cliché, it's dumb, but it's true: we're all doing what we can. Believe me. And because we're human, it's almost never enough, just how I wasn't enough for . . . Sarah. I wasn't. Because . . . Jane, as much as it hurts, after she was gone . . . I realized I couldn't live with the past and with all the things I hadn't done or I would have to kill myself. The best way to make up for it is to tell the story, to prevent people in a similar situation from going down the same path, if I can . . . I never forgave my father for so many things – he was a cruel, isolated man, he never admitted to any mistakes, never apologized, never let other people know there was a problem – that's how his era shaped him. You can only be better than them if you love and forgive them. If you don't admit you carry them inside you, you become them.'

'I don't know what to tell you,' I say after a little while. He nods.

'No need to say anything. If I said something wrong, just chalk it up to an old man's ramblings. The older you get, the more you're afraid of carrying things to the grave.'

The orange sun comes out from behind the houses and drenches us in light. A silver Honda stops at the corner and catches a gleam of the sunset. The window opens, a little kid runs to the car, exchanges a few words with the driver, goes back, crawls under the steps of one of the houses, digs for something underneath them, gets up and goes back to the car, taking something from the driver's hand and disappearing back into the streets. The Honda takes off and disappears as well.

The sunset burns for a bit longer, then the day dies a lilac death, the kids and teenagers on the corners are replaced by other kids and teenagers, loud bass booms somewhere, interrupted by a dog's barking.

Night falls on Philadelphia, on the northern parts where the present lives; on the perfect past displayed in Center City; the darkness swallows the suburbs with their strings of cookie-cutter houses, windows illuminated by the evening news.

As we become one with the road again, Tim and I laugh at something silly, but we've already grown apart, as you do with people who have fulfilled their purpose in your life and it's time to part ways; our paths were meant to cross exactly here, on this sweltering afternoon. Somewhere in Jersey we stop for a break and as I watch the white smoke on the canvas of the black sky and listen to the pulse of the highway, I finally make peace with my nostalgia. Maybe someday I will find my home. Not now, but someday. Someday.

Lily

The banal strangles life. Toilet seats, dirty dishes, the smell of the overflowing trash can, the bills piling up, the nasty sludge in the drain of the kitchen sink, the cockroaches. They're to blame, Lily thinks. If only her life could be . . . different. The rumble of the train takes her back in time, to the years when she regularly traveled to the Medical School in Pleven. When she told her mother she wanted to be a doctor, her mother had urged her to think it over carefully, saying it was no profession for a woman, that she should be a homemaker and mother first, a wife and a woman. Back then she had thought that, after twenty years with her father, there was nothing else her mother could say. Back then she believed she was not like her mother. And she wasn't. She did not stay with the drunkard. She made the brave decision. What happened? Where did she go wrong?

Her daughter calls her grandmother every time they fight, and on the other end of the line the grandmother always says *I warned her even back then that she wouldn't be able to handle it*. They are ashamed of her divorce. Surely they wouldn't be as ashamed if he had killed her and her child. Her father is constantly sniveling down the phone about her divorce, mourning her as if she were dead. She hasn't set foot in her hometown since the separation. And things aren't going well at work, either. She thought that once they were no longer together, everything would be different. But he still lives in her thoughts; he disturbs her dreams. She still works the same twenty-four-hour shifts, she keeps quiet the same way she's always kept quiet. And the grind of everyday life crushes her: she wants to pay the heating bill but can't. No, that's a lie, she refuses to pay it because he's not paying a penny of child support. Or rather, both things are true – they keep living to spite him for his absence. She's glad the court let them stay in the apartment until Yana turns eighteen, never mind that the roof leaks and the girl's bedroom is moldy and the neighbors won't pay for repairs; never mind that they have to line the windows with duct tape in the winter to keep the wind out; never mind that she only pays off the interest on the loans. Would it be better to return to the countryside? What could her daughter become there besides a layabout or a drug addict? The train stopping interrupts the eternal sermon of her own thoughts. She gets off at Sofia North Station and catches the Number 11 tram. She looks at the gray slag on the pavements and buildings, the old signs, unchanged since the Socialist era, the sad prefab apartment buildings. She rummages in her bag and pulls out the small folder the nurse had pushed into her hands before the end of her shift.

FINLAND URGENTLY SEEKING DOCTORS

A blonde beauty smiles against a backdrop of snowy mountains. Lily's eyes roam over the names of places she has never heard before. They offer more for specialists, but even as a generalist she would make ten times her Bulgarian salary there. She remembers what day it is and her stomach churns; she now divides up the months according to her creditors and what she has to pay . . . *The employer will pay for the Finnish language course* . . . She almost misses her stop. They say Bulgaria has not produced anything since the Transition, when all the factories shut down, but some smart-arse said that wasn't true – they'd produced emigrants, and she had liked that idea. Her eyes close on their own. She leans against the wooden paneling in the lift as she loosens the straps of her sandals. It dawns on her that she hasn't missed her daughter – that little girl, who used to cling to her legs and wouldn't let her go to work, whose bed she used to sit on at five in the morning to drink her coffee before work, is long gone. Her daughter hasn't called her once while she has been at work. But Lily doesn't want to call her, either. Another habitual thought surfaces in her mind – she's a bad mother. The stairwell, the ugly wood paneling in the lift, the grate you have to force open – she's coming home to her ex-husband's apartment.

'Yana?' she calls from the door.

She kicks the trainers sprawled in the middle of the hallway toward the wall. She glances into the living room, then into the girl's bedroom, where she is sitting in front of the computer. She looks at her watch – 10.45 in the morning. Every day around the clock, that fucking computer.

'I only hope you've got your homework done, otherwise . . .' she calls over her shoulder.

She goes to her room, tosses down her bags and strips off the clothes soaked with the stench of the hospital. The bed calls out to her. She heads to the kitchen to wash her hands. Some dirty cutlery and two plates are sitting in the sink, with crumbs and a dead cockroach swimming on them.

She fought with him because of the sink. She slept with another man because of the sink. This very same sink that he used to piss in. Why is this sink never clean? Why can't everything be OK, just for one day? She doesn't even touch the tap, instead she heads straight to the girl's room. Yana is wearing headphones, she doesn't hear her coming, the mother digs her fingers into her scalp, feels the hair tearing in her hands.

'Ooowww! What the hell are you doing! What is this about?' the girl shrieks.

'You'll see for yourself what the hell I'm doing. Come into the kitchen.'

To her co-workers, she is the kindest, most polite colleague. To her patients, she is the most patient doctor. To her friends, she is the most heroic, determined single mother. To her daughter, nothing is ever enough. Her daughter is eternally unsatisfied. So distant. So alien. To her daughter, she has nothing left to give. To her daughter, she is a monster. Fine, now she may as well give her a good reason to believe that.

'Mom, please,' the girl whines.

'Shut up.'

It's not a child's responsibility to clean the house, her mother tells her every time they talk on the phone. *While I missed out on my whole childhood thanks to cleaning, harvesting and digging*, she thinks to herself.

In the kitchen the girl tears away from her grasp and stands in front of her. She looks more like her grandmother every day. Her eyes are red, full of the tears she is trying to hide.

'How many times do I have to remind you about the dishes? Hm? Do you know what long hours I work and how dead tired I am when I get home?'

'I was just waiting for there to be more dishes so I could wash them all at once, and not one by one . . .'

'You lazy little bitch! How many times have I told you?'

The dead cockroach makes another lap around the dish. Fucking dishes, it's their fault everything has died. If anyone loved her, they could wash a few goddamn dishes.

'It makes no difference whether I wash them or not! You'll just find something else to latch onto! What about how you throw your clothes all over the place? Or how you leave your papers everywhere? It's not like you're so tidy yourself! But you're always blaming everyone else. I could do the dishes ten times over and you'll notice the one time I don't! So I'm not going to do another fucking thing from now on, because it doesn't matter!'

'Don't talk back to me.'

'Aren't you asking me? I'm answering!'

'Watch your mouth.'

'Leave me alone!'

'I'll leave you alone when I send you to a home for juvenile delinquents and let you fend for yourself. We'll see how smart you are then.'

'Fine, do it.' The girl steps back. 'Better there than here with you.'

'Really? Really? So the fact that you eat, sleep and study on my dime means nothing? Is that why your life is so terrible?'

'What, are you keeping track of the expenses? When I grow up and get a job, will you expect me to pay the money back? That's all you think about, money! Money, money, money! Money and numbers, that's the only thing you care about. Money and grades, money and grades. You have never once asked me about anything else, you have never once acted like a real mom!'

'You little shit.' She takes a swing, but her hand meets resistance.

The face screaming in front of her looks like a mask from a horror movie: red, shiny with tears, sticky with snot. 'If you have a kid, aren't you supposed to take care of them and spend money on them? How is it my fault that you can't? That you didn't think about that back when you should've? Did I give birth to myself? Did I ask to be born, you . . . you . . . fucking monster!'

Her daughter shoves her squarely in the chest, and she stumbles back – at the last moment she grabs the edge of the cupboard, which shudders, jangling the jars inside.

'You don't deserve anything,' she hears herself saying, 'and you'll never amount to anything. Fs at school, you ditched the piano that I sacrificed so much for. You'll end up exactly like your father.'

'Then surely you'll finally be satisfied,' the snot-slicked mask replies. 'You never expected anything else.'

The girl races past her and bangs the door to the kitchen shut. Lily goes to follow her, then decides against it, instead sliding down the cupboard and staying there on the floor. She hears muted sounds from the living room. A few minutes later, the front door slams. She closes her eyes and leans back against the cool wood.

The world still exists – someone on the floors above flushes the toilet, two pigeons land on the windowsill, their feathers rubbing against the rusty sheet metal, a tram crosses the junction.

Has she dozed off? She doesn't know how much time has passed when she stands up and glances at the dishes one last time, where the cockroach is still swimming its laps. A pile of dirty clothes is heaped near the washing machine. She opens and closes the refrigerator door absent-mindedly. It's almost empty. The fight they just had seems like a dream to her. Why was she so upset about the dishes? What's the big deal, really? Washing them would take all of five minutes. She does a final round of the apartment. A documentary film is paused on the computer. The girl is gone.

She takes a quick shower. She wraps her hair in a towel, ignoring its musty scent, and puts on her pyjamas. She opens up the medicine cabinet and disappears inside until she finds what she needs.

The sleeping pill works instantaneously – she falls asleep and does not dream.

16

The unpleasant tickling I get in my stomach when I see a message from my mother on the screen has lessened over the years. But her unpredictability frightens me as much as before. I never know what mood she's in.

Back then, when we didn't have any money, I thought I'd sell my kidney. Fifty thousand euro for one.

Or jump off the big balcony, from the eighth floor, but then I thought I couldn't do that to you.

I lock the phone and put it away in my pocket. I pretend I've heard Ken's joke and try to laugh.

In 2004, Frank Warren sent three thousand postcards to strangers, asking them to write one secret they hadn't told anyone on the card and send it back, anonymously. As of today, he has received over a million postcards. On one of Frank's cards, you can see four children in their bathing suits, the sandy waves of an endless beach rising and falling in the background. They are all standing with their hands over their eyes for shade, looking for something invisible in the distance, in the water behind the photographer.

That card comes back to Frank Warren with a single sentence written in black Sharpie in the sky above their heads:

My family is like a foreign country to me.

Yana and Lily

'Hey, Mom, I've saved some pictures here, this is what we'll do in Finland when we have a nice house.'

Silence.

'Mom, don't you want to see?'

'Of course I want to see.'

'OK, so look, we'll have a kitchen like this, with a big window, and here's where we'll cook. And we'll serve everything in beautiful dishes. And there'll be lots of flowers.'

'Very nice.'

'And we'll also have a room with lots of books, mine and yours. And I'll study there when I get home from school, so it'll be quiet for you.'

Silence.

'Mom?'

'Hmm?'

'Do you like it?'

'Yes, very much.'

'And we'll have a dog, too . . .'

'Come on now, a dog? And who's going to take care of it? You?'

'Yeah, why not me! There'll also be places to walk it, and I won't have to worry about packs of strays like we do here . . .'

'Fiiiine, we'll get a dog, too. Although you can barely take care of yourself, let alone a dog . . .'

'Enough already, Mom. OK, so look, you'll have a bedroom like this, with a big bed, and it'll be just for you. I read that in Finland in the winter they ski and go ice-skating, they also love saunas and a lot of houses even come with saunas built in. Can you imagine us having a sauna?'

'Sure.'

'And we'll have nice clothes, both me and you, and we'll go to eat fish – there's tons of fish there – and we'll go to the seaside as well . . .'

'Do you ever think about anything besides having fun?'

'No, I just wanted to show you . . .'

'Where'd you find those pictures anyway, the internet?'

'Yeah.'

'Do you really think people like us live in houses like that?'

'People like us?'

'Exactly. Go do your homework.'

She can't admit to her daughter that she failed the Finnish language test.

* * *

The girl brings the dog home on a rainy November afternoon. Late that evening the rain turns to snow. The puppy is small and black, with a white collar and orange boots on his paws. She found him tied to a tree in West Park, one of the largest parks in Sofia, and the most dangerous, too.

'What were you doing in West Park?' her mother asks, seemingly nonchalant, after she has given a firm 'no', which – as is usually the case with her firmness – quickly melts into resignation.

'I was just walking around.'

* * *

The dog bonds more with her mother than with her. Her mother buys it special food. She cooks eggs for it. They sleep in the same bed. Her mother walks it in the park and makes friends there, to whom she complains about the girl – how bad her grades are, how she never studies, how she drives her crazy. When the girl runs into them, her mother's friends give her that look. The girl also takes the dog out, but it runs away and doesn't come home for days. One time, she catches it in the park and lays into it with a heavy steel chain. The animal whimpers. Then the girl cries for a long time, buries her face in its fur and apologizes.

*   *   *

'I'm going to Germany,' her mother tells her one day. 'Through Katya at the hospital, I found a company and was approved. I just need to get a B2 language certificate from the German Institute. My exam is in two weeks. I can't stand it here anymore.'

The girl shrugs and goes back to staring at her laptop. She's used to her mother's empty words and threats. To all her failed plans. This, too, shall pass.

*   *   *

'I'm not coming with you.' She repeats what she has already said a hundred times; her mother pretends not to have heard her.

'What do you mean you're not coming?'

'There's no point. I don't know German. I've only got two years of high school left. Why should I go there and waste my time, instead of just graduating here so that when I turn eighteen, I won't be a burden on you anymore.'

'You're not a burden. It's not a question of being a burden . . .'

'Yeah right, I'm not a burden on you.'

'Yana, please, honey . . .'

'I'll get a job and go to university wherever I want.'

'You'll have far better opportunities in Germany than here in this shithole of a country . . .'

'If you know the language. All my friends are here, my school is here. I'm not coming with you. Besides, I don't hate Bulgaria. I don't blame the world for everything.'

'You're being self-centered again.'

'You never support me unless I do what you want.'

'How can you be this way?'

She stares at her mother without saying a word.

'I simply can't understand why you're acting this way. Why are you always trying to sabotage me? You're coming with me, at least until you're eighteen, I've got parental rights . . .'

'You can't make me.'

'We'll see.'

'There's nothing to see. You can't make me go. I'm not a baby anymore, you can't just do whatever you feel like with me.'

'It's easy to spout all this nonsense when you don't know what it takes to earn a living. I'm the one supporting you—'

'And two years from now you won't have to support me anymore. And then your life will be rainbows and unicorns and everything will be perfect. And one day I'll pay you back all the money in one go and you'll never see me again. You should be thanking your lucky stars I don't want to come with you. After all, I'm your biggest problem in your life, right?'

* * *

She leaves at the end of summer. Eva has come to the city to stay with the girl. The three of them go to the airport, with her mother's co-worker. They check in her only suitcase. They're early as always, so they mill around in front of the escalators, chatting. Katya gives Lily endless pep talks, babbling on and on about what a hero she is, how much a daughter should respect her mother, how it will be hard for her, but that she must not give up.

'Fix your shirt,' Lily tells the girl.

She looks down at her T-shirt in confusion. Her mother sighs sharply, pulls her over by the sleeve and starts tucking in her shirt in irritation.

'Cut it out!' the girl cries, pushing her away.

'Honey, there's nothing wrong with her shirt, leave her be,' Eva cajoles Lily.

'We can't look like idiots in front of everyone,' Lily replies.

'Everyone who? And what's so idiotic about us? Are you out of your mind?'

'Lily honey, Yannie, don't fight right before the trip.'

'Fine, just leave,' Lily tells them. 'I'm going to the gate.'

Eva hugs her daughter hard, strokes her hair and whispers to her that everything will be fine. Then it's Katya's turn.

Mother and daughter exchange glances. Neither takes a step toward the other.

'Have a good trip,' the girl says. 'Call when you get there.'

Lily shows her boarding pass at the checkpoint, takes out her ID, the security guard double-checks it, lets her pass and wishes her a pleasant flight. The three others watch as she goes up the escalator – first her hair disappears, then her shoulders, finally the high heels of her sandals. She does not look back.

'You need to have more compassion for your mother' – the grandmother turns to the girl as they reach the revolving glass doors – 'she still can't get over the divorce.'

17

The fall brings a golden chill. The temperature drop is often more extreme along the coast, and sometimes as you walk along the beach you cross an invisible boundary between warm and cold, you physically feel the weather changing. The number of tourists diminishes with every passing day and come October, the town dozes off under a blanket of auburn-tinted leaves.

This summer's co-workers leave one by one. During cigarette breaks I scroll through their pictures from California, Colorado and New York, from the plane, from the return home. The rest – Laz, Norma, Bruce, Harry, Tim, the cashiers, Mary from the front desk – expected me to leave at the end of the season, the question ripening in their eyes as the days went by. Finally, Lazlo told me he didn't expect me to stay, he blurted it out like a question to which I didn't provide a response. The sous-chef Norma officially introduced me to her husband, Almandeto, who shook my hand and whispered in my ear that he could provide me with a fake driver's license and even a green card for a certain price. I politely refused.

This year, once again, Tim will leave for Florida where the season is only just beginning but he has told me that he'll probably stay there this time around. As we say goodbye he gives me a few concert tickets in frames with dates on them from the end of the sixties and the seventies. We promise each other we'll write and call.

Alina fires me after I refuse to clean the toilets twice in one day. The next morning, when I come to open the store, I see my name crossed off the schedule with a fat Sharpie. The restaurant is on my case, too. Greg the manager tells me to figure something out with my papers, they're tightening things up – he stares at me intently – and gives me a deadline that he pushes on a week at the end of each week. I see him talking to Almandeto, the two of them look at me, Almandeto says something in Greg's ear and he shakes his head, lips pursed.

For a long time, I have been a member of the large family of people with flight in their blood. I tell Sylvia and Dancho what has happened, and they not only give me more shifts but teach me how to look for work as an illegal immigrant: everyone has a relative or an acquaintance who works somewhere else, who's involved in some sort of scheme; everyone gives different advice, sends me somewhere else, promises to call a friend for me. I go to countless parties in countless houses that have been turned into eternal student rentals, where the furniture stinks of cigarettes and weed, the mattresses lie on the bare floor and the pictures on the walls show smiling, ageing parents in front of identical Soviet-era bookcases with identical books inside. Norma shows me photos of her entire family – modestly dressed in front of a shack, the only thing that makes them different from us are the palm trees and their darker faces.

At the end of the month, I am the only person left at Tony's. He stops by several times, aimlessly opening and closing cupboards, looking at the holes in the walls and picking at the grout in the bathroom. He calls his visits 'inspections', but what he's really implying is that I have to get going. I hear rumors he's decided to sell the house. I pretend I haven't heard anything. I can't rent a house without papers, Sylvia and Dancho's house is full, and I don't want to tell the American. Many nights have followed that first one, but so far I've always made him drop me off in front of the supermarket so I can walk home – I don't want him to see where I live, I don't want him to meet the endless succession of roommates. Yana and Jane. Jane and Yana.

I get a message from Tony a few days before Halloween. He gives me a notice to vacate in two weeks, during which I am not to forget to pay the rent. I immediately call Sylvia, and she promises me I can move in with them at the end of November. I have to find something until then, she says. That same day at work, Greg announces they can't keep me any longer without papers. I gather my things quickly and leave without saying goodbye. I spend the rest of the day with the insects in Tony's house, sobbing, smoking and swearing.

On Halloween I move out. Dancho drives my luggage – two suitcases – to their house. He gives me a key so I can stop by and get stuff, if necessary. He assures me they'll give me as many cleaning shifts as they can.

I start spending the nights at the American's place, trying not to think of the days, which begin when he leaves for work at eight in the morning and stretch until nine, sometimes ten o'clock at night. I helplessly watch the money in my bank account dwindle, even though I'm not spending much. Nevertheless, I don't reply to my mother's messages asking me whether I need any money. *Money has a price*, she used to say when I was little. Hers is expensive.

I roam around the resort – I know every street and every shop. Americans don't only decorate at Christmas, every season is a hurricane of tchotchkes hanging from doors, wrapped around porches and peeking out from behind curtains. The scent of pumpkin and cinnamon emanates from coffee shops and bakeries, the outlets prepare for the winter holiday season, careless summer words are replaced by other pleasant nouns, adjectives and verbs: *cozy*, *wholesome*, *festive*, *cheer*, *merry*, *jolly*, *magical*, *wonder*, *share* . . . The supermarket – one of my main shelters from the ruthless November rain – becomes the most accurate calendar: after the ice cream cones and shakes come gummy spiders and worms, skull cookies and molasses kisses, which are quickly moved to the reduced-price aisles a few days after the holiday, only to be replaced by all sorts of turkey- and pumpkin-shaped desserts, candied apples and giant bags of candy corn. The last aisle has the Christmas candy, which will soon take over the entire section. I look at everything as if I were at an exhibition: I touch and read labels but don't buy anything. When I can, I go and eat at the church where they have community lunches. If someone asks me a question, I pretend I don't speak English – they're used to it. After a while I get used to it, too.

I befriend Anelia while cleaning. She has a deep, husky voice and a twin sister who joined some religious cult six months ago and doesn't speak to her anymore. We drink beer in her room, when I sleep over for the first time.

'Why don't you marry the American?' she asks out of the blue. I'm so startled I take a bigger sip and part of the liquid comes out my nose. I shake my head and blow beer boogers into a piece of toilet paper.

'Because it's not that kind of situation.'

'What kind of situation?'

'I don't want to be a citizen, I don't want to stay. I don't want people to think that I'm with him just for the documents. I really want to be with him. I feel like it would taint everything.'

Anelia scoffs. 'What the hell do you care what people think? Everyone here does it.'

'You didn't.'

'Yes, but you're not gay,' she says with confident pride.

Anelia's from Pazardzhik, which is where she left her one true love. She tells me about this mysterious unnamed girl with the enthralling orientalist pathos of a Balkan pop-folk *chalga* song. But it gets me every time, and I really feel for her. She considers herself above everyone else because she isn't in a sham marriage. Instead, she applied for refugee status in California, where she told the interviewers she was persecuted back in Bulgaria for being a lesbian. When I ask her how many of the horror stories she tells are true, she admits to having altered and added details here and there.

'What was I supposed to do?' she asks me.

I don't have an answer.

She lives in a small two-story unit above some garages and pays rent to Vassil, a pizza delivery guy who shares the adjacent room with his high school girlfriend, Tanya. Some American guy lives in the third room, but he never comes home. Vassil is a weed dealer and people are constantly coming and going from his apartment. The bellman from the hotel is a regular and when I see him there he tries to explain how it's actually for medicinal purposes. When he asks what I do now, I say I found a better job for more money in another town. That I'm waiting for my papers. Everyone in town tells me how happy they are for me.

I stay at Anelia's a few times. I'm running a bit behind one day, so she leaves for work and lets me finish getting ready. I'm at the door when I hear Vassil's voice behind me.

'Can we talk?'

We've exchanged no more than a few words, we've barely seen each other. Most of the time when I hang out with Anelia, they're both at work.

I walk with him over to the glass coffee table in the living room. He sits on the leather couch, and it squeaks. Vassil spends his mornings coughing and hacking up phlegm over the kitchen sink, before rolling his first joint. He pulls out a small bag and arranges its contents on the table without looking at me.

'I hear you're sleeping here.'

'Yeah, I've stayed with Annie once or twice, we got close and . . .'

'Don't you have a house?' He continues to twist the grinder, staring at his hands.

'I do,' I stutter. 'I usually stay at my boyfriend's, he's . . .'

'Uh-huh. Tanya tells me you take showers here. You sit around all day with Annie, you've taken over the TV, you eat from the fridge.'

He sets the grinder aside. He takes a thin piece of rolling paper from the small bag, opens the round box and empties its contents into the paper. The back of my head starts burning, like when I was a child. It hasn't happened in years.

'We don't eat anything from the fridge,' I tell him. 'We buy stuff and we . . .'

'What about the showers? Where do you think the water comes from? And you dye your hair, too, and then who do you think cleans this toilet, huh?'

'I haven't showered, I asked Annie to help me dye my hair and she suggested doing it here, then I had to wash it, but we didn't leave any trace. Other than that one time I've never showered here, if she hadn't suggested . . .'

Vassil adds the filter. He then licks the paper and carefully rolls the joint.

'Look, I don't mind. But you have to pay if you're going to be visiting. This ain't a roadhouse. This ain't Bulgaria, where we come and pay visits to each other. This is A-me-ri-ca,' he stresses. 'Dollars, dollars. I pay rent, I pay bills. Every time you piss and flush, that's dollars. When you wash your hands, what flows from the spout? Money. The rent is eighty dollars a week, if you want to visit your friend.'

I look at my knees. He lights the joint and the living room is filled with the bitter smell that has penetrated the entire apartment. I want to defend myself, but nothing comes to mind.

'Your cat has worms,' I say.

'What?'

The gray cat is soaking up a sliver of sun on the windowsill.

'Your cat has worms. A huge white worm crawled out of . . . you know, the other day, and Annie and I cleaned him, pulled the worms out . . . Maybe you should take it to the vet . . .'

I get up, my legs shaking.

'Wait, what are you . . .'

'I won't come around anymore, since it's a problem. I'm sorry for making the wrong impression.'

'That's not what I wanted to say, look now—'

'I think I get your point.' It takes a tremendous effort not to start crying. Why am I such a piece of shit? 'Sorry.'

I quickly go down the stairs. It's raining again outside, the rain is freezing. I walk down the highway, the sky is dark, like it is before dusk. I realize I've forgotten my phone at Annie's. And my wallet. The warm lights of the cafes, gas stations and houses are reflected in the wet asphalt. I let the water run down my face; my clothes are soaking. I walk through the city. I pass by the few open restaurants in the center, where the locals have sheltered from the rain over some hot food. No one sees me – I'm a shadow, even on paper I don't exist,

I'm not supposed to be here. I'm an intruder, trespasser, invader. *Illegal alien.*

I almost run to the shore, I walk on the wet sand, away from people. The ocean is frightening and gray. I pass the last house, turn to the roaring water and scream in response to its growls. I scream and I cry – my voice tears my lungs and my throat, breaks free, hurls itself toward the water and crashes into the white crests of the furious waves.

Lily

Two flies chase each other beneath the chandelier, interweaving in flight and continuing their mad whirling. She tears her eyes away from the lamp, types out the final notes in the patient's case file – the writing goes slowly, she's still not totally used to the German keyboard – then she switches the computer off. She'll tape the rest on her voice recorder and give it to the secretaries to finish.

A breeze blows, the leaves of the birch trees twitch. The trees are old, the roots of their white trunks have dug into the soil, lifting the paving stones in places. The sun shines through their crowns. This part of Germany reminds her of her home region, except that here the broad plain is full of life – combines reaping the last remaining ears of wheat; wind turbines whirling in the distance, like giant mechanical flowers; cars darting between picturesque villages; in front of the cafes in the small squares, retirees savor their last afternoon coffee while waiting for the church bell to announce the end of the day. Here her grandmother's generation is still alive, and often her patients recount their memories of that wounded Europe whose poorly healed scars she and her mother and daughter have inherited.

She runs through the mental list of what she has to do by the end of the day: she has to drop her white coat off to be cleaned, she needs to run to the bank to send money to Yana and the old folks, she needs to go grocery shopping. She puts off going home to her empty flat, where only a bare mattress is waiting for her, along with a red armchair she salvaged off the street on bin collection day. She wavers between the belief that she is a good mother sacrificing herself to provide a better life for her child and guilt for being a failure, that she was wrong about everything. With her departure, she lost her closeness with her mother, she lost the few friends she had left in Bulgaria. It's just not the same over the phone. She has even lost the security of language, which she had taken for granted: her high school German is clumsy, the terminology is different, the hospital equipment is different, she has so much to learn at an age when other people are kicking back and preparing to quietly reap what they sowed in their youth. And perhaps she is reaping as well, it's just that the seed was bad.

'Heading home, Frau Doctor?' Lily lifts her head from her white clogs and meets Nurse Helene from the ER's blue eyes.

'Yes, Helene, I'll be going. I have some things to do before . . .'

'Frau Doctor, I'm very sorry to bother you, but a young girl came into the A&E who doesn't speak German, and I didn't know who else to turn to.'

Lily nods. Besides her, there is one other foreign doctor, a Greek woman who lives in Berlin with her husband and two children, but she is not on shift at the moment. When Lily arrived in the country, the Greek woman helped her with all the paperwork and told her that no matter how much she was being ground down, no matter how much less they paid her, she had to be patient and not speak up until she had learned the language perfectly and completed her specialization, then she could tell them all where to stick it. The Greek woman tipped her off that West Germans look down on their fellow Germans from the East, and on Eastern Europeans in general. At first Lily didn't believe her. But only at first. The only thing that's the same as at home is their shared dislike of Turks and Arabs, with whom they often compete for jobs. The locals have softened toward her since the refugees came. They say the men refused to let women treat them and wouldn't let male doctors examine their wives. Many of them didn't speak German. She stays out of politics, but still engages in conversations about current events with her colleagues from time to time, albeit carefully.

We prefer you to them, the head of the department once told her. *The lesser of two evils.*

She follows Helene down the hallways, their clogs squeaking on the clean floor. The hospital is run by an evangelical order, and out of habit in the main lobby Lily glances up at the convulsed Jesus hanging from the ceiling, an exceptionally ugly sculpture thanks to which the children's ward has a special entrance, otherwise the children scream and cry when they see it and won't go any further into the hospital.

'She's over there,' the nurse quietly directs her. 'She arrived this morning, seriously dehydrated, unconscious. With vomiting and a high fever, plus fainting spells.'

'Why didn't they bring her in earlier?'

'I don't know. They brought her in early this morning, at about six o'clock, in a white van, two men, they didn't speak German, they just handed us her ID and drove off before we could even figure out what was going on. When I looked at the passport and saw where it was from, I decided to call you, thinking maybe you could help. She just came to a little while ago.'

Lily takes the reddish passport from her co-worker. She looks at the girl and feels the familiar instinctive shock of relief she has learned to accept over the years: this is not her daughter. The girl has the same dark hair, but is very thin. Her hands are chocolate brown, her farmer's tan traces the outline of her vest top. She glances at the passport – the girl is Croatian. She looks over the notes on the intake forms the nurse has handed her. Severe dehydration and heat stroke.

'Moram se vratiti na posao,' she hears a voice from the bed. 'Molim vas.' Croatian is a distant Slavic cousin of Bulgarian, so some of the words sound familiar to her. *Molim vas*, I beg you.

The girl struggles to sit up. Lily starts speaking in German, then catches herself and switches to Bulgarian: 'Please lie down and stay calm. You are not well and you need to rest. What is your name . . .' She looks at the intake card. 'Sanja! Sanja, it's all right, do you understand me? You are in good hands.'

'Izgubit ću posao ako nisam tamo,' the girls says in a hoarse voice and grasps Lily's hand. 'Molim!'

'Izgubit . . . loses . . . you've lost . . . What have you lost there? Or are you lost?'

The girl nods, a sweaty lock of hair falls across her forehead. She goes to push it out of her face and grimaces, feeling the IV catheter in her arm.

'Sanja, where did you come from? How did you end up here? Tuka, here . . .' Lily points at the ground, then raises her hands as if asking a question.

'Beelitzer Spargel, Beelitzer Spargel, Beelitzer Spargel . . .' the girl says over and over in bad German.

'Frau Doctor?'

'Yes, Helene?' she replies, angry that she can't understand anything.

'Can I speak to you for a moment?'

The blonde nurse leads her out of the room and closes the door behind them.

'We think she is a seasonal worker.'

'A worker? If she has other documents, let's see them, there might be contact info there, so we can get in touch with her co-workers if . . .'

Helene shakes her head.

'Frau Doctor, there are no documents.'

'What do you mean, there are no documents?'

'In Beelitz, they grow lots of asparagus and strawberries. The farmers often hire people like y— people from abroad to work for the summer. Often without . . .'

'Without what, Helene?'

'Without documents. They're from Europe, they're easy to transport, they don't have to pay any insurance or benefits for them, so it's cheaper . . . They're poor people, they don't speak any German, they've come here for treatment before, but there's always been someone to help us figure things out?'

'What do you mean, figure things out?'

'We treat them, then we send them back. Most often they haven't drunk enough water or have been out in the sun too long, so sometimes they bring them here. Sometimes they even pay their bills . . .'

'But what do you mean "send them back", Helene? Where do you send them back to?'

'We don't send them back, I didn't put that quite right, we just release them from the hospital. Otherwise there's a lot of bureaucracy, lots of headaches, back and forth with the police. Afterward they end up working it out on their—'

'Out of the question,' Lily cuts her off.

The nurse is stunned.

'What do you mean they haven't drunk enough water or were out in the sun too long, Helene? Have you ever stood out in the sun until you fainted?'

Without waiting for an answer, she goes back into the room.

'Sanja! Sanja, do you have anyone you can call, to let them

know you are here? Friends, family.' She points at the girl, then at herself, making a gesture as if she is rocking a baby in her arms, then pretends to dial an imaginary telephone.

'Jesam li trudna?' The girl's eyes flood with tears and she starts to howl: 'Joooj!'

Trudna . . . didn't that mean pregnant? 'No, no, no, no, Sanja, Sanja! Wait, wait! No, I mean your mother, not that you're going to be a mother! Your mother! Yours!'

'Moja majka?' Sanja stares at her through her tears. 'Nema šanse. Ne, ne, ne!'

'You don't want to call your mother?'

The girl shakes her head.

'Sanja, what do you want?'

'Želim se vratiti na posao. Kad se mogu vratiti na posao?'

'I don't understand what you're saying. Vratiti, that sounds like vrata. You mean door?' She points at the door, and the girl nods. 'I don't understand, Sanja. What do you want with the door?'

The girl raises her hand, the palm parallel to her body, then clenches it into a fist, as if she is ripping something out. She repeats this movement several times, then wipes her forehead with the back of her hand.

'Kad se mogu vratiti na posao?'

Helene comes back into the room.

'I think she's asking when she can go back to work,' Lily tells her, then translates Helene's answer back into Bulgarian. 'Pet dena. In five days at the earliest, Sanja. You need to rest and recover.'

'Pet dana? Pet dana?'

Lily nods.

'Nemoguće. Pronaći će nekoga drugog. Moram se vratiti!'

She tries to get up again but fails. Her face spasms, and she vomits on the blanket.

Helene presses the button and one of the younger nurses arrives immediately.

'Helene, what's the procedure in cases like this?'

'We could call the police . . .'

'Nemojte policija! Nemojte policija!' The girl's whisper grows into a whimper. 'Molim vas! Molim!'

'We won't, we won't.' Lily rests her hand on the girl's arm. 'Calm down, just calm down.' Then she asks Helene in German. 'If . . . they are called in, what happens?'

'She'll definitely have to pay a fine and perhaps even go to court, then they'll send her back to wherever she came from.'

'And won't her employer have to pay fines, too?'

'If they can find him.' The nurse shrugs. 'It also depends on what he says. He could claim she lied to him, gave him fake papers, that she threatened to do something to him if he turned her in . . . Frau Doctor . . . these things are an open secret. And it's nothing new, it's been going on for years. If you ask me, and I beg your pardon if I'm overstepping, but I really don't think it's any of your business.'

'Rekao mi je da ako kažem nekome, tužit će me. Molim vas, doktore, pustite me. Pusti me, molim te,' the girl keeps whimpering. *Ako kažem nekome* – if I tell anyone . . . *Molim vas, doktore, pustite me* – please, doctor, let me go.

She must be only a little older than her own daughter, nineteen or twenty at most. She looks at the passport again – she hasn't even turned nineteen yet. She sits down next to the girl, brushes the hair from her face and strokes her cheek. The girl permits this, her eyes half-closing.

She remembers sitting next to Yana in the hospital when she got her appendix taken out. They let her sleep with the little girl in the hospital room, since she herself was a fellow doctor. The first night she woke up and saw cockroaches crawling across her daughter's forehead. At first she thought she was dreaming, then she looked around and saw they were crawling over all the children, as well as the sink, an open sleeve of crackers, around the rims of the plastic cups half-full of juice. She screamed at the nurses in desperation, knowing full well that they were every bit as helpless as she was. As if the brazen disregard for these little humans was not bad enough in and of itself, they had to be further humiliated, crushed, turned into food for cockroaches.

She felt like crying with fury. Why now, holding the hand of this unknown girl, does she again feel this helplessness? Why does she feel backed into the very same corner?

'Sanja,' Lily begins. 'We'll let you go, Sanja. But promise me' – the absurdity of the words weighs heavy in her throat – 'promise me that you'll drink more water, voda.'

'Ja ću piti vodu.'

'Promise me that you'll eat, and you'll stay in the shade in the hottest hours of the day, and wear a hat and sunblock . . .'

'Neće nas više natjerati da radimo toliko naporno.'

'And promise me that you'll think about whether what you're doing is right, not only for you, but for your family. No amount of money is worth what has happened to you.'

The girl nods.

'And you'll still have to stay here for five days. Do you want to call anyone?'

She makes a telephone gesture with her thumb and pinkie and holds it to her ear. The girl nods again.

Lily looks at the nurse, who goes to get the hospital phone.

She comes in each of the five days, even when she's not on shift. She is glad that in a fit of sentimentality she slipped *The Wonderful Adventure of Nils Holgersson* into her suitcase, the first book she read to Yana. She reads it aloud as the girl looks out the window or at the muted TV screen, before she finally falls asleep.

On the sixth day she stops by to see if everything is OK, but the bed is empty, the sheets are blindingly white, the equipment has been sterilized.

'The same van came back and picked her up,' she hears the nurse Helene's voice behind her. 'I watched her go from the window.'

She finally makes it to the bank to send money back to Bulgaria. That evening she calls her mother.

'Her grades are good, she's doing fine, sweetie,' Eva tells her daughter.

They talk almost every day.

'I'm afraid to let her live on her own. I don't know what she spends the money on, who she's with, what she's doing.

I'd really prefer for you to be there.'

'We can't keep her under house arrest anymore. And besides, we didn't get along, she's already all grown-up, a young woman, while I'm old . . . I've got a lot of work to do here with the gardens, the animals, your father . . . We don't see eye-to-eye and I've accepted that. You can't keep her under your thumb her whole life.'

'She's sixteen years old, what does she know about anything?'

'You yourself lived on your own in Mihaylovgrad when you were sixteen. You left home at fourteen.'

'It's not the same thing.'

'You've got to let go of your obsession with controlling everything. You take after your father in that regard.'

'Mother, please.'

'Listen to me just this once. Leave her alone . . .'

'Do you go to her parent-teacher meetings? Have you talked to her class teacher?'

'All her report cards have been excellent, except for maths, but that's how it's always been . . .'

'I don't believe it.'

'I'm telling you what they told me and what I've seen of her report cards. I also ran into Didi's mother,' the old woman says.

'And?'

'And she asked me how Lilia could have upped and left and abandoned her daughter here.'

Silence.

'And what did you tell her?'

The older woman shrugs.

'Well, just like that, I said. What else can I say?'

'Mother . . .'

'Don't worry, you've got to be brave, the kid will be all right. Every night before I go to bed, I pray to the Lord God – once for you, once for your brother and once for Yana. You think it's not hard for me, with all of you so far away, your brother in England, you in Germany . . . ? God forbid if anything were to happen to us . . .'

'Nothing's going to happen, Mom.'

'But I grit my teeth, sweetie. What else can we do, since this is how our life has worked out?'

'There's nothing we can do.'

'Nothing at all. So I grit my teeth and keep putting one foot in front of the other. Let people say what they will – that's the only thing they know how to do in any case.'

Lily is silent.

'Lily, honey, why don't you come home for a holiday? Your father is also really hoping you might visit, how long has it been since you've been home, even before you left for Germany . . .'

'My job is intense, Mom. I send you money and then save the rest for an apartment and a rainy day. We'll see.'

'Fine, honey.'

'We'll see. I promise.'

Eva

Her leg has been hurting for several days now, every day it seems a bit worse – in the morning it's numb, asleep, it's not there at all. By the time she manages to wake it up a bit it's already getting dark again.

'I must've banged into something, who knows what happened. It'll pass, honey,' she tells her daughter over the phone. She doesn't want her children to worry. She only talks to Yana about the worst things, about those that weigh the heaviest on her, but the girl hardly ever calls anymore – it's nothing to get upset about, she's a young person, with her own life to lead.

Ignat is doing crossword puzzles on the couch, the news is droning on on the TV again. She's sick of hearing the same thing over and over all day long. Do they really need to rehash every tragedy a hundred times over, don't they make enough money from covering someone else's misfortunes only once? She tells him to change the channel.

'What's that?' He lifts his eyes from the newspaper. He's deaf as a doornail by this point. Why did Lily bother buying him that hearing aid, he's never once used it.

I'm telling you to change the channel on the TV, we've already heard this before, she repeats. Why is he acting so strange?

Ignat suddenly turns toward her.

'Eva, what the heck are you trying to say?'

Change the channel, she shouts.

He tosses the paper down and grabs her by the shoulders, looking her over, staring at her left side.

'Eva, do you understand what I'm saying?'

Of course I do, let me go, what's wrong with you?

'Eva, do you understand what I'm saying?'

I understand you, damn it! She nods.

Why is she dizzy all of a sudden?

'Just stay there, Eva. Stay right there.'

What are you doing? What's wrong with you?

'I can't understand what you're saying, I can't understand what you're trying to tell me. The words aren't coming out of your mouth, something's going on.'

What do you mean something's going on? What could be going on?

She wants to get up, but can't. Her body just stays there on the couch. Clenching her muscles, propping her hand on the armrest, standing on both feet – all of this happens only as a thought.

Ignat . . . she tries to say, but her lips will no longer obey her. He's already got up and he's making a phone call. Purple flashes are swirling around the room.

'Just take it easy, Eva, just take it easy, let's not get scared now.' The old man has started to cry.

Even now, in her old age, she still gets annoyed with him – why is he always crying?

'Hello, send an ambulance quick, my poor old wife . . .' This is the last thing she hears before the world disappears entirely.

18

Somehow our parents move into our phones, we keep them there at a safe distance. Could we be condemning them to this prison as punishment for all their mistakes?

I was expecting one of the three meaningless questions:

'What are you doing?' (the same thing as yesterday)

'How are you?' (if I told you the truth, you wouldn't understand)

'Is everything OK?' (if it weren't, you'd already know it)

But instead, I see three simple sentences:

Your grandma had a stroke. You might think about coming back. I already have a ticket.

My mother has not been back to her hometown for more than twenty years. This time I take her seriously.

'It's a good thing you're going,' Norma tells me. We see each other one last time in the restaurant before I fly back to Bulgaria.

'Humpf,' Almandero scoffs. 'As if anyone would give *her* a hard time.'

'What do you mean by that?' I ask him.

'Nothing.'

'No, tell me.'

'He doesn't mean anything by it. He's just worried.'

'Why is he worried?'

'Well, because of . . . the president.'

'What, you don't really think Greg and Welch are going to lose their staff? Who would do the work?'

Norma's English stumbles over her Spanish. The result is almost always in the present tense, singular, a mosaic of accents and words.

'Oh, cariño mío, they think about you the same way they think about me . . . You even look like one of our girls, from down there. 'Cept you're a little whiter. If you don't say nothin' to an American, they won't know what you are. But they always see you as a . . . there's a saying, you know? Pajaro de mal aguero.'

I shake my head, I can't decode that phrase. I take out my phone, and Google Translate spits out: *Bird of ill omen*.

'I don't know. I don't know nothin' no more,' she goes on.

'No one's gonna catch you, Norma. You'll see. You know what Tim always says – in America, profit always wins out.'

'Travel safe, and say hi to your grandma from me,' she responds.

'I'll tell her.'

* * *

'Where are you coming from?' The question interrupts the airplane's monotonous roar.

I reluctantly open my eyes. The woman to my right is leaning over in her seat to get a better look at me.

'America,' I rasp. The trip plus the air conditioning have dried out my throat.

She's satisfied. 'Ah, that's nice, that's nice. You coming back?' She doesn't wait for my answer. 'I was visiting my son and daughter-in-law, went to see the grandkids, they live in Holland, I'm on my way back home now.'

I smile, nod and go to close my eyes.

'Do you come back to Bulgaria often?' She doesn't give up. 'My kids spend a week or two with us in the summer, plus a week at the seaside . . .'

'No.'

I hear her sharp sigh.

'I'm sure your mom and dad miss you. Will they be waiting for you?'

I nod again.

My mom and I have agreed to meet at Grandma's place. Diving straight into everything at the airport would be like jumping into icy water with an overheated body.

'I could barely stand to say goodbye to the grandkids. It's really hard.' She sighs again.

Such a tiny woman, where is she storing all these sighs?

'My dream is for people like you, young people, to come back.'

I wonder if young people anywhere else are expected to sacrifice their freedom to pay off debts accumulated over generations?

'Lots of young people stay in Bulgaria.' I can't help myself, and instantly regret it.

She shakes her head.

'It's not the same . . . they're not the same. The best ones leave.'

I think about Sylvia and Dancho, about Emo, Stan and Anelia. I think about that girl who was run over at that intersection. Why are the ones who leave saddled with all the blame for this unhappiness? What if they hadn't gone? After all, for half a century nobody could run away anywhere, could they? But for the first time I don't feel like arguing. Why not leave her with the idea that if I hadn't left, if her son hadn't gone to seek his fortune elsewhere – her life would be better.

'I'm gonna try to nap,' I tell her. 'I didn't sleep well on the other plane.'

She nods, smiles and stares out the window on my left side, while clasping her hands in her lap, her smile gradually growing into a worried grimace that I recognize from my mother's and grandmother's faces.

We descend into the familiar labyrinth, with the National Palace of Culture and the golden domes of St Alexander Nevsky Cathedral at its center, the sunset bathing Sofia in orange. I expected to feel something special, but all I can sense is exhaustion and my desire to go to bed. Bulgaria hits me in waves, people's faces are different, the colors too, as if someone had switched out pieces of my reality. I've lost the little reflexes: how people wait in line, how they call out to each other, how they look at each other, how they jostle and shove to get on the bus. The air is different, lighter, the ocean's lethal humidity is missing, which I only now realize I'd gotten used to. The edges of the sidewalks and roads look gnawed on. The taxi drivers look like ghosts floating in clouds of harsh cigarette smoke; I recognize the old cars, the dust that sticks to everything, the rust on the trash bins, on the lamps, on the sheet metal. Grass, weeds and cigarette butts sprout from the cement flower pots sitting on crooked paving stones. As if in a dream, I see the hundreds of glowing eyes lighting up the panel-block apartments in Mladost neighborhood. At the bus stop by the big mall a group of kids get on the bus, two girls are holding hands and sitting next to each other, the elderly woman nearby gives them a dirty look. I smile at them, one of them smiles back. I get off at Eagles' Bridge and change to the subway.

'Now look, with the subway I can go all the way out to Druzhba, to the other end of the city, to see the kids . . .' I overhear a conversation between two elderly women in identical brown skirts and black coats – they look familiar, perhaps I've dreamed of them? – before the doors shut behind me with a hiss.

The maw of the subway spits me out at the southern end of Vitoshka; my hotel is in one of the little side streets that criss-cross the pedestrian zone and make up the ribcage of the city. It's a Tuesday in November and the cafes and restaurants are full – here, no one waits till Friday night to have fun. The only sound is the quiet clamor from the restaurants and dogs barking in the distance.

Distracted, I exchange pleasantries with the receptionist, she helps me with my suitcase, I leave her a tip, she tries to refuse it, I insist. There are no towels in the room, I call down again, another woman picks up. Bulgarian has a kind of blunt ease to it, something I haven't noticed before, a lightness and a directness.

Before I fall into an exhausted sleep, the hazy thought crosses my mind that returning is a myth, a lie; once you've run away, even for a short time, you carry all your wanderings within you.

* * *

I decide to walk around Sofia, to follow the routes we used to take as kids – from downtown along Pirotska, then to the intersection of Konstantin Velichkov, the garden around the Holy Trinity Church, Tsar Simeon Street, West Park. These are the hors d'oeuvres, the beginning of the next several days in which I have decided to throw myself a feast of nostalgia. On Pirotska, I pass by a few new stores and a bakery. In a little arcade selling underwear and cheap knitted clothes, a woman tries on pajamas under a sign made from the cardboard backing of an old calendar with 'This is not a dressing room!!!' scribbled on it. In the distance I see the orange 22 streetcar. I catch up to it and what do you know, the little store for snacks, banitsa, rolls and so on is still there, in the foundations of a half-ruined old building that has been frozen in eternal renovations since my school days. I cross Botev and continue down the old part of the street. Some of the buildings have been renovated, the new ones have been smeared with graffiti. I pass by my old high school, the usual crowd in front of the doner shop, the same smell, the schoolkids still smoke in front of the post office, just like we used to smoke, along with a few of the teachers. A group of heavily made-up girls, every single one of them zipped into black leather jackets, gives me a critical once-over. I smile back at them – this startles them. The druggie cafe in front of St Nicholas Church is closed, and in place of the abandoned building next to it there is now an empty lot for sale. As I pass by the Jewish school, I remember how we would hurl ourselves into piles of freshly raked autumn leaves, we would wade through them with our new sneakers. I also recall the scent of rain and chestnuts: it smells the same, but now something is missing. I get angry, I cling to the past, I struggle to impose it onto the facades and sidewalks of the empty street, but it doesn't fit, the present peeks out from underneath. I should feel at home, safe, but instead I feel rage and an indeterminate weightlessness, that life has gone on without me. The little market has been renovated, the park has new jungle gyms, young women push strollers along the smoothly paved asphalt in the cold, some of the old chestnut trees have been cut down, the church has been repainted in bright colors . . . I feverishly make a list of all the changes, checking off what is the same and what is not.

I left Sofia at sixteen. After my mother went abroad, I couldn't live in my father's apartment anymore. I now realize that your hometown lives most vividly in your childhood memories: Sofia will always be the old green booths of the Dimitar Petkov Market that have since vanished; it is scrambling over chunks of dug-up asphalt on Konstantin Velichkov Boulevard; the rusty jungle gyms in the weed-choked parks; roaming the streets early in the morning and late at night; the chestnut blossoms on the gray asphalt in the rain; the endless idleness of the teenage years . . .

Are these the first signs of getting old? Is this me refusing to see how the world changes over time and struggling to force it into the mold of memories, gradually becoming a foreigner in my own life? Is this why adults strike us as strange? I think about my grandma and her stubborn refusal to use a smartphone, I think about how she only went to the seaside once in her life and she didn't want us to take her anywhere, she didn't like leaving her hometown, maybe she really was frightened . . . she *is* frightened, she is still scared because the world she knows is changing piece by piece until one day what she sees before her will turn out to be incompatible with what she remembers . . . I step in shit and scrape it off on the edge of a crooked paving stone. I walk among the familiar old panel-block apartments, heading toward my childhood home. Near the building I notice a scrawny horse tied to a tree by the dumpsters. I scrape off the sole of my shoe one more time and go into the entryway. Everything is exactly as I remember it.

I won't go up to the apartment, I just open the door to the elevator and see something new – the light bulb is locked up in a tiny cage with a microscopic padlock. I am in awe of whoever created this device – it shows that Bulgaria is the real land of opportunity.

I get tired of walking and get on the metro. I eat out for every meal – for lunch, I choose a hole-in-the-wall *kratchma* restaurant near Five Corners; I order everything I've been wanting to eat over the last few months and years. I wonder if Bulgarian restaurants will create a special menu for returning emigrants – *tarator* soup, meat balls, *shopska* salad, fried cheese, banitsa, strained yogurt with walnuts and honey. In the evening I choose a modern place, decorated with retro signs and everyday objects and photos from the Communist era. I eat the same food, only it's served a different way, as more modern 'fusion', the waiter explains to me. The food comes in those old metal dishes, just like the ones my grandma used to make porridge in, and I find myself wanting bowls like this, too.

That same night I have my recurring childhood nightmare: I'm in the old wooden elevator in the apartment building on Tsar Simeon Street, which, like most in that style, doesn't have internal doors, and I press the button for the fourth floor. It starts going up. First, second, third, it skips the fourth floor and goes on to the fifth, sixth, seventh . . . I start pressing everything wildly, but the stop button doesn't work and an endless film reel stretches out in front of me – door-concrete-door-concrete-door-concrete . . .

After a terribly long time, the elevator finally stops, I slip out and start going down an endless staircase, I come across dozens of unfamiliar doors, but I can't find my home. I wake up.

As always, the aftertaste of the nightmare stays with me the whole day.

*   *   *

I get to the train station early – I've inherited the habit of showing up unnecessarily early. This complete immersion into memories is possible only with Bulgarian trains, which have not changed. Look, here's one more detail I had forgotten – people are always rushing because they are afraid the train will leave without them; and they always ask the conductor if this is the right platform, because of another eternal fear – of getting on the wrong train. I buy pretzels, water and *ayran*, the salty yogurt drink we love so much in the Balkans. I pass several banitsa stands – the baked goods in the windows look greasy, pizzas with crusts three fingers thick, bottles of brownish *boza*, another classic Balkan beverage. Everything is old and new at the same time, I both remember and see it for the first time. Perhaps the only way to truly love your homeland is to leave it.

The train leaves on time. It's an open car, almost empty: apart from me there's only a Gypsy kid whose earphones are buzzing with the oriental strains of chalga, and an elderly man sitting near the door – he is so old that it looks like he is in pain from the very fact of being alive. Now and then he wheezes and grunts, but soon the clacking of the train swallows up his unpleasant rumbling. I open a book, which I end up not even glancing at. The Sofia basin outside gathers speed, before gradually folding and shattering against the Balkan Mountains' colorful slopes. There are few passengers, the Gypsy kid gets off in Svoge, the elderly man falls asleep. Amid the autumnal landscape I see the familiar disintegrating factories; sheds with windows that are papered over with faded posters of busty chalga singers or failed politicians; shabby stations and prematurely grayed faces. I catch a glimpse of a statue of a partisan, his stony gaze keeping watch over the surrounding area.

I silently observe people hefting bags and carts onto the train's luggage racks, afterward unloading their stories. I listen to two elderly voices coming from behind me, their words weighted with the familiar local accent.

'Sell while you can, just sell. That's what I keep telling him. Now no one and nothing's left. And all these bad years . . .'

'Haven't I told you, I've been here since the sixties, I'm getting on eighty, been here my whole life . . . I've never had to water the crops in March! To say nothing of the summer . . .'

'Summer, what summer? The whole winter is summer now!' the other voice protests. 'The wife waters the tulips, scrappy little things, only yay big' – I imagine how he shows the size with his thumb and pointer finger. I'm dying to turn around and look, but that'll give me away – 'barely twenty centimeters. The trees are flowering like crazy, but they don't have any fruit . . .'

I imagine them in their wool socks, their black rubber galoshes, their faded visored caps, their knitted sweater-vests.

'I cut back the vines, must've been a month ago, then I watch and watch and watch, nearly went blind from watching . . . but they're not crying! They're not crying at all, let me tell you! Not even a drop. I've never seen that before . . .'

'You hear what they're sayin' on TV?' the other breaks in, his voice padded by the authority of the television. 'You don't think it's just us, now, do ya? The whole damn world is going crazy . . .'

I know from my grandfather that they call this train the 'greasy train'. As a child I thought they called it that because it was dirty, but later I found out how the Northwest fed starving Sofia during the world wars and then again in the Transition years. When I was a kid, my mom and I would go to the cargo area at the station, looking for the packages my grandma sent – soaked in the scent of the village house, tied with white string, addressed in spindly, grandmotherly handwriting and almost always including a pair of hand-knitted slippers inside.

The peaks are adorned with a delicate fog, the grass alongside the rails is covered in frost, the meanders of the Iskar river toss bright glints of sunlight back at me. After Mezdra, the hands of the clock turn with the train, which switches engines and tracks, now heading backward and northward; time starts creeping in reverse as well, the landscape turns to rust, dust, sandy clay and dark soil. Men in soccer jerseys and frizzy-haired women loaded down with those cheap plaid plastic tote bags get on. The train car fills with folk music, sunflower seeds and pistachios. Time stretches out even longer, we now measure it in hands of belote. Traffic to and from the last toilet, at the very end of the train, is brisk – that's where you can smoke.

'Deal them, boss!' I hear.

'Let the other boss deal,' an offended voice replies.

'This card game, I invented it, you know,' a third chimes in.

A round of 'cheers' follows.

'Oh, for fuck's sake, I messed up, I didn't count the spades.'

'That's why you shouldn't play cards when you're drunk... I'm talking about myself, of course,' one of the players clarifies.

I chuckle along with several other passengers who are listening to the card players. Everything gradually quiets down – we're approaching Vratsa.

'Thank God for the kids, let them keep sending money, then let them talk about democracy all they want.' I hear a few final words before we set off again. There is no one left in my train car.

The doors open – two men are looking for a warmer car toward the back of the train.

'I kept quiet then, but now I won't!' They are clearly in the middle of an argument.

'Even if you don't keep quiet now, who's going to listen to you?' the other man replies, before continuing down the aisle.

We plod toward the edge of the world. Three stations before the end, I remember Charlie Chaplin – I wonder if he's still alive. I search for his name and town in Google, which immediately spits back an article from the newspaper *24 Hours*, from which I learn that *Charlie Chaplin now has a new shtick – impersonating Hitler.*

* * *

The train slowly enters the station. I slip my phone into my pocket and catch sight of a woman on the platform who is anxiously peering in every window, clutching her purse nervously, shifting her weight from one foot to the other. At that exact moment my mother's gaze finds me and the tired smile she saves only for me floods her lips.

We ask each other the usual things – how was the trip, are you OK, have you eaten. She has lost weight, she doesn't look like a fifty-year-old woman.

'How's Grandma?'

'They're sending her home tomorrow. I went to the hospital, cleaned the room and the cupboard, brought new sheets – the old ones were completely filthy. There's no neurologist, he only comes on Thursdays, so we're waiting for him to see her.'

'Did she recognize you?'

'Yes, she's constantly asking about your uncle.' She shakes her head. Her steps are rushed, just like my grandma's, as if she is running late. 'Pavel this, Pavel that. Your grandpa has completely lost it, he's just bawling and getting on my nerves. You need to help me clean the apartment, I almost had a heart attack when I set foot inside. It hasn't changed a bit since I left to study in Pleven. They live like hoarders.'

She chatters away as we walk toward the apartment building – about her job in Germany, about her patients, about money, about all kinds of things. For the first time, I don't feel any urge to argue with her – on the contrary, I enjoy listening to her.

'Will she recover?'

'The test results will come back tomorrow, but the stroke affected several parts of her brain' – she launches into a detailed explanation full of medical terminology and diagnoses that I won't remember.

The town's main street has been renovated. I recall that while I was in the States, Grandma was always telling me about the construction, happy that the town would finally be spruced up. But the paving stones are already starting to crack, rust is gnawing at the lamp posts, weeds and grass have sprouted up between the sidewalk and the curb.

'It looks like Syria,' my mom says. 'I don't want you bringing that boy here.'

She glances at me. I haven't told her much about the American.

'Why shouldn't I bring him here?'

She is silent.

'It's a part of me, just like it's a part of you. Warts and all. I have nothing to be ashamed of.'

Graffiti on the side of the building reads GYPSIES TO THE MOON. We unlock the door under the stern gazes of all the deceased neighbors – the entryway is covered with death notices. Yet another forgotten instinct – looking to see who has died since the last time you were here.

'Grandma doesn't want us to make a death notice for her,' I blurt out. 'She's told me that a million times.'

'She's not dead yet, so that's neither here nor there,' my mother replies offhandedly. 'Plus, you know your granddad.'

The entryway smells like a musty cellar. The elevator is smaller than I remember. My mother grasps my hand and smiles at me. This gentleness between us is awkward – I would feel much better if she yelled at me about something. I stifle the urge to push her away.

My grandfather hugs me and bursts out sobbing. I pat him on the back. I am made of guilt, just as bread is made of flour, and he knows it – he scolds me for staying in the States, for not calling, for not acting the way I should, he does not approve of these years of no schooling, with only work, with a foreigner, with nothing. To my surprise, my mother tells him to shut up and go lie down until he can get a hold of himself – my mouth drops open in shock when he complies. I realize that as an adult I have never seen them together in one place.

'He's been spouting nonsense non-stop,' she confides while giving me orders in the kitchen, which I silently carry out. 'He says he dreamed that aliens came and brought his mother back, that old bat who made my and your grandma's life a living hell. Good thing you were born, so she could finally kick the bucket. Go wash those dishes, please.'

We spend the rest of the day sorting through old junk. When deciding whether to throw things away or not, I try to see them through my grandma's eyes – I had jealously kept all her stories, I greedily hoarded her memories. My mother is merciless, she doesn't allow me to keep anything she deems unnecessary, so I hide things – under the bed, in the cupboards that we had already cleared out, in my suitcase. When my mother grabs the long stick I know the old folks use to open the curtains, my grandfather starts to protest.

'Shhh! I don't want to hear a peep out of you,' she snaps at him.

He retreats to his room, cursing: 'This is how you clean out a house after a death, goddammit . . . But we haven't even died yet . . . This is my life's work, for fuck's sake . . .'

'Give it here, I'll throw it away,' I tell her, and she thrusts the stick into my hands and disappears into the kitchen.

I knock on the glass door, even though I know he is too deaf to hear me. I open the door a crack – he's sitting on the edge of the bed, his head in the hands that I was so afraid of as a child.

'Grandpa?' I say.

He raises his head. He is so wrinkled that his eyes are mere slits. His gaze is clouded, that's how it is in the final years when a person is trapped between this world and the next one.

'I'm going to hide the stick here under the couch,' I tell him. 'You'll take it out once Mom leaves. OK?'

'Huh? What're you doing here with that stick?'

I repeat myself a second and a third time until he catches on. I leave him shaking with sobs and quietly shut the door.

'I can't believe it,' I tell my mother. 'For as long as I can remember he was always yelling at her, putting her down . . .'

My mom starts sprinkling a spiced mix of grated pumpkin into the phyllo dough crust and rolling it up carelessly, with her typical impatience.

'He took me out to the vineyard,' she says. 'He was complaining that you didn't want to go.'

I nod.

'You know, your uncle and I hauled the bricks for that lozé. We didn't have a childhood, we were always hauling bricks and digging. And now when I went there this time – he's got two dogs, he's chained them up with a wire, they shit at one end of the wire and sleep at the other, a total nightmare. So I told him: "Let those poor creatures go, people in the civilized world don't treat animals that way," and he answered that he knows what they're up to, they've been raised that way, they've gotten used to it . . .'

Her voice shakes slightly, but she doesn't lose control.

'And I'd gotten used to it, too, Yana. I didn't know things could be different.'

I fiddle with the edge of the vinyl tablecloth and look out the window: the daylight filters toward the horizon, the fog mixes with the harsh smoke from the chimneys, a dog's barking floats in from the hills. I recognize some of the neighbors who are crossing Main Street, heading home, a little more tired than before, but otherwise the same. The rest we've already met in the death notices on the wall.

'You need to go to bed early,' my mother announces, with complete certainty that this is exactly what will happen. 'We need to move all the books from the shelves in the living room so we can put your grandma's medicine and diapers there. And we have to get rid of all her houseplants – there's no one to take care of them.'

Shortly before they bring her home, I start getting rid of the plants. Something makes me take a picture of them in the hallway in front of the elevator. In front of the building, I run into Auntie Nellie from the apartment across from ours. Yet another forgotten reflex – *prikazavne*. It doesn't mean just talking; the *pri* prefix added to the action of speech implies going toward somebody and evokes the intimacy of touching, hugging, confiding. My mother complains that here people have no concept of personal space. Auntie Nellie looks at the flower pot in my hands in horror.

'What're you doing with those plants?' she asks me.

I tell her.

'Auntie Nellie, what if I just leave them here in front of the building . . .'

'Leave 'em, leave 'em! I'll give Lozinka and Tsetsa a call

right now, we'll take 'em in, one or two each, least we can do We're not gonna toss 'em, and when poor Evie gets better, she can take them back . . .'

I arrange the others on the staircase; the three floors above and below us promise to water them. I tell my mother, who always chats politely to the neighbors, calm, smiling. She has always been like that to everyone except her loved ones.

They bring Grandma home in the late afternoon. My mom sends us into the other rooms so she can change her diapers and catheter, and get her settled in the bed. When I come back into the living room, I see her from behind and I recognize her messy white hair, which is sticking up in tufts of all different lengths, since my grandfather has cut it. My mother is sitting at the other end of the bed, doing exercises for my grandma's right hand, which keeps shooting chaotically into the air.

'Mom,' my mother says to her loudly, slowly, 'look who's here.'

I cross the living room and come closer so she can see me. The woman lying in the bed is much older than I remember.

'Y . . . a,' she wheezes, 'yyy . . . aaa . . .'

'Ya-na, Mom, Ya-na,' my mother replies. My grandma clucks her tongue and shakes her head sharply. 'You're not going to pout, Mom, you're gonna talk! Come on, you've got to try. Come on.'

'Yee . . . n . . . a. Yaa . . . a. Yeea-n-a.' Every letter costs her enormous effort, her tongue flops out of her mouth, slips back in, then out again.

'Good job, Mom. Bravo.'

I sit down at my mother's feet, next to the bed. My grandpa comes into the living room with a plate and a plastic bag of sliced bread. *You can't sit down to eat without bread*, that's the Bulgarian saying. My mother gives him a tired glance.

'Dad, she can't eat on her own yet. That means that before you sit down to eat, you need to ask her if she wants something, if she's hungry or thirsty. When we leave, you'll need to take care of her. Are you going to sit down to eat and just leave her there to watch?'

My grandma taps on the blanket with her left hand to get my mother's attention. My grandma shakes her head.

'Eva, do you want something?' he asks her. She continues to shake her head. 'Never thought I'd live to see the day when they treat me like an imbecile in my own home,' he says to my mother.

I huddle closer to my grandma, leaving them to argue over my head.

'I brought you books,' I tell her. She smiles, her left hand clumsily rubs against my shoulder. 'And I'll tell you about America. Grandma, you ought to think about going back to Germany with Mom or . . .'

She shakes her head.

'He can't take care of you, Grandma. Remember when you were in Sofia and he flooded the apartment, or when he washed all your clothes in boiling water, or when he forgot to plug in the freezer and you had to throw away all the meat, or that bottle of cooking oil he dropped, the splashes are still all over the wall in the kitchen, or that time when he forgot the pot of beans on the stove and started a fire . . .'

No, no, no, she would say if she could.

'I never thought I'd see the day when he met his match' – I glance at him and then at my mom as I whisper into my grandma's ear – 'but he needs someone just like him to shut him up.'

We giggle. Her left hand squeezes my shoulder.

'How . . . how . . . hoooww . . .'

'What is it, Mom?' my mother cuts in. 'Do you need to use the bathroom? Food? Are you hungry?'

She shakes her head, her eyes fixed on me.

'How . . .'

'Water? Yana, go get some water . . .' She starts giving me orders.

'Wait a second, Mom! How . . . Do you mean house, Grandma? The house?'

She nods.

'Relax, Mom, Uncle Georgi agreed to water the garden,' my mom replies.

'N . . . n . . . no!' my grandma stutters, her right hand shoots up, then falls back onto the bed. 'How . . . D . . . D . . . n . . . no!' She gives up, clicking her tongue and sighing deeply. I realize that every sound exhausts her. What must it be like to carry all the words in your mind without being able to say them aloud?

'Mom, wait.' I rest my hand on my mother's knee. She doesn't have the patience to hear my grandma out, to delve into her thoughts, to piece together the puzzle of sounds.

'Grandma . . . do you mean to say "house"? Is that the word?' I ask her.

She nods.

'The house across the street?'

She shakes her head.

'This house?'

No.

'The vineyard?'

No.

'Your brother's house? The apartment downstairs?'

No.

'Come on now, leave her alone, she doesn't know which way is up,' my grandfather butts in, smacking his lips. My mother opens her mouth to reply, but I squeeze her knee even harder.

'Grandma . . . do you mean the house in Dolna Riksa?'

She inhales sharply, nods.

'You want to go there?'

Another 'no'. Her left hand drops away from my shoulder.

'Shh . . . shn . . . s . . . y . . . y . . . yuh. Yuh. Yuh. Y . . . oo. You!'

'You want me to go there?' I interrupt her.

Nodding, a tear falls from her right eye. I'm not sure whether she's crying or the effort is exhausting her.

'Mom, Yana needs to help me clean, she doesn't have time to go traipsing around—'

'No, I'll go,' I cut her off. 'It won't take long, I'll help you. Uncle Pavel can give me the car keys.'

'You're not driving anywhere!' my grandfather squawks behind me. 'What with all the maniacs out on the roads, so many folks gettin' killed—'

'Fine, Dad,' my mom interrupts him. 'Nobody's going anywhere.'

She turns to me and my grandma.

'Yana, I'll call your uncle now. You'll go when the old man heads to the vineyard so he doesn't have a fit. Mom, do you need something from the house? You remember, don't you, that we sold it years ago to your cousin Valya?'

My grandma nods.

'I think she just wants me to see it.' I glance at my grandma. 'You just want me to see it, right?'

Yes.

I quickly get used to the bulky torso of the old Mercedes. Inside it reeks of pine air freshener, so I leave the window open despite the cold. I revel in the fresh air outside of the dome of coal smoke that covers the city. *Crisp October air* – the phrase pops into my head in English, that other language butting in, meaning something between crunchy, fresh, lightly covered in frost, carrying both fall and winter within itself, a cold blessing, an aromatic death . . . The road, brand new or patched over in places, riddled with potholes in some spots and completely missing in others, passes through the local villages in a steady rhythm: wasteland, dilapidated houses on the outskirts of the village, a few nicer homes near the center, a kindergarten or a community center, a little village square, a town hall, the mayor's house – always the biggest with the sturdiest fence – several more nice houses, dilapidated places on the outskirts, wasteland. The further from the city, the more deserted the villages become, kindergartens and schools either gape empty or are locked up. In the distance the Balkans look even more massive than they did from the gorge; here the mountains carry the weight of a border beyond which lie the lost homelands of our forefathers.

How will I even find the house at all? I've written down the exact address, but the names of the streets, the towns and the heroes of this country have changed three times over since my grandma was born – from the monarchy through Communism and now to 'Democracy'. Her brother explained it more simply to me: after the fork at the village square, it's the third house before the end of the village. I pass by the rusty sign for 'Dolna Riks' – the final 'a' has been burned off – and park in the square. I head up the road, toward a big building with gaping broken windows, through which I can see rooms full of weeds, chunks of plaster and sagging wallpaper. My gaze is drawn to the red star on the wall next to me. There is a marble plaque beneath it:

LEGACY FOR FUTURE GENERATIONS
BURIED ON 24 JANUARY 1987
TOO BE OPENED ON 24 JANUARY 2037

I wonder how it's possible to engrave a spelling error into stone. There is a memorial plaque to the partisans nearby as well – surely this is the monument whose history I have heard countless times: before the Communist coup on 9 September 1944, later celebrated as a national holiday, there was a group of Communist partisan fighters in the village, and my great-grandfather warned them to run, because he'd gotten word that the gendarmerie was coming. They dug in their heels and said they wouldn't listen to a fascist mayor. The next day the gendarmerie really did show up and shot them all in the forest.

When they built that monument – what heroes, what praise! Beneath the monument lie dried-up carnations.

'Looking for someone?' I hear a voice behind me.

I turn toward a thin old woman who is two heads shorter than I am.

'Uh no . . . I . . . I'm the granddaughter of a woman who used to live here.'

'That so? Whose girl are ya?' she asks me.

'Eva? Eva . . . Lazarova?' If they know my grandma, they'll remember her by her maiden name. It flashes through my mind unwittingly that this was the last place she was happy.

'Lazarova . . . Lazarova . . . can't say it rings any bells.' She shrugs. 'But I'm not one of the locals, I'm married into this place.'

'You don't say?'

'Yup, I came here fifty-odd years back.'

'Well, you can't get much more local than that,' I joke. She looks at me in confusion. 'Her father was the mayor . . .' I hesitate. Which side was she on? Actually, what does it matter anymore? '. . . mayor before the changes. Georgi Lazarov . . .

'After the fork, the third house from the end?' I make a final attempt.

She thinks for a moment.

'You mean one of Vani's folks?'

I throw up my hands in a show of helplessness. I don't know the name of a single cousin, nor any of my cousin's cousins, aunts, uncles . . .

'Well, lemme show you where the fork is at least. It's on the other side, there's just the school here. Nobody left down that way.' She waves to show me.

We head back past the locked-up town hall. There's a small store next to it, a wrought-iron table and benches under a dried-up trellis, and on the wall behind it a faded but otherwise untouched slogan about 9 September with a female worker looking confidently into the future. The old woman follows my gaze.

'We still celebrate the Ninth,' she tells me proudly. 'Ya ought to come next year.'

I smile.

'My name's Plamka.' She offers me her bony hand, her skin is almost translucent.

'Yana,' I say.

'From Sofia?'

'Yes, from Sofia.'

'Ev'rybody from around here skedaddled to Sofia,' she

concludes. 'My kids're gone there, too. Some foreign people turned up in summertime,' she tells me. 'From America. With a little one, must've be about your age, young, but Bulgarian. They stopped, had a gander. Then the girl came over, all polite-like, good manners an' all that, asked me if I knew where the ghost village was. Them people were on a hunt for a ghost village. So I told her: just look around, here's a ghost village for ya.'

She chuckles, showing the two teeth left in her head.

'That's just our luck, I guess,' she goes on. 'But what do you know, the Party up and fixed our road. Maybe somebody'll come, like you did.'

'I'm sure they will,' I reply.

She stops at the edge of the sidewalk – in front of us the road splits in two. I had come from the right fork, she points to the left one.

'You've got to head that way.'

'Thank you,' I tell her. 'If there's anything . . .'

'Don't mention it, I gotta go now, 'cause I have a pot of beans on the stove, stop by after and have a bite to eat, if you aren't in a rush,' she tells me. Then reading the excuses on the tip of my tongue, she cuts me off. 'Or some other time, if not now. But come, come on back. It's nice to see a young person around here, to have a little chat.'

She doesn't wait for my answer, only waves, and I watch her totter back down the sidewalk until I lose sight of her down one of the side streets.

After the fork the third house from the end.

The rusty door is locked, the dried grass in the yard is

nearly waist-high. I find a place where the barbed-wire fence unhooks from the post, lift it and slip underneath. The ground is covered in rotting apples, beneath the tree lies a crooked concrete trough filled with dirt and weeds – I've heard about this trough that provides water for the animals, while in the summer it's a place for the kids to bathe. Whoever owns the house now has not been here in years. The house is still standing, my grandma loves to tell us how it was built that way – *even if a bomb were to fall, it'd still be standing*. The eaves are filled with swallows' nests: I count at least twenty. Nothing else gives away the house's age: I've imagined it differently, the house – much older, somehow almost in the Bulgarian Renaissance style. In the backyard there are only weeds and more ivy. There is a gaping hole between the beautiful wooden railing and the wall, as if the house has slumped slightly to one side of the steps. Cracks creep up the back wall.

I cut a path toward the small veranda out front, a few steps from the gate. I know that my great-grandmother left bread here to cool; that when Russian soldiers passed through, someone snuck into the yard and stole her just-baked *tikvenik*, her pumpkin pastry, and my grandma had cried once for the tikvenik and once again when the Russian soldier came back several days later to apologize that he hadn't eaten anything for days and to leave money.

They'd all really enjoyed the tikvenik, he told her.

Ivy has overtaken the entire staircase, as well as the wall to the left and the door – I step carefully onto the orangish-green carpet. I can't see anything through the little window, beneath it is a chair – I wipe off the dust, check for giant spiders and whether it is rotted through, and decide to sit with time for a while.

I've brought my grandma's photo album from her childhood and teenage years with me.

I open it up and immediately recognize the wooden door and railings. My grandma, age two, in a woolly sweater with a hood, is standing in front of the very same door I'm sitting next to. The next brownish photo: again in the same place is a pile of unfamiliar aunts and cousins including my grandma and her brother as children. My great-grandmother is in a blindingly white dress holding a child in her arms – it must be somewhere out back, it's hard for me to connect the current jungle with the well-tended little yard surrounded by a wooden fence in the photo.

Another in the backyard – deep snow that two big dogs have waded into.

Springtime – the yard has turned white with tiny daisies, my grandma and her mother are playing in the grass near the steps, a blurred white spot runs toward them.

The four of them – my grandma, her mother, her father and her brother, smiling, my grandma's hair is long, her expression is mischievous, they are standing under the apple tree.

One of the last photos is of her and her brother, perhaps after their high school graduation – my grandma looks a lot like my mother – it must be from when the house was sold? I don't remember her telling me they had come back. Another on the veranda: he is in a military jacket and wearing a cap, while she is in an elegant black coat looking off into the distance. A scrap of paper falls from the pages. I pick it up, something is written on the back, which I don't read – I'm more interested in the man in the photograph, young and handsome, with a serious, almost gloomy look in his eyes. I've never come across him in the photo albums. I turn it over and read:

Keep me in your heart?

That I can't require.

Keep me in your dreams?

That is my desire.

My phone rings, sharp and loud – it is only then I realize how quiet it is here.

'Come back,' my mother barks at the other end of the line, 'your grandma's taken a turn for the worse and I think the end is near.'

In the car I call the American. It's morning there, I hear the seagulls in the distance. I miss him.

'My mom thinks she's dying,' I say.

'How are you?'

I don't know. I don't answer.

'When I was a kid, everyone started wearing white sneakers. "Brandies", that's what we called them because they were brand-name: Adidas, Nike and so on. They were expensive, around two hundred leva. My mom's whole take-home pay for a month was around six hundred. From one of her jobs. Her other job paid less, it wasn't a private hospital. I really wanted shoes like that. I was sick of being poor, of being sad, of everything. I wanted to be like everyone else.'

A horse cart jumps out from around a bend – I slam on the brakes.

'My mom bought me the shoes. She bought me everything and was always saying how she didn't have nice things as a kid, so that's why she wanted me to have them.'

I blow straight through an intersection, only seeing the stop sign at the last minute. Good thing it takes more than one person to make an accident.

'*Fuck*,' I curse.

'What happened?'

'Nothing, nothing... what was I saying... ? Oh yeah, about my grandpa. I was dying of boredom out at the vineyard, so he put up a swing for me. Then my grandma started laughing her head off because when we put the swing up together, she saw he had bought a brand-new one – and he never bought anything new, ever – and we got into a fight, I called him a Gypsy, but half an hour later we made up. That's how it always was. My grandma explained to me that he needed to explode to blow off steam, and then he'd be as soft as warm bread. He always cried when he had to slaughter a chicken or a rabbit, always. He raised his animals as if they were his children, he'd talk to them, I remember how he'd be holding the axe in one hand and the chicken in the other, and tears would be running down his cheeks . . . And he always fixed my bike for me, pumped up the tires and greased the chain . . . He would go shopping in the morning, you know, I've told you . . . He would go to the market while she did the housework . . . And even now, even though I grew up long ago, and he doesn't know . . . He always buys something for me that he knows I like. I don't even eat that greasy stuff anymore, banitsa, donuts, but he's always buying tons of it, bringing them home for me, saying hey, Yannie, look what your granddad got for you, your favorite . . .' My voice is shaking.

I hear his even breathing. Or maybe it's the ocean.

'He drives my grandma nuts, 'cause he's always buying her hats' – I laugh through my tears. 'At home we've got a huge bag of hats, all kinds of hats. Hats with visors, ear flaps, stocking caps, beanies, with pom-poms . . . And she doesn't even wear hats!' He laughs, too. 'She hates hats. My mom would always sign me up for all kinds of field trips. Summer camp. And I'd always come home and tell her that the other kids had more pocket money.'

'I'm sorry I'm not there,' he tells me after a pause.

'Do you mind if we're just quiet while I drive?' I ask.

'No problem.'

I head back into the plains. The windows of the village pubs are already lit up; I imagine bloodshot eyes watching the lone car pass.

'Here there are only two things you can do – work or drink,' I tell him.

'Just like in Delaware,' he replies, and we laugh.

Four Gypsy neighborhoods surround the city; a wedding is taking place in one of them and the belly dancing rhythms echo in the surrounding hills.

'I forgot to take a picture of the house!' I exclaim. 'If you could only have seen the mural I saw . . .'

I tell him about Granny Plamka, the monument and the time capsule.

'Maybe someday we'll come back and go inside,' his voice on the other end of the line grows enthusiastic as I park in front of the apartment building.

Maybe.

'I have to go upstairs,' I tell him.

'OK. What is it again in Bulgarian?' he asks.

'What?'

'Och . . . iba?' he stutters.

'Aha . . . Obicham te.' I love you.

'Yes. Obicham te.'

'I az te obicham.' I love you too.

Yana

'I tried pointing out individual letters to her, but she couldn't recognize them,' my mother tells me in the hallway. 'And to think, just this morning we were joking about your grandfather and his dreams about aliens . . .' She shakes her head.

The new books I brought her are lined up next to my grandma's bed. More than anything in the world she loved – *loves* – reading. And knitting.

My grandpa is howling.

My grandma is staring blankly into nothingness, saying my mother's and my uncle's names, searching for them. My mother is once again sitting at her feet – she has grasped her by the ankle. My grandfather and my uncle are standing around the table – it is the first time I have seen them so deflated, so shrunken from helplessness.

'Pa . . . vel,' she utters.

My uncle goes over to her, strokes her face, jokes with her. She gives the slightest of smiles, only her left cheek twitches.

'Ya . . . Ya . . .' Her gaze is again searching. 'Huh . . .' she starts to say.

I grab her hand. 'I went to Dolna Riksa, Grandma. The house . . .'

I stop. And all four of them look at me.

'The house is fine. The apple tree really blossomed this year, actually there's still fruit on all the trees.'

My grandma's expression changes to a grimace – she's smiling.

'I changed the water in the trough' – I go on, my mother starts to interrupt me, but I shoot her a pleading glance and thank God, she catches on – 'so the animals can drink nice clean water. I gathered up the hay with the thresher, fed the chickens – and found a ton of eggs, I'll boil one for you in a bit.'

Her gaze releases me, scatters, drifts off into the distance.

'I let the mare Martha out to graze in the yard and also untied the buffalo, you remember them, Belcho and Sivcho? Then I did some weeding in the garden and took the bread down from the kitchen window – it had already cooled – so nobody would take it, right?'

They've all fallen silent, even my grandfather.

'If only you could see how beautiful the garden is! The hollyhock's grown almost two meters high, I pinched back the geraniums a bit, and your favorite primroses are doing fine as well. The daisies in the meadow are already blooming for the second time around, probably because it's been so warm lately, so all the grass is covered in little white medallions. I hoed the vegetable garden a bit, too, turning over the soil just like you taught me when I was little. If you ask me, it'll be perfect for peppers or cucumbers, as long as it rains next year, God willing. Or maybe tomatoes . . . The windows were dusty, so I wiped them down and opened them up to let in some fresh air. The first blanket you knitted is still there, so are the cross stitches, the embroidered cloth is up on the wall, it just needs a good wash . . .'

'Yana.'

'. . . and the dogs are fine, the big white and gray one barked at me at first, but . . .'

'Yana . . .'

'I let them out to run around . . .'

'Yana, you can stop now.' My mother grasps my hand.

I look toward my grandma's half-closed eyes. I am about to tell her that I love her, but I'm too late.

* * *

Migration, life, death – everything passes from one drawer to another. My mother signs the death certificate, they carry the body out like a piece of old furniture. My grandma always said she didn't want me to cry when she died, that death is not the end of anything, that the world is much larger than a single shell. My mother starts cooking, because that's what's done: from the cradle to the grave, every milestone is an excuse to stuff ourselves. I add several crocheted things, chosen at random, to my bag, along with the photo album – I've never liked them and surely I will never use them, but she really loved them.

'Did she show you the big suitcase?' I ask my mother, while picking away at the vinyl tablecloth.

'The one full of knitted stuff?' She smiles.

'Yeah. She always said that she knitted to stop herself from killing him, it gave her something to do with her hands. And then she would take out the suitcase, God, I can't even imagine how many scarves and doilies must be in there . . .'

'At least two hundred . . .'

'If not more! That's sixty years of suffering in silence.'

'Don't just stand there like a bump on a log,' she says and hands me several empty plates.

I take everything out into the living room. My grandfather has gone to lie down in the bedroom, after announcing he would not live to see the morning. My uncle is out somewhere.

I keep emptying out the cupboards. I discover old-school appliances, made in the USSR, with the kind of plugs they don't even make anymore, once upon a time they hooked right into the wall, their boxes are pristine, while all their parts are perfectly shiny – they have never been used. In the spice cupboard I find a packet of tapioca from 2002, along with twenty-three packs of sugar sprinkles – I open one up, they've turned to dust; a jar of savory full of moths, and a bar of chocolate long past its expiration date. Next come several brand-new sets of dishes, a broken soup tureen – we take out a second one, which is intact – three huge plastic bags of lids to jars, a plastic bag of metal twist-ties, a beat-up box full of all kinds of plastic forks, spoons and knives, straws and toothpicks. In the bedroom my mother takes out bags full of sheets that still have the tags on them – 1988, 100 percent cotton, made in the USSR. We pull out three boxes of unused cloth handkerchiefs, my grandpa's favorites, so my mom throws away the old ones. My grandma's cabinets are full of unlived life – everyday products that the Socialist authorities released onto the market in limited quantities and that she dutifully collected, since she never knew when they might be available again. My mother calls me from the kitchen. I wipe away the tears and go to her.

'Has your uncle come home yet?'

'No.'

'Can you finish up here? I have to call the undertakers, I promised. Your grandpa won't listen to a word anyone says, he just keeps grumbling and howling, I'm going to go out where I can talk in peace.'

I nod.

'Mom?' I call after her. I'm thinking she must have already left, but she comes back.

'What is it?'

If only I'd managed to grow up faster, so I would've understood.

I'm sorry I was so difficult.

I'm sorry you had a daughter, and not a son.

'Yana?'

'Nothing. I'm just happy to see you.'

She comes over to me, hugs me and strokes my hair.

'I don't know what I would've done if you hadn't come.'

I keep an eye on the oven and take out the tikvenik, carry it into the living room. My grandfather is watching the news over the top of his glasses, a newspaper open in front of him. It's some local channel; they are showing burning fields.

'Just look, what a wasteland.' He points at the TV, lisping – he's taken out his dentures. 'They've ruined ev'r'thing, the bastards.'

'In America, too, there's nobody left in the villages and small towns, Grandpa. People go to the cities.' I shrug apologetically. 'That's just the way it is.'

He looks at me. Then he waves his hand.

'Yeah right, what do you know about the way things are, you little brat.'

He adjusts his glasses and buries his nose in the newspaper, gives a satisfied grunt and circles something. The page is covered with circles. He reaches out and pokes me in the shoulder with a fat finger.

'Listen, here's one that might work for her!'

I let him read me the urban poetry of obituaries. A flock of crows winds around the setting sun, their thin spirals grow, the dark cloud seizes the sky and flies off north toward the Danube.

day

I help my mom check her luggage. Our flights are a couple hours apart, so I'll have to wander around the airport, but that's fine with me; the pointlessness of the everyday – shopping, stuffing your face with nasty food, stupid conversations – it all reassures me that the world is still here.

We talk, we joke, I listen with resignation to the unwanted advice and recommendations she gives me before going through security. I will do barely any of what she says. Finally, I give her a long, hard hug.

'I'll miss you,' I tell her.

'I love you too,' she answers hastily, her eyes flicking nervously around the airport – she's overwhelmed by the fear of missing her flight or getting on the wrong plane.

'Take care of yourself,' I add.

'Good luck with your studies. Let me know how it goes. Well, bye for now!' She waves.

I watch as she goes up the escalator, turns around and blows me a kiss. A soft autumn light glows through the terminal's glass ceiling; I sit down in a patch of sunlight and listen to the sounds of the airport. Those who are leaving tear themselves away from the grasping hands that remain outstretched behind them a moment longer than they would if the parting were a happy one; at the other end of the terminal those waiting at arrivals tap their feet on the tiles in impatient anticipation.

'Last call for Flight SJE1583 to London, Heathrow,' the metallic voice says.

I am the stories of all these women, I am the story of none of them.

The final thread connecting my grandmother's past to my daughter's future.

I am the generation torn between yesterday and tomorrow.

How do I compose the sentences of my own self?

The airplane lifts off the ground, my heart sinks into my stomach before again returning to its place. November explodes into a final sunset and I see the city, which could be

Sofia or Berlin, Paris, New York, Calcutta, Shanghai – dirty, burning and overcrowded with people shopping at the same stores, watching the same movies; with people who laugh, love and go their separate ways, who are cruel and kind, disoriented in their eternal flights. The airplane gains altitude, the network of lights disappears, giving way to an impenetrable darkness beneath the red sky.

'Heading home, huh?' the young man in the seat next to me asks.

I hesitate for a moment, then smile: 'Yes.'

Author and Translator's Note

Tucked away in the south-east corner of Europe, Bulgaria is easily defined as a 'small' European country with a 'small' language. Just ask Bulgarians how small they are, and they will be happy to tell you all about it. That said, Bulgaria is not quite as small as they might lead you to believe – it is larger in size than Hungary, Portugal, Austria, Ireland and Switzerland.

If you look at how Bulgaria is depicted in the press, you will find headlines claiming it is 'the saddest country in the world' (labeled as such by *The Economist* back in the 2000s, an expression later popularized by author Georgi Gospodinov). It has also been described as 'one of the European Union's poorest countries',[1] 'the most corrupted country in the European Union'[2] and even 'the fastest shrinking population in the world'.[3]

Bulgaria is at the crossroads of Asia and Europe, a land between continents and cultures. It bears the scars of every

1 https://www.nytimes.com/2025/12/11/world/europe/bulgaria-prime-minister-resigns-protests.html

2 https://transparency.bg/ti-bg-in-medias/bulgaria-on-air-ti-bulgaria-bulgaria-is-the-most-corrupted-country-in-the-eu

3 https://www.bbc.co.uk/worklife/article/20190913-how-to-slow-down-the-worlds-fastest-shrinking-country

ancient empire: in the capital city of Sofia one can walk among Roman ruins, see Byzantine mosaics, catch Turkish words in someone's sentence – leftovers from half a millennium as part of the Ottoman Empire – stroll amid Viennese-style architecture from a time when the country had a German prince for a king, and finally explore the dystopian leftovers of Soviet brutalism.

It is through this palimpsest of landscapes that young Yana, the protagonist of *Born of Guilt*, wanders in search of meaning, oblivious to the 'large and small history' which molds us all. Although Yana manages to reach the United States, she carries her past with her, a past that haunts the rest of her family, too. She is a part of what Timothy Garton Ash calls 'the born frees' – the generation born after the fall of Communism in 1989, when many formerly Soviet-aligned countries underwent an often disastrous transition from planned to market economies. In time, Bulgarians (and most Eastern Europeans) understood that 'free market economy' didn't automatically bring freedom of mind or spirit; that 'democracy' was not a fail-safe against corruption and injustice; and that the journey was bound to be much longer, and harder, than anticipated. They also realized that freedom could not be obtained by simply replacing 'People's' in the 'People's Republic of Bulgaria' with 'Democratic', or by erasing the Soviet figures from the names of streets, cities and stores.

In a way, the regime change created a mirror-world for the generations who grew up under dictatorship, as they were all of a sudden told that the 'Luminous Future' of tomorrow, promised by the Socialist Party and turned into a propaganda slogan over the years, was no more. A better future now awaited them, in the form of democracy. For Yana and the rest of her generation, the promise implied by this new and better democratic future is laden with the expectation of living the life denied to her parents and grandparents over half a century of Communism: she should learn English instead of Russian, go to study in Western Europe or the United States – and run away from what they see as this small, godforsaken land, because, they were led to believe, in the West everything is better.

For many families, the memories of the years under dictatorship linger: of budget deficits both during and after the fall of Communism, when many didn't have enough to eat and relied on their private gardens and animals; of meagre meals like 'popara' – just bread soaked in tea; the broken promises of the democratic government for a utopia that never manifested; the dilapidated socialist panel-blocks that rise like coral reefs in Sofia and every Eastern European city – these fragments of habit and memory keep unfolding like fractals, creating a claustrophobic desperation – in the end, there is no running away from history. Every departure is an illusion. But so is every arrival.

'Everyone wants to be Russian or American,' the narrator says, 'no one wants to be Bulgarian.' For the born-frees, there is a new empire in town, this time far subtler, but with a much stronger gravitational pull: American culture – with its cartoons, movies, dreams, objects and promises – captivates not only Yana's generation, but also those who have only glimpsed the American Dream through the Iron Curtain.

The 'Work and Travel' program through which Yana arrives in the US as a seasonal worker still exists today, and American resorts still rely on their labor. From what I hear from Bulgarian students ten years after my own Work and Travel experience, parts of which have inspired the fictional story in this novel, working conditions remain largely the same. Young students still die in accidents on American highways, and many still use the program to see the country while earning money, sometimes then extending their stay illegally to become a part of the American experiment. During the labor shortage caused by the COVID-19 lockdowns, most businesses in the Delaware beaches area had posted desperate signs for hiring 'J1s', as these students are known.

The challenges of crossing cultures described in the story are also evident in the translation process. Where the plot takes place in the US, the American spelling, expressions and slang have been kept. In other cases, we have decided to introduce Bulgarian words to the reader, especially when there was difficulty in translating rich regional dialects. I believe that, while English has changed the 'smaller' languages it touches, there is a secondary 'world' English, which is also changing and reflecting the colors of its many multinational speakers, becoming a sort of iridescent chameleon, a beautiful hybrid. Angela and I have tried to reflect this in the text.

Finally, the presence of a note like this one suggests that non-English texts need 'explainers'. While I understand this,

I'd like to believe that Yana's story is above all a human story and could be understood as such despite an unknown word or circumstance here and there. After all, this is the very purpose of art and literature: to offer a safe place to face the unfamiliar in all its forms, from its beauty to its horrors. I hope that this note enhances the novel and the full, diverse polyphonic world that it is trying to reflect.

Sofia, Paris and Amsterdam,
January 2019 – September 2020

Acknowledgements

A book doesn't really belong to its author, or if it does, it's only for a short time.

An author is indebted to the people who made him, her or them, with whom they have shared their stories – to these people I express my gratitude, and this book is for them:

For Stephen.

For my family at home, in Bulgaria, and in the United States.

For my chosen family – An and Yovko, Bozhana and Karlo, Vessy and Emo, Viktoriya, Joanna, Kat, Marina and Nik, Roumen, Tsveta, Andy, Julian, Clara, Louisa.

Many thanks to all who nursed this book until she was ready:

To Boryana and Didier Orland, who never left me alone during the hardest time.

To Rosemary, without whom I would never have been able to finish it.

To my Bulgarian publisher, Janet 45, for giving us both a home.

To the magical Laurence Laluyaux, unmatched and irreplaceable; and Katharina Volckmer, Niktaa Amirkhalili, Sam Coates and everyone else at RCW Literary Agency – because of them this story speaks in more than ten languages and counting.

To Angela Rodel for her boundless talent and professionalism.

To my editor, Aisling Brennan, Jo Stimfield and everyone else at Faber & Faber, where the novel finds a home in my second language.

Born of Guilt hatched from the cocoon of a short story in Zurich, during a spring afternoon in April 2019. I am grateful to the Cultural Perspectives Foundation, to whom I owe meeting Georgi Gospodinov. I am also grateful to the Elizabeth Kostova Foundation for their support within the Sozopol Fiction Seminars in 2019 and beyond.

And to Georgi – for the freedom, for his patience, for his honesty; for being the first to notice. For his words which kept me afloat in the loneliest moments of writing.

Reader, now this book is yours. I thank you for your trust and time.